THORN IN MY SIDE

DI Mike Yorke is coming home. After three months in London, he's looking forward to being back in the north east – but he's barely off the train before he's deep into the most bizarre case of his career. A viciously flogged corpse. Children disappearing the length of the A1. Horrific new street drugs. And buried somewhere is a deadly secret that will lead him down paths so dangerous, he will question the very fabric of society.

THORN IN MY SIDE

THORN IN
MY SIDE

by

Sheila Quigley

Magna Large Print Books
Long Preston, North Yorkshire,
BD23 4ND, England.

British Library Cataloguing in Publication Data.

Quigley, Sheila
    Thorn in my side.

      A catalogue record of this book is
      available from the British Library

      ISBN   978-0-7505-3517-5

First published in Great Britain 2010 by Burgess Books

Copyright © Sheila Quigley 2010

Cover illustration © Roy Bishop by arrangement with
Arcangel Images

The moral right of the author has been asserted

Published in Large Print 2012 by arrangement with
Sheila Quigley

Magna Large Print is an imprint of Library Magna Books Ltd.

Printed and bound in Great Britain by
T.J. (International) Ltd., Cornwall, PL28 8RW

DEDICATION

For Michael Quigley

ACKNOWLEDGEMENTS

For Heather Cawte, one of the best editors in the business, and for Aarron Forrest – thanks for the hands. And as ever, Paul Lanagan.

PROLOGUE

FRANCE 2007

'Non.'

One word of defiance. Spoken quietly but with an unbreakable finality. The French word for 'no' winged around the room, bounced off the walls and echoed in the heads of those gathered there. A thick, cloying silence descended as fear took hold of their hearts and quickly spread.

Every face turned to the front.

The man known simply as The Leader stared at the youth. His face flushed from red to purple with anger. He turned to those gathered there. 'Get out,' he yelled. He spun back round to the youth. 'Not you.' He put up his hand to stop the young man from leaving. Behind him the room emptied.

Knowing he'd said the wrong thing, the youth froze, his heart pounding in his chest. But what had been asked of him was impossible.

Two others stayed behind, both of them over six foot with steroid-hyped bodies rippling with each movement. One, of obvious Chinese descent, smiled a predator smile, while the Caucasian's face showed no emotion at all. He stared in front of him like a well-bred fighting machine awaiting instructions.

'You dare to defy me?' The Leader, tall, thin,

with long flowing black hair, asked with more than a touch of amazement in his voice.

Quivering, the youth hung his head, not daring to answer. The Leader snatched a bamboo stick off the table and poked the silent youth hard in his stomach, punctuating each word with a vicious thrust. 'You will do as I say... Answer me.'

Sticking to his native tongue, the youth muttered quietly but stubbornly, 'Absolument pas.'

'You dare to tell me "absolutely not"? You dare to say those words to me?' He had spoken quietly, amazed that this skinny, stupid, ugly peasant had the nerve to defy him.

His next words though, spoken to the two heavies, were loud and very clear. 'A lesson needs to be taught here, so that others may not catch the fever he so obviously possesses.'

He glowered once more at the youth before striding to the corner of the room, where he stood with his hands clenched in front of him, his eyes unblinking and a sarcastic curve on his mouth.

The Caucasian guard grabbed the youth from behind. Quickly he stripped him, his thin cotton shift like so much tissue paper in the huge guard's hands. A moment later he hauled him naked to the centre of the room. The captive, beyond terror, had barely struggled. His will sapped, knowing his fate, he gave up. Not even a sob escaped from his dry lips.

His wrists were tied above his head to a large thick wooden pole, where a metal ring had been fitted for this purpose. Then the Chinese guard tied his feet to another set of metal loops

14

concreted in to the floor. His face pressed tight against the wood, splinters already digging into his cheek and drawing tiny spots of blood, the trembling youth did not see the huge wooden-handled whip the Chinese guard had taken from a cupboard, set flush in the wall at the right-hand side of the room.

He felt the first lash though, felt his flesh being ripped from his body in nine different places, and screamed for mercy.

His tormenter looked across at The Leader. He was the only one who could give clemency, the guards would only do what he told them. The youth's pleas fell on deaf ears.

Leaving the wall, his hands still positioned in front of him, The Leader moved up to the wooden post, circling it once, sniffing at the youth's ravaged back, before suddenly grabbing the youth by his scalp and savagely yanking his head back. His face close to the captive he said, 'No one defies me, peasant boy. You are a cancer that I will eliminate.'

Slowly he shook his head at the guard. 'Finish it.'

The second lash, criss-crossing the first, brought more agonising screams as blood ran down the young man's back and legs before pooling on the floor.

Thirty-eight times he was lashed, with a whip that had nine tails. Each time the whip landed, the tips found an unspoiled piece of flesh.

It took the youth two days to die. During his time of dying he had hours to reflect on the reason why he was here. His biggest regret was

15

the pain his mother and the rest of his family would go through when she found out what had happened to him. Every minute of the forty-eight hours was taken up with prayer, prayer that begged God for her not to see his body.

PART ONE

PART ONE

CHAPTER ONE

LONDON 2008

It was the wrong side of midnight, the wrong city, and Detective Inspector Mike Yorke was pissed off. Bad idea to leave the car at home this morning, he thought, as his feet swam in a pair of shoes he would have sworn were a good fit this morning. His dark hair was plastered to his head and hanging over his eyes. He pushed it off his forehead so he could see where he was.

'Yeah, right street,' he muttered.

Mike had been in London for a few months now and still he mixed the back streets up, they all looked the same to him. He quickened his pace and could hear his feet squelching in his shoes. Shit! Eighty-five bloody quid down the drain. He reached the steps to his flat. He was halfway up when he raised his head and saw the bundle of rags lying at his door.

'What the...?'

Angry that someone had dumped the rags on his doorstep he reached them and lashed out with a hard kick. A moment later he cringed when his foot was met with a solid resistance. With a bad feeling in his gut he bent over and quickly yanked at a damp moth-eaten blanket, dragging it down to the next step.

The security lamp, lazy since the day it had

been installed, finally decided it was time to go to work, exposing not a bundle of rags as Mike had first thought, but the body of a child. And the dampness on the blanket was not just rain. It was blood, blood that was still flowing from the large gaping slashes in the kid's wrists.

'Jesus Christ!' Shocked, Mike jumped back. Whipping his phone out he dialled for an ambulance. Phone still in his hand, he opened the door and stepped over the kid. Inside he took the stairs three at a time. Reaching the airing cupboard, he shoved the phone into his pocket, grabbed a sheet and a blanket, and hurried back outside.

He placed the kid in the recovery position, tore the sheet into strips, and quickly wrapped them round the bleeding wrists, noticing how deep the cuts were. He recoiled for a moment when he saw just how many healed scars were already on the thin arms, each vicious groove an obvious attempt at death.

To preserve what little body heat the kid had left, Mike covered him with the blanket, and got as close as he could by lying down next to him. Resting his left arm over the boy, he snuggled in as tight as he could, the bitter cold stone steps digging into his side.

Is it a him? Mike wondered.

Leaning over, he studied the pale face, then winced when he saw the deep slash marks on each corner of the kid's lips, marks that created a permanent false smile, a heinous parody of a circus clown.

'Jesus!' Overwhelmed with pity, Mike shook his

20

head. The scars looked fully healed and had obviously been there for some time. Why the hell would a kid do this to himself? He sighed, unable to tear his eyes from the terrible ruin of the kid's face.

He heard the sound of an ambulance in the distance and prayed it was the one he'd called for. Sirens were two a penny in London. It made Durham, where he lived, and Newcastle, where he worked, seem pretty quiet in contrast. A friend who had lived here for ten years had told him that soon he would be able to block them out. He figured he was getting there, but tonight there would be no chance of sleep until he found out the story behind this poor kid.

Gently he covered the boy's head with the blanket. It was a boy, he was convinced of that, although how old is the poor little sod? He shook his head. Rough guess, he could be anywhere from ten to fourteen, fifteen at a push.

A few minutes later the ambulance lit the street up with its flashing lights. 'Thank God,' Mike muttered, as he put his cheek next to the boy's lips. For a moment Mike's heart sank. There was nothing. With an overwhelming sadness, he was about to pull away when he felt a gentle caress of air against his skin. Heaving a sigh of relief he rocked back on his heels, convinced he'd done everything he could for this poor forgotten piece of humanity.

The ambulance pulled in close to them, and quickly the paramedics got the boy into it. While they worked on him, Mike took the opportunity to get out of his sodden clothes and changed into a pair of black jeans and a white T-shirt. Dumping the dead suede shoes into the bin as he passed, he went to the cupboard and found a pair of trainers.

'Amazing!' he muttered. He'd searched for the same elusive pair for over a week with no success. Shaking his head, he grabbed his car keys and hurried outside.

Running to the ambulance, he was about to hop on board when he spotted his neighbour from the flat below among the small crowd that had gathered, all of them wondering what had gone on in this quiet little back street where nothing ever happened. Where you bump into a neighbour after a couple of years and wonder when he got those lines on his face.

'Catch you tomorrow,' Mike said to the tall, bald man. He had moved into the basement flat the week after Mike had taken up residence. Keith Stotter was a friendly American from Atlanta. They had shared a few pints at the local pub and often put the world to rights when walking Keith's dog.

'OK,' Stotter said, as he gave a small wave.

They arrived at the hospital with the sirens full on. Quickly the boy was taken out of the ambulance and rushed into Casualty. Watching the trolley being pushed away, Mike looked up and noticed the ward sister staring sadly at the kid. She lifted her head and Mike caught her eye.

Walking over, he introduced himself, explained he was the one who had found the boy, and said, 'You seem to know him?'

She sighed, then smiled sadly, her chubby

cheeks dimpling. The smile stopped short of her blue eyes just before it faded. 'Yes, I know him, just about everyone in here knows Smiler... Would you like a coffee?'

'No thanks.' Mike said. Coffee wired him up to the ceiling, and by the time he got home he would need some shuteye.

The sister ushered him into her tiny office, offering him one of two seats, then said over her shoulder as she headed back out the door, 'Won't be a mo.'

Mike looked around the small space, the usual office paraphernalia scattered around – a pile of clip boards on the desk, an assortment of pens, posters on the wall proclaiming to the world the perils of sharing needles and unprotected sex. Not that anyone seems to take any notice of them, Mike was thinking, as the sister came back in carrying a cup of coffee in one hand and a cream bun in the other.

Knocking the door shut with her hip, she put the coffee and the bun on the table and sat down. 'Smiler...' She fell quiet for a moment as if choosing her words. Taking a sip of coffee, she looked at Mike and sadly shook her head. 'Smiler is the most damaged person I have ever met, and trust me, we get some damn sad cases through these doors... He was abused from early infancy. His alcoholic drug-addicted mother...' She shrugged. 'That's if you can call her a mother. I certainly wouldn't.'

Mike froze. Doors slammed shut in his head as her voice droned on. He tuned back in a few minutes later as she was saying, 'What she did to

23

that boy was unforgivable. He's been sectioned more than once for his own good. He either escapes or behaves for the recommended period of time, then he's back on the streets again selling himself to feed his habit.'

Mike tutted. 'So where's the mother now? Any other family?'

'No one. His mother's been dead seven years, an overdose. Smiler's been on the streets ever since... She... She...' The nurse shuddered, looked up from her coffee, met Mike's eyes and paused a moment before saying, 'She had been dead for weeks before anyone found her.'

Frowning, Mike asked, 'So how old is he?'

'Seventeen.'

'Good God! So the kid's been on his own since he was ten years old?'

'He's had whatever becomes available. Half a dozen council homes, ran away from them all. As for foster care...' She shrugged. 'There's not many out there with a heart big enough to take on the likes of Smiler, especially when they see his face.' She shook her head sadly. 'It sort of turns them off.'

Slowly Mike nodded. He could well understand why.

She held her hands up in a helpless gesture. 'The shame of it is, when he's stable he's such a likeable kid, not a mean bone in his body. He'll do anything for you.'

'So you, er...' Mike frowned. 'You said she'd been dead for weeks?'

'Sadly, yes. It was summer, a hot spell. They were living in a caravan. It was the smell that

24

alerted people. I shudder to think what state she was in. I was on holiday at the time.'

Grimacing at the thought of a ten-year-old sharing a home with a dead body for all those weeks, Mike went on, 'How the hell was it left so long?'

'From what I've been told, she never came out of the caravan from the day she went in until the day she was carried out. Smiler wouldn't open up to anyone. From what we could gather he'd spent his days in the library, and his nights on the street selling himself for food.'

'Jesus Christ!' Mike rapped the chair arm with his fingers, and the sister could see the anger in his eyes.

Perhaps, she thought, it's a good thing the nasty old cow's already dead.

'So how's he managed to eat since then?'

Sighing, she went on, 'The poor soul still begs. Not much else he can do, is there? In the beginning, after his mother died, he used the only way he knew to make money... He stopped selling himself when he was about thirteen, after a pretty nasty character gave him a hell of a beating. Someone found him in a dustbin, got him here just in time. He'd been in the bin for over forty-eight hours. We patched him up, a few broken ribs and a broken arm. It was the pneumonia that nearly saw him off.' She shook her head, her eyes in the past seeing Smiler's broken and bruised body.

'Jesus,' Mike muttered, more to himself than to the sister.

She nodded, 'Yes... You could actually see the

footprints on his back and chest.'

Mike's voice was rough when he asked, 'Anyone pay for it?'

Looking Mike in the eye and understanding what he meant, she said, 'Not that I know of.'

Inside Mike was seething. Whenever he heard of abused kids, it made him want to reach out and crush with his bare hands whatever depraved creature – he could never bring himself to call them human – had perpetuated the crime.

'OK... It's obvious why he's nicknamed Smiler, so what's his real name?'

She shrugged. 'No one really knows. The night he was rescued from the bin he was hand-cuffed.' She paused for a moment, then said angrily, 'The handcuffs were woven from a thorn bush.'

'What?'

'Yes, painful indeed.' She bit her lip, and sighed before going on. 'The wounds became infected. We reckon it was some sort of ritual that he'd refused to go along with.'

Becoming more angry the more he heard, Mike clenched his fists. For a moment he stared at the floor. When he lifted his head, the sister went on. 'For administration reasons, because he was not expected to live, the clown who was on duty that night gave Smiler the surname of Thorn.'

'A bit insensitive.'

She shrugged. 'Computers, they have to have a surname and a forename. That's why a lot of babies who are found in the winter get Winter for a surname, and so on... But Smiler is all he'll answer to. And trust me, he doesn't do a hell of a lot of smiling.'

Used to the brutality of the depraved, it still never ceased to upset Mike when he heard tales of such horror. He was about to ask more when the door opened and a doctor looked round. Mike and the sister both looked at him, the same question burning behind their eyes.

He smiled. 'He's going to make it.' He turned his head to Mike. 'Well done – you got him here just in time.'

Mike smiled his relief. 'Oh, great.'

Smiling back, the doctor nodded at the sister, and closed the door.

CHAPTER TWO

It was Thursday, the last Thursday that Mike would be spending in London. After nearly three months working undercover, tonight should see everything finally sorted. The last meeting had been a pure waste of time, along with the previous two. He felt like he was being led down the garden path, big time.

Mike had found out nothing he didn't already know. For the last couple of years the list of missing people, mostly teenagers, had grown out of all proportion, and lately most of the missing seemed to be connected to the A1 corridor from London to Berwick-on-Tweed.

In a typical year, over two hundred thousand people go missing in the UK alone. Quite a lot turn up, mostly teenagers, who have run off in a huff. But lately the volume, and where they were missing from, had the police totally perplexed. Not one teenager from the towns and cities up the corridor had ever been seen again.

Mike smiled as he hurried down the stairs, ten flights but damn good exercise. He was thinking of the night six weeks ago when he'd kicked what he'd first thought was a bunch of rags on his doorstep.

A few days later, Smiler had turned up at the station. Since then Mike had seen quite a lot of Smiler, enough to know he was going to miss him when he went home.

Mike walked out of the office, and Smiler was standing in his usual place, talking to an old woman who regularly fed the birds on that spot. Even in this heat she wore the red belted coat she was never without, prompting most of the officers to nickname her Little Red Riding Hood. A few half-hearted attempts to chase her over the years had come to nothing and she was now a regular feature. She knew all of the detectives by name, and, despite Mike telling her over and over that he was not a Geordie, but had been born in Durham, she still called him Geordie, insisting that them strange folk up north all sounded the same.

'Hello, Nancy,' Mike said as he approached them.

'Hello yourself, Geordie... Nice day.' She threw a handful of seeds at the birds around her feet.

'It sure is, Nancy. Be seeing you.' He smiled when she nodded at him then, as if dismissing him, turned and went on feeding the birds.

Winking at Smiler, Mike moved closer to Nancy. Shoving a ten pound note into her pocket, which he had to bend to do, he said quietly, 'For the birds, love.'

'Thank you, Durham lad,' she whispered back.

Mike laughed loudly as he and Smiler went on their way.

Half an hour later they were sat at a table in MacDonald's, tucking into cheeseburgers and fries. After spending most of the day in the library, Smiler was sounding off about wars going back as far as the thirtieth century BC. Mike was only half-listening, thinking about tonight. He'd had enough anyhow with the daft idiot who was part of the Laurel and Hardy duo in the office. He'd been spouting off all day about reports due, reports overdue, reports not finished. God, the tit thinks I'm a bloody secretary.

Then, half a dozen fries on their way to his mouth, Smiler suddenly froze.

'Choking?' Mike asked, picking up Smiler's drink to hand to him. 'Sip it.'

Slowly Smiler shook his head before saying in a hushed voice, 'Don't go.'

Puzzled, Mike frowned. 'What?'

'Don't go... The meeting tonight... The car park... The high rise one... Don't go... Please... It's a set up.'

'What the hell?'

Smiler put his head down.

Mike frowned again. No one outside of the office knows about tonight's meeting, so how on earth...? 'What are you talking about, Smiler?'

'There's a woman, a big woman with red hair,

29

wearing a red dress and red shoes.'

'And?'

'She's there... It's dangerous.'

Mike sighed. 'So where the hell is all of this coming from?'

Smiler lifted his head, looked Mike in the eye. 'You know I see things,' he answered in a quiet voice. 'I know you don't believe in what you call mumbo jumbo, Mike, but you should keep an open mind. Actually...' Smiler suddenly stopped talking and began counting his fingers as he looked furtively around.

Mike's heart sank, remembering what the doctor had said when he'd had a few words with him about Smiler. Quietly Mike asked, 'Smiler, have you been taking your medication?'

Smiler stopped counting for a moment, stared at Mike as if he was a stranger, then said, 'What?'

Mike felt a chill run down his spine. In total contrast to the warmth of the day, he shivered. The sun streaming in through the windows only made it more surreal as he repeated, 'I said, have you been taking your medication?'

'You know I have.'

'Look Smiler, I haven't got time for mumbo jumbo.' Mike held his hands up. 'OK... But you know as well as I do where it's coming from, don't you?'

'You think it's drugs.' Smiler said slowly, and barely above a whisper.

Exasperated, Mike's voice rose as he snapped, 'What the hell else could it be?'

'I've told you, I haven't done them since we met. I promised and I've kept it.'

30

Mike sighed and, as if he hadn't heard what Smiler had just said, went on, 'You promised you would keep away from that shit. You know it fucks you up.' Mike slapped his palm on the table. 'For God's sake, Smiler, don't you ever want to get better? Do something with your life instead of wasting it? Smiler, I still don't think you realise what you're capable of. You have the intelligence to do just about anything you want. You know this for a fact, you're the smartest kid I ever met... You're certainly intelligent enough to know that much more of that shit will leave you with no way back ... at all ... ever.'

'I've said I haven't touched it.' Smiler's voice was growing louder with every word until finally he was shouting. 'But you don't believe me, do you?'

Mike didn't have to say anything. His face held the absolute disbelief and disappointment he felt. Smiler had shown a marked improvement lately, but now it looked like they were heading back to square one.

'Where did you get it?' Mike demanded, vowing silently to personally rip the throat out of whichever dirty fucking creep of a pathetic arsehole dealer had coaxed Smiler back onto drugs.

Smiler glared back at him, the silence between them lengthening. Then suddenly, as if an explosion had gone off in his head, he jumped up, shouting. 'Should have known you were no better than the rest! Why would you be, eh?' There were tears in his eyes as he went on. 'Here, keep your fucking food.' He threw the half-eaten cheeseburger at Mike, and swiped everything else onto

31

the floor before turning and running out of the restaurant. At the door he looked back and, glaring at Mike, yelled, 'You'll be sorry... I hate you... Bastard, that's all you are, just like the rest of them... I should have known... I should have known. I hate you... I fucking hate you. Tosser. Just like the rest.'

'Shit.' Ignoring the curious glances from the people around, Mike wiped the tomato sauce off his shirt, dropped the napkin on the table, kicked the remains of their meal to one side in case anyone slipped on the mess, then quickly headed after Smiler.

Outside, he looked first up then quickly down the street. Not a sign of him. The pavements were crowded, people hurrying past each other in a frantic effort to catch the tube, grab a taxi or find their car and get out of the city. He hurried along to the corner, pushing past the tide of people. Still no sign of him.

'Where the hell...?' He sighed. He hadn't really expected to see him. Smiler was small enough to totally disappear in any crowd.

Tutting, he turned back. The last thing he'd meant was to hurt the kid's feelings. Christ, people have been doing that more or less since the poor sod was born.

'And now I've gone and put me big fat foot right in it. Shit!' he muttered, receiving an odd look from an old lady who picked up her pace and hurried past him.

Feeling lousy, Mike headed towards the car park. I should have listened.

Should have trusted Smiler instead of condemning him right off, damn it.

Trust me, and my fucking big mouth! Sounding off without any real proof.

I hope he doesn't do something stupid. It'll be my fault if he does, The poor kid trusted me. Must have been a flashback. It's not like I haven't seen him have them before.

He ran his hand across his thick dark hair. Tired, that's what it is I'm too damn tired.

Damaged, the sister's words echoed in his head. Smiler is the most damaged person I have ever seen.

Of course he's gonna have flashbacks.

Not paying his usual attention to what was going on around him, Mike hadn't noticed the man who had followed him out onto the street. Just another bloke hurrying home, mobile phone glued to his ear, he stepped behind Mike to cross the road.

CHAPTER THREE

What Smiler had said chewed at Mike's conscience later as he lifted his weights. Unable to concentrate, and after doing way below his usual count, he put them away and took a quick shower. His eye on the clock, he dressed – black jeans, black v-necked jumper, black leather jacket, fake gold chain, his usual drug dealer front.

Satisfied and giving his reflection a nod, he decided to get there earlier than usual, protect his back by having a good look round.

Just in case.

He laughed at himself as he went down to the car. 'In case of what?' he muttered. 'A psychic vision? Get real.' He pressed the fob that would open the car door.

Inside the car, an unmarked maroon Ford Focus, on loan to him while he was in London, he rummaged in the glove compartment, his fingers finally closing around a hard metal object. Pulling his hand out, he looked at the knuckledusters. The metal had a slight reddish colour that was more than likely dried blood. It was the first pair he'd seen in years, taken a few weeks ago off a stupid third-rate low-life dealer who'd fancied his chances. Well, the punk's learned a hard lesson.

Another junkie peddler waiting for trial. He'd turned out to be a good squealer though, and now the daft idiot expects a deal.

Fat chance!

He'd put the knuckledusters in the glove compartment to hand in. He was pleased he'd forgotten now. No harm taking precautions, especially not with this evil scum. Tonight should see them all in the bag. But there was a niggle still in Mike's mind, a niggle that said things were much deeper than they looked on the surface. A niggle that wouldn't go away, a niggle that connected this business to the other one he was working on.

He looked at the knuckledusters, shrugged and slipped them in his pocket. Not wanting to admit just how much Smiler had spooked him, he muttered, 'Won't need them.'

A whole load of nonsense, of course. Just Smiler's brain trying to rewire itself. He paused a moment before starting the car, his mind on Smiler. God, I've become so used to having him around, I'm certainly going to miss the kid.

Hope he keeps safe.

Sighing, and putting Smiler at the back of his mind, he set off and reached the high-rise parking lot nearly fifty minutes before he should have. Parking on the ground floor, he took the eight flights of stairs to the roof, the last two flights slowly and in dead silence. Keeping to the shadows he crept around the perimeter, his rubber-soled shoes making no noise, telling himself that he would have done this anyhow.

Of course I would.

Don't I always cover my back? Shrugging, he smiled to himself. Of course I do, only just not this early.

A third of the way round he heard a sound he swore was that of metal being dropped on concrete, followed by a series of profanities in a man's deep voice that, although muffled, rang a bell in his head. But no matter how hard he tried, he couldn't quite place the voice. Quickly he slipped behind a thick square concrete pillar, risked a few quick looks, saw nothing and decided it was time to move. Slowly, silently, using the cars to shield him, he wound his way to the spot the sound had come from.

Lifting his head above the nearest car bonnet he saw a man wearing a black balaclava. The man was crouching down and assembling what looked suspiciously like a submachine gun.

Christ almighty! Mike could barely believe his eyes. He ducked back down, his heartbeat up and his blood feeling like ice as it coursed through his veins. He pictured his body lying on the cold concrete floor riddled with bullets, his blood draining into the gutters.

The bastard, he sure wasn't gonna miss!

Mike looked around. The place was devoid of people, and only half full with cars, probably just arrived for a night on the town, not cars whose drivers would come from work to claim them at any minute, the rush hour being long gone.

Unless there were any unpleasant surprises, he figured that he should make it over to the gunman in twenty seconds. Not long enough for him to finish assembling the machine gun, nor long enough for the bastard to get up and run.

His body poised and ready, still scanning the space around him, he suddenly froze.

Bloody hell! he mouthed silently, his dark brown eyes wide open in amazement.

The car park had wide window spaces. Through the space opposite him he could see a huge billboard. On the billboard, posing seductively on a couch, was a woman promoting perfume. She had long red hair and was wearing a red dress and red shoes.

He felt spiders crawl down his back, but only for a moment. Turning from the woman in red, he rid his mind of her, of Smiler, and everything else. Concentrating on the job in hand, he slipped the knuckledusters on, pleased that they were a good fit. His eyes locked on the gunman who was quite calmly preparing to blow him away. He counted

36

down from five.

Twenty seconds had been a generous estimate. He reached the man, who must have become aware of Mike by a disturbance in the air and certainly not by any noise, in half the predicted time. The man turned. Bringing his fist down hard, Mike caught him behind the ear in the exact spot he intended. The man's eyes had less than a moment to register fear before they closed.

Quickly, and constantly looking around, Mike shoved all the parts of the gun into the shabby black sports holdall they had been brought in, threw it over his left shoulder, then picked the man up and none too gently tossed him over his other shoulder, before heading for the stairs at a run, thanking God as he reached the first step that they were going down and not up.

Pushing him into the front seat of his car, Mike quickly yanked the man's trouser belt off and tied the would-be assassin's wrists behind his back. Without wasting another moment he ran round to his side of the car, jumped in and, with the engine screaming, got out of there as fast as he could. The man was more than likely working alone as assassins usually did, but Mike did not intend to hang around long enough to find out. Hitting the street, the first thing he saw towering above him was the poster of the woman in red.

'No way!'

He made it to the police station car park in thirty minutes. It should have taken half that time, but he needed to assure himself that he wasn't being followed. He was tempted to go back and see if the contact turned up, though he strongly doubted he would, and he had to get this murdering bastard sorted first.

The main thought he couldn't shake was, why would some one want me dead?

What – who? – am I getting close to?

Parking as near to the door as he could, he cut the engine, then turned to the man who had been moaning and wriggling about for the last ten minutes. A hard thump in his stomach from Mike quickly shut him up.

Then Mike whipped the balaclava off.

'You! Bastard... Lying fucking toe-rag.' Mike gritted his teeth, tried to control himself, but it wasn't happening. 'Bastard,' he said again as he punched him, splitting the would-be assassin's bottom lip wide open.

The man spluttered, spitting out a chunk of flesh and half a tooth.

CHAPTER FOUR

Smiler shuffled towards Westminster, his hands in his pockets and the hood of his blue top hiding most of his face. The night was warm but he felt cold inside as well as out.

I should have known Mike was no better than the others.

Why would he be?

What was the first rule?

Trust no one.

Why have I broken it?

Why have I let Mike in?

Fool. Stupid fucking fool, that's what I am, a first class idiot for leaving myself wide open. Fool for thinking that I could have, or even deserve, a friend.

Got what I deserved all right!

They're all the same, every fucking bastard one of them, out for what they can get. The only difference between fucking Mike Yorke and the rest of them is that I just haven't found out what Mike wants yet, and now I don't want to. I couldn't care less, Mike Yorke can go to hell as far as I'm concerned, I wouldn't piss on him if he was on fire.

He knuckled water out of his eyes and hated himself for even thinking that Mike was different, for letting himself be fooled. He jumped in shock a moment later as a guy wearing a black hoodie over a white baseball cap stepped in front of him.

'Haven't seen you around for a while, Smiler... Need something to chill with? I've got the lot, just ask.'

Looking closer at the hoodie, Smiler recognised him as Snakes, a kid whose eyes were nearly transparent, but turned to a shimmering green in certain lights. He was also a thief and a liar and just about the nastiest piece of scum around. Not one person that Smiler knew on the streets liked Snakes or had anything good to say about him. Mostly he was avoided like the plague.

Smiler judged nobody – on the streets you did what you could to survive – but Snakes was way past mean. He would do you a bad turn just for the sake of it and laugh in your face. He'd dealt horse shit to kids who had never come back up, never made it back to the living hell, but who were locked forever in the burning hell that Smiler dipped in and out of, and Snakes had never batted an eyelid. Even cracked sick jokes about it. As far as Smiler and a lot of the homeless clan were concerned, if evil had a face and was walking the streets, it was Snakes.

'No, I'm cool... Thanks.' He tried to keep the wobble out of his voice, but it would have been easier to stop his heart from fluttering with fear. Feeling anything but cool, he tried to step past him, but Snakes stopped him.

'Whoa, Smiler, hang on a mo. Got some new stuff here, blow your head off, guaranteed, just down from the north. Man, is it special. Strong enough to wipe every thing else off the market.' He giggled, an insane sound that belonged behind a locked door.

'No.' Fear trickling down his spine, backing away, Smiler shook his head.

Snakes stepped closer. 'Come on... Try it... You know you want to... Need to.' He grinned at Smiler. 'Come on, touch your new friend for the readies... Good to you, is he?'

'What do you mean?'

Snakes laughed. This time it was a bitter hollow sound totally devoid of humour. 'You know what I mean. Got your self a cushy number there all right, ain't you, boy?'

'It's not like that.'

'Isn't it... Pull the other one.'

'He's a friend.'

'Yeah.' Snakes nodded knowingly.

'Fuck off and think what you want.' Surprising himself and amusing Snakes, Smiler stuck his chin out as he went on, 'Mike's a good bloke.'

'Ohh.' Snakes laughed. 'Truth hurt a little... Stop fucking kidding yourself and get wise, Smiler... Also,' he moved closer and Smiler could smell the stink of fish on his breath, 'nobody gives a fuck what you do, they're all too busy earning their own readies... Here, try this and chill. Come on man, you remember how good it is, don't you, eh, don't you? Course you do... It's not that long ago that you were fucking begging for it... I swear, man, you are seriously gonna love this. Here, have the first one on me... Go on... It's like what you've been chasing since your very first hit. The place you thought you'd never find again.'

Smiler stared at the small plastic bag in Snakes' hand. Yes, he remembered, missing days, missing nights, where the pain of living and the memories of horrendous abuse stretching as far back as I can remember, disappeared on a magic cloud. He hesitated. It would be good to forget.

To go away.

To the land of no pain.

Mesmerised by the small yellow pill, he slowly reached out.

41

CHAPTER FIVE

'You fucking dirty sly bastard.' Mike dragged the hitman up the stone steps, giving him a hefty shake strong enough for his teeth to jar together on every step. Into the police station, past half a dozen giggling prostitutes milling about, obviously waiting for their pimp to show, who would without doubt, with the help of a do-gooder, talk his way out of the thousands of pounds' worth of tax-payers money that it had taken to catch him and his stable. Then, still dragging the man behind him, he ran the gauntlet of a handful of drunks, all snarling and making threatening gestures to each other. Now that was something he wouldn't like to sort out.

Sometimes Mike wondered if it was all worth it.

'Hey there, big boy, meet you later?' a tall leggy blonde shouted after him.

Ignoring her, Mike shoved the now protesting man into a side room and left, quickly locking the door, not trusting himself to be alone with him for a moment longer.

Hurrying down the corridor he barged in to the commander's office, the door swinging behind him. Two other people were in the room, Detectives Tom Berriman and Anthony Driver. One had been a good friend, almost a brother, since they were boys with the same burning ambition. He had moved to London ten years ago and ranked with Mike. The other was not much better than the grey-haired bespectacled prat in front of him. The same prat who hid behind everyone in the department and managed to come out smiling each time he bungled things. Commander Ross Simmonds, alias Oliver Hardy.

Well, not this time, mate.

Throwing the holdall on to the desk and scattering papers every which way, Mike shouted, 'Clean sweep of the area, eh? Eh? That's what you said, isn't it?'

Commander Simmonds spluttered, but Mike wasn't letting him have the chance to say anything and wriggle out of this one.

'Nice quiet little backwater you said, decent people earning a decent living. No one will know who or what you are, a safe cover... Yeah, right.'

The commander frowned, his small square gold-framed glasses slipping down his nose, the same glasses that Mike was itching to snatch off the pompous prat's face and stamp on. 'I don't understand, Yorke, what seems to be the problem? And aren't you supposed to be out on a bust?' Shoving his glasses back up his nose, he glanced at the clock on the wall above Mike's head.

Without mincing words Mike proceeded to tell him exactly what the problem was, demanding to know, in the process, what the fuck the man who had lived in the flat below him for the last three months, the very man who had pretended to be his friend, was doing with a fucking machine gun in his possession, and lying in wait for him to show.

43

CHAPTER SIX

Smiler grabbed the bag of goodies, held them up to the light, looked at them for a moment, then slowly studied Snakes. You could tell right off that this fool was addicted to the shit he sold.

Not so long ago I would have had the same look on my face, a look of pure worship.

'Go on, man...' Snakes' eyes glittered. He knew how much Smiler had been dependent on him before, how much money he'd cost him this last month or two, when he'd somehow managed to wriggle out of the net, and just how far Smiler would have gone in past times to get his fix. Marks like Smiler, you didn't like to lose. 'I fucking promise you, kid, there's nothing like it.'

'Nothing like it, eh?'

'Yeah, man, they've only hit the streets this week, and already everybody's raving about them... Going crazy for the little yellow fuckers... Don't know how you haven't heard, it's all the buzz... Oh yes, been shacked up with your new friend, haven't you.' He sniffed loudly and wiped his nose on his sleeve.

Smiler watched, then his eyes were drawn back to the packet.

Just one. That's all, so I can remember.

One more time.

Seeing Smiler's fascination and sensing his growing weakness, Snakes went in for the kill.

'Take some for him, why don't you? Go on man, chill out together.' He threw his head back, exposing the filth in the creases of his neck, and laughed, 'You know it's not a party on your own.'

He leaned forward smirking in Smiler's face now, close enough for Smiler to see his manky green teeth and realise that's where the smell was coming from. Quickly, trying not to gag, Smiler moved his face away from the smell.

Snakes laughed, confident that this fish was hooked again, and counting the quids already. He couldn't keep the smirk off his face. He got a shock a moment later though, when Smiler threw his wares back in his face, and the bag burst, scattering the contents all over the path and into the gutter.

'Thanks, but no thanks.' Wondering where he'd summoned the courage to walk away, Smiler turned and headed quickly back the way he had come, leaving a cursing screaming Snakes to pick his goodies up out of the gutter.

I owe Mike an apology. I've been stupid, bloody stupid.

He knew that Mike didn't go for 'mumbo jumbo' as he frequently called it, but Smiler knew the visions weren't coming from the drugs. He'd been having them for as long as he could remember, and been terrified from the beginning.

He stuck his chin out, a stubborn look on his face. If Mike could only see inside my head, see what I see.

But it's because of Mike that I had the strength to walk away. Without him I would have caved, and one more hit would probably see me in a straightjacket for life.

I owe him big time.

CHAPTER SEVEN

Mike was nearly at the safe house when his mobile rang. Pulling over to the side of the road, he opened it. Caller id said 'Tony.' Mike was amazed to find he was a little miffed at his old friend. He hadn't given it much thought until now, but he'd stood there and said nothing the whole time he was in the prat's office.

'Hmm.' He put the mobile to his ear. 'Yes, it's Mike.'

'Hi, where are you?'

'Why?'

'Thought we might have a nightcap, seeing as you're leaving in the morning.'

Mike hid a sigh. It would be churlish to say no. He guessed that Tony was probably aware that he was pissed off with him. 'OK, where?'

'The Clachan?'

'Right, ten, fifteen minutes.' Mike put his mobile away and, taking the first right, headed towards Soho.

The Clachan, a quaint Victorian pub with a lot of its main features still intact, was in Kingly Street. It still had its original ornate ceiling, rich woodcarving and pretty tiles in the entrance. It was a place Mike liked to relax in. Also it had the

46

added attraction of serving real ales. When he got there he found Tony already seated at the back with two pints of ale in front of him.

On the surface Tony looked calm, his blond hair cropped close to his head, the usual pale grey suit and blue tie, always the perfect match to his eyes. He had dozens of them and demanded them for presents, and God help you if you bought the wrong shade. But Mike knew Tony well. He'd thought for weeks that something was bothering his old friend and had tried in round-about ways to get it out of him, but nothing had worked. Sitting, he picked his pint up and took a long swallow. As he put the glass back on the table, Tony said, 'So I guess that's it, then. Back home tomorrow.'

'No thanks to you.'

'Look, Mike, I did everything I could to help. You just rubbed each other the wrong way.'

Mike raised an eyebrow, 'Strange, I don't re-member you ever being in my corner, even when you knew he was wrong... Which was, come to think of it, most of the damn time.'

'You didn't know how to handle him. If I had stuck up for you in front of him, believe me, you would have been sent packing long ago.'

'So you're saying you worked behind the scenes?'

'How do you think you lasted this long? I did my best, not that you made it easy for him to like you with quips like, "How about never, is never good for you?"' Mike grinned as Tony went on, 'And "Your cry-baby whiny-arsed opinion would be?" And what about, 'This isn't an office, it's hell with

47

fluorescent lighting!"' That one made Mike wince, as Tony carried on, 'And how about, "Wait a minute, I'm trying to imagine you with a personality."' Mike shrugged. 'But the humdinger just had to be, "If I throw a stick, will you leave?"... Jesus, Mike! Simmonds has about as much a sense of humour as an upside-down tortoise.'

'Hmm. Well, all I can say in my defence is, it seemed like a good idea at the time.' He looked at Tony. A second later they both burst out laughing.

'Guess I'm better off up home... And,' he pulled a face, 'an upside-down tortoise?'

Tony nodded, 'Picture it... And I guess you are... Better back home.' He picked his pint up and took a good long drink, smacking his lips, a habit Mike remembered from their school days. Tony used to do the same whenever they got their hands on a glass of pop. Putting the glass down, Tony said, 'OK, he's a prat, you're right. But better the prat you know than the one you don't... He only got promoted to the top spot because of his connections.'

'The old boy network?'

'Something like that. One of his cousins is a count or an earl, what you might call very highly connected.'

'Huh.'

Tony shrugged. 'It's the way of the world, Mike. You should get used to it.'

'Huh.'

'Are you gonna sulk all night?'

Mike sighed. 'Guess not.' He did believe that Tony would have protected his back. They'd

48

looked out for each other for as long as he could remember, the three of them, him, Tony and Dave, the three amigos. 'OK.' He smiled, drained his pint, and put the empty glass on the table. 'It's your turn, mate.'

'Er, I don't think so, didn't I just get them in?'

'Yeah, but I've been very upset,' Mike laughed.

'You'd make a damn good conman, Michael Yorke,' Tony said, as he got up and went to the bar.

When he returned Mike said solemnly, 'So what do I tell her? You know she's gonna be hounding me for news.'

Tony frowned. Looking genuinely regretful, he said, 'Tell her I'm sorry but I will be up north soon, I promise.'

'Yeah, really?'

Tony couldn't disguise the look of guilt as he said. 'I do phone often, you know, and I never ever miss a birthday.'

Mike turned his head and looked Tony full in his face. 'It's not the same though, is it?' But the thing that bothered Mike the most was that Tony had said, 'up north', and not 'up home'.

CHAPTER EIGHT

Mike switched the TV on in the hotel bedroom. Half a dozen policemen had been sent to his flat to collect his belongings. He'd left them packed. No sense in unpacking for one night, he was on

49

the nine o'clock train home in the morning.

And personally he couldn't wait. Most of the guys down here had been pretty much all right. A couple of them had even taken him home to meet their families and provided a cooked meal, more than once. And it had been great meeting up and spending time with Tony, whose visits home lately had been rare, as well as working on the same job as him. But, like everywhere, there were always tits and prats and the commander was the biggest cock-up he'd ever met.

He laughed at himself as he channel-hopped. He watched the depressing news for a minute wondering if commentators were brainwashed to ignore anything good that ever came over the wires, instead choosing the worst shit they could find to depress the world.

He threw the remote on the bed. Inside he was still seething, though he'd never let on to Tony. Three months' work down the drain, and that bastard downstairs had my number all along.

'Nice night, just going over the common with the dog, fancy tagging along?' Mike mimicked, then growled, 'The cheeky twat... Oh, shit, the dog!'

Jumping up, he shrugged into his jacket. He'd been told to keep away from the area for his own safety, but the idea of the dog left to starve he couldn't live with. It could be days before they got round to searching the flat. He could phone it in, but the dog was no cutie that would easily be rehomed. And he knew that he would only be kept so long before they put him to sleep.

It took a few minutes to climb down the fire

escape at the back to avoid the patrol car outside, then twenty minutes to drive back to his old place. Parking two streets away in a dark patch where some toe rag had conveniently smashed the street light, he quietly made his way to the flat. There was only one house light on in the whole street, and that was an old lady who lived alone in the middle. Rumour had it that she'd been a big star in the fifties, though no one knew what name she'd used. Mike thought she'd probably started the rumours herself. She always smiled and said hello very regally when Mike bumped into her in the corner shop on a morning. She also reminded him very much of his Aunt May. Now, she would be quite capable of concocting something like that.

He reached his flat and went down the basement steps. Silently he opened the letterbox and put his ear to the empty space. He heard a snuffling then a thumping noise as Tiny's tail beat off the wall.

'Shh, boy... Get back,' Mike whispered as he straightened up. Turning sideways, he caved the door in with his shoulder. A moment later he was pounced on by one of the biggest German shepherd-cross-Irish wolfhounds he'd ever seen, his face soaked in moments by dog kisses.

'Come on,' Mike whispered, as he wiped his face with his hand and reached up for Tiny's lead from the hanger on the back of the broken door.

Two more minutes and they were in the car. As Mike pulled away, a car with three very unhappy-looking men pulled into the street. Jumping quickly out of the car, two of them ran up to

Mike's flat. The other one headed towards the basement flat.

Stopping at a twenty-four hour Tesco, Mike bought dog food, let Tiny out of the car and fed him. As Mike watched the dog wolf the food down, his thoughts turned to Smiler, wondering how to let him know he would be gone tomorrow. It doesn't seem right to just up and go. I would at least like a chance to talk to him again, maybes get him to come up north sometime for a holiday. It would be good to keep in contact with him.

Opening a bottle of water, he filled a flask top to the brim. When Tiny had drunk his fill, he walked him round the car park, noticing cars leaving and cars arriving. It seemed as if a hell of a lot of people shopped on a night. He shrugged. This was in a busy part of London. He put Tiny back in the car, where he sat regally on the front seat next to Mike. Mike opened the window and Tiny hung his huge head out. Having scanned the car park repeatedly, Mike drove off and went to look for Smiler.

He tried the Embankment first. No one had seen him for days, but Mike got the feeling that even if they had, he would be the last to know. As he was walking away from a bunch of black kids, a stunning young woman in a very short skirt and high heels, blonde hair piled Amy Winehouse-style on top of her head, pouted at him and offered him a very good time in a deep masculine voice. Mike smiled, and muttered, 'No thanks.'

'You sure, you beautiful man?'

'I'm sure.' Still smiling, Mike walked on.

Behind him he could hear the kids greeting the transvestite. 'Hi, Rita.' Mike turned his head to look at them, a hint of amusement on his face, as a police car pulled up.

A huge policeman with a barrel chest jumped out of the passenger side, as a smaller bored-looking policeman got out of the driver's side and rested his arms on top of the police car. Shaking his head, he let his chin fall on his arms.

'You bothering these kids, Rita?' Barrel-chest asked, glowering at the transvestite.

'Like you're really, really bothered,' one of the kids quipped.

Barrel-chest took a step forward as the other copper lifted his head and, catching the kid's eye, shook his head in a warning. Getting the message, the kid had the sense to back off. With a satisfied smirk, Barrel-chest turned his attention back to Rita.

Mike knew he should move on, not get involved. He had too much going on at the moment, but he'd never been able to walk away from a bully. If Rita wanted to dress like a woman that was his business, nothing to do with this Neanderthal dressed as a policeman.

'What's the matter, Mr Cop?' Rita asked, 'Trousers too tight? Dying to try a skirt on, is that it?'

'Ohh shit,' Mike muttered. 'Wrong thing to say, Rita, wrong thing to say.' He slowly started to walk back to them.

The cop leaning on the car put his head down again and resignedly shook it, as his partner launched a huge fist at Rita's chin.

53

Rita wobbled on his high heels, and the kids jeered and booed at the copper.

'That's enough.' Mike shouted as he reached them.

Barrel-chest turned, a snarl on his face. 'If you know what's best for you, you'll piss off and mind your own fucking business. This perve was about to molest these innocent kids.'

'No, she wasn't,' one of them plucked up the courage to shout, and was quickly echoed by the others.

Mike took his badge out. 'I think it's best if you piss off, don't you?'

The bored copper quickly jumped into the patrol car as Barrel-chest backed off. 'I ... er ... I was only doing my job,' he spluttered, getting into the car.

'If I ever find out that you've come back and bothered this lot again, I'll personally make sure that you're out of a job. Got it?'

Staring straight in front of him, not daring to meet Mike's eyes, he nodded as the car drove off.

'Thanks, mister.' Rita held his hand out as he rubbed his bruised chin with his other hand. 'I owe you.'

Mike took the offered hand, noticing the red manicured nails. What the hell, he thought shaking Rita's hand, if this is how Rita wants to live, then it's up to Rita.

After leaving messages again that he would be on the nine o'clock train to Newcastle in the morning, this time he was greeted with promises from all of them that they would go seek Smiler out. He tried a couple of other places, leaving

54

more messages with a lot more people that they promised to deliver if and when they saw him.

As a last resort Mike tried the hospital. The doctor on duty was the same one he'd met to talk about Smiler.

'Hi,' Mike said when they met up in the corridor. 'I was wondering if you'd seen Smiler lately?'

'No, not for a while. I'm told he popped in a few weeks ago and read some stories to the kids. Everyone was so pleased at how well he looked, actually putting a bit of weight on... I believe we have you to thank for that.' He smiled.

Mike shrugged. 'Well, actually we had a bit of a falling out today, and I have to go away tomorrow. I would hate for him to think I've just sort of abandoned him. So if he does happen to call in some time, just tell him I'm sorry. And if he ever needs me, he knows my number.'

'Of course I will. You've done so much for him that I can't see him turning his back on you over a row, he's probably gutted that you're leaving... So take care.'

'Yeah, you too.' Mike nodded then turned and walked away.

CHAPTER NINE

As Mike was finally putting his head down for a few hours sleep, three hundred miles away in a nightclub a young girl gasped, frightened. She left the nightclub in a frenzied hurry, the bouncer, (usual issue, medium height, muscles bulging, bald head, dressed in black) said a pleasant, 'Good night.'

She ignored him, moving as quickly as her huge amazingly thin heels would let her, sweat breaking out on her brow in tiny little beads. Her hair whipping around her face, and full blown panic waiting in the wings, she tottered down the road.

Tonight was not a good night!

Tonight she'd heard the whisper.

Amongst the crowds, in the dark, bodies pressed and heaving against each other, the flashing neon lights turning every move into a jerking, old-fashioned cartoon motion.

Then in the midst of the jumble, a voice she didn't know had spoken softly in her ear, a breath, a kiss, a dire warning.

The brothers were coming for her.

Fear in her eyes, she'd looked around. It could have been anyone of the dozen or so closest to her, but no one was looking her way. And she daren't ask, couldn't ask, fear had sealed her mouth. She'd barely been able to breathe, never mind speak.

Heart pounding, she reached the corner of the badly lit street. Which way... Which way to go. Left? Right?

Think... Think... For God's sake, think.

She chose to go right, not because she'd thought it through – her mind was a mess of panicked jangled thoughts, thinking straight was virtually impossible. It was slightly better lit, though, and would lead to a place she could take sanctuary in. Five yards on and the heel of her left shoe caught in the crack between the paving stones.

'Bastard,' she screamed as her foot twisted. Teetering forward she fell crashing to the path, taking the skin off her palms as well as her knees. The pain made her yell again, even though she knew she should be quiet. How am I ever gonna escape them making so much noise? Her heart was pounding so loudly in her ears she thought it was going to burst at any second.

Grabbing the shoe with both hands, her fingers slippy with blood and rain, she pulled as hard as she could, but the shoe stubbornly refused to budge. She pulled and twisted but it was stuck fast.

'Shit, shit, shit.' Tears of frustration and fright were streaming down her face now.

Why did I ever got involved?

Stupid... Stupid idiot that I am, thought I was so cool. Get in, get a story, get out.

There was only one thing she could do. Flicking her black hair out of her eyes with an irritated gesture and kicking off her other shoe, she jumped up, ignoring the pain in her scraped knees. Tattered strings of flesh dangling and blood running down her shins, she legged it as fast as she could.

She was of small build but had been a good runner at school. That was eight years and God only knew how many fags ago though, and long before she had inherited this terrible debilitating disease.

Fifty yards along the deserted street, the pavements shining with the rain that seemed to have been falling for weeks, and she was fairly feeling the strain. Chest heaving, her breath rising in clouds before her, she knew she had to slow down.

She couldn't stop though.

She daren't stop.

To stop would be the death of her.

She cut her foot on a rusty bottle top, the jagged edges going in deep. Each step she took drove the bottle top deeper and deeper into her flesh, but in her utter panic she felt no pain. She felt nothing but sheer dread. She knew what was coming for her, what the consequences would be. Terrified, she pounded along the pavement towards Mary Street.

Why the hell had did I choose Berwick-on-Tweed of all places to run away to?

Why didn't I run to London or Edinburgh, like just about everybody else does?

People have rows all the time, say things they don't mean, sometimes out of sheer pig-headedness trading insults, they run away. Families, who bloody well needs them!

She'd come up with a grand scheme to make money, when she'd heard the story. Oh yes, hadn't I just!

I should have ignored it, gone down south, that was the first plan. Why the hell did I listen to the drunken ramblings of a fool?

Only the fool had been right!

Warned to keep the secret, told what would happen if she didn't, she ignored the warnings and went about everything the wrong way, trusting the wrong people.

Now she would pay, and pay with her life if they

caught her.

Get the story, sell it to the papers, that had been the plan. She would make a good life as a journalist, show them at home a thing or two, a dream come true. Move to London, a bigger paper, a grand life. That would definitely show them.

Huh, some dream. I couldn't even get a job washing friggin' teacups on the local rag, not enough qualifications.

Wow! Like what qualifications do you need to wash a bloody teacup?

Nothing in the last year has run true.

She was running now, though. Running for her very life.

A car turned into the top of the street. 'Oh Jesus, sweet Jesus.' She was so frightened that she lost control of her bladder. Terrified and ashamed, she stood there shaking with terror, a cornered creature, knowing there was nowhere to run, nowhere to hide.

Then she gasped, a tiny flame of hope lit in her heart. It was a taxi.

'Thank you, God.'

A chance, a lifeline had been thrown her way.

'Help,' she yelled, moving quickly into the middle of the road. 'Stop... Stop.' She frantically waved her arms up and down, refusing to move out of the road.

The taxi slowed to a halt. Very near fainting with relief, she jumped in, gave her address to the driver, an oldish grey-haired man who looked like a kindly uncle, begged him to be as quick as he could, then collapsed back in the seat.

She closed her eyes and tried to control her breathing. She would be all right now, she would get away from here, as far away as possible.

Everything will be fine.

I will never even think about the brothers.

Never again!

They will be dead to my mind.

And what I know will die with me.

I am going to be fine.

She opened her eyes a few minutes later and gasped, 'Oh my God.' They were heading in the wrong direction.

'Is he fucking stupid or what?' she muttered.

'No, no... It's the wrong way,' she said loudly when she realised they were heading for Sally-port, the last place she wanted to be. 'Turn round, turn round.' Her voice rose with every word.

But the driver either couldn't hear her or was deliberately ignoring her.

The last was unthinkable.

She pounded on the glass partition with her fist, shouting now, straining her throat, that he had to turn, go back, go the other way.

'Turn around,' she yelled.

The driver increased his speed. She was flung into the corner, her face pressed up against the side window. The panic she'd felt before was coming back with a vengeance. Spotting four youths in regulation hoodies walking up the street, she banged as hard as she could on the window, screaming, 'Help... Help me. Please help me.'

Of the four, two laughed and pointed at her, a third was so far gone he was on the moon, and the other grinned evilly at her. 'Enjoy,' he mouthed as the taxi sped past them.

At the port the taxi finally stopped. She squashed herself into the corner, eyes wide and staring, her whole body trembling as the door opened and an arm reached in.

CHAPTER TEN

Evan Miller looked at his watch. 1.30 am. He glared at his friend across the round metal bar table, which was really silver plastic in disguise. The music was loud enough to deafen even the strongest pair of ears, so loud that he could feel the bass vibrating through his body. What was even more annoying were the stupid repetitive lyrics. He hated coming here. What was the point of a night out when you couldn't even talk to your mates without shouting? And the place stank of stale beer. The smoking ban had caused that, just shows how much the smoke used to mask the smell.

But something was wrong with Danny. He'd been mates with him long enough to know when something was bugging him, which really could be anything from a glass of spilt milk to England's shores being invaded by every country on the planet.

The very first day at infant school was when he'd met Danny. A lot of the other kids had shied away from him because his skin was a few shades darker than theirs, but not Danny. Danny had come bouncing over, an exact replica of the Milky Bar Kid with his white-blond hair and face full of smiles. Over the years Danny's hair had darkened to a dull gold, but he smiled just as much and still had the gift of the gab.

Evan sighed. He'd bet every thing he had that he could probably guess just what was wrong this time.

Evan counted. One, Danny was half cut by nine o'clock.

Two, he's had a face like a slapped arse all night.

Three, he only wants to come to this dive when he doesn't want to talk.

Four, put money on it, the daft sod's had a major row with Shelly.

Evan tutted under his breath as he watched Danny down the remains of his drink then stand up and stagger dangerously to the bar for a refill.

Bet he's even forgotten that I'm here!

'Knew it,' Evan said a few minutes later, as Danny, with the exaggerated care of a drunk, put one drink in front of his own seat.

'What?' Danny slurred, practically falling into the seat. Struggling to sit up, watched by a frowning Evan, he said again, 'What?'

Evan raised his empty glass, 'Drinking on your own, like?'

Shrugging, Danny put his hands in his pockets and stretched his legs out in front of him, crossing his right foot over his left and staring glumly at the floor.

'That's it, I've had enough.' Putting his glass down on the table, Evan jumped up and hoisted

Danny out of his chair.

'Oi, what do you think you're doing?' Danny slurred, as he struggled with Evan.

'We're going outside for a walk until you tell me what the hell's eating you.'

'But, but it's … it's pissh … pisshing down.'

'Good, you'll sober up that much quicker.'

'Really don't wanna go,' Danny protested, slowly shaking his head as Evan practically dragged him to the door.

Outside the rain had eased off and the fresh air hit Danny like a shock wave from a bomb blast. 'Oh, oh, gonna be sick.'

'Not over me you're not.' Quickly Evan spun him round so that he was facing the gutter.

Danny emptied the entire contents of his stomach into the drain. Then, head still spinning and muttering under his breath, he allowed Evan to steer him back into the nightclub where, thank God, Evan thought, the toilets were near the door.

Fifteen minutes later they were back outside. Danny was semi-sober and feeling lousy. Evan had practically drowned him under the sink taps, and now he was starving. 'Kebabs?' he asked, raising his eyebrows.

'Aahh… How could you, sicko? I can still smell the bloody garlic you had at tea time, even though most of it's on the way to the North Sea, or wherever the hell it goes to from the drains.' He held his hand up. 'And really, I'm not that interested before you get into detail.'

Danny allowed himself a small smile, before sighing deeply and saying, 'She didn't come home last night.'

'Thought it was something like that. Had a row?'

'Sort of.'

'Sort of?'

Grimacing, Danny headed towards a wooden bench. When they had both sat down he went on slowly, still slurring his words now and again. 'Well, you know what it's like. It's these new people she's been hanging around with, filling her head full of nonsense, babbling on about the Lindisfarne Gospels and how much more important they are than people realise. She said I wasn't interested in anything she does... Don't listen enough.'

'Do you?'

'Do I what?'

'Listen to her, thicko.'

'Not when she's babbling on about that bunch of raving loonies, and spending most of her time on bloody Holy Island.'

Evan winced. It was his girl friend Alicia who had introduced Shelly to those weirdoes, as Danny so nicely called them.

Not feeling inclined to remind Danny of this, he fell silent as a group of drunken youths appeared, all of them carrying cans of beer and swigging from them as they walked, the noise they were making preceding them. They had been amiably laughing their way along the street when they suddenly started arguing. Within moments the arguing changed to fighting. Danny felt Evan tense beside him. He put a restraining hand on his friend, who all their lives had seemed to have a compulsion about helping people. All well and good but not if it puts you in danger, was Danny's motto.

'Leave it,' he hissed at Evan.

For a moment Danny thought Evan was going to let it go. There were after all plenty of them to sort it out amongst themselves, and it looked like they were going to do exactly that, as one tall, thin lad, his blond hair spiked a good three or four inches out from his scalp, stepped forward. 'OK, Jase, he didn't mean it, come on. It's been a fucking good night...'

Suddenly Jase, who had another boy pinned on the ground with one foot on his chest and was about to kick him in his face, spun round. Before Blondie knew it there was a knife at his throat, and most of his friends, including the one on the ground, had melted away into the night.

'Hey,' Evan shouted, jumping up from the bench.

Danny groaned loudly. 'You just had to, didn't you? Eh, just leave it alone. Evan, come on.'

Ignoring Danny, Evan moved closer. 'Calm down, mate, and let him go.'

'You talking to me, mister?' The boy with the knife snarled, his features twisted in a drug-induced rage. 'Well, fuck you, and I ain't your mate...'

Suddenly he jumped back dragging the other boy with him. Planting his feet in a boxer's stance he yelled, 'Come on,' as he gestured with his left hand for Evan to move closer. 'Come on.'

Even though he felt nervous, Evan's voice was calm and slow. 'Yes, I'm talking to you, and OK,

65

I'm not your mate but he is and I'm sure if you think about it that you don't really want to hurt him.'

'What's it to you? Hu, fuck off and mind your own business, prick face.'

Evan moved forward, his empty hands outstretched in front of him, as Danny, agitated with worry that the druggie might do something stupid, shouted, 'Come on, Evan, leave it.'

'Yeah, Evan, leave it or you're next.' Grinning he dug the blade into his friend's neck – not hard enough to do any real damage, just a nick, but big enough to cause Blondie's blood to flow.

Ignoring the danger, Evan shook his head and moved closer. 'Just let him go, man. Come on, don't be daft – he can't be worth a life in the nick.'

'Evan, come on, leave it. The bastard's drugged up to his eyeballs, he's a friggin' psycho nut.' Danny was becoming more nervous by the second. After all, he thought, you hear every day of someone stopping to help people and getting their heads kicked in for their bother. And their lives are never the same again.

The extra adrenalin rushing through his system had certainly fully sobered him up and he was now thinking straight.

Evan knew Danny was right, but Blondie's eyes were pleading with him to help. He couldn't walk away and leave the lad on his own, not with this crazed fool. He'd never be able to live with himself if something happened. His heart beating a little faster, he moved closer.

That was the moment that Psycho Nut chose to

slash out with his knife.

Side-stepping neatly, Evan jerked his body to the side, but the blade caught his arm, ripping it open nearly to the bone.

'Bastard!' Danny screamed, rushing forward to defend Evan who was clutching his arm in shock. The youth, his blood lust fulfilled and in shock himself when it sank in just what he had done, backed off, then, turning quickly, ran away. His blond friend, hand pressed over the cut in his neck, followed him.

'See, see what happens.' Danny was agitatedly bobbing about. 'I'll get you, crazy fuck bastard!' Shaking his fists in the air, he screamed at the retreating figures.

He led Evan over to the bench, whipped his blue T-shirt off and pressed it against the wound. 'Sit down and don't move, promise you won't move, mate.'

Evan nodded, his eyes glazing over in shock.

'I'm gonna get help, phone from the club.'

'No, no need.' Evan groaned, the pain biting in.

'Yes, there is, mate. The blood's pouring out of you, and God knows where that blade's been. Ohh, the druggie bastard!' Danny ground his teeth together and clenched his fist, staring up the now deserted road.

'Danny, use...' Evan shook his head slowly as Danny took off before he could stop him. Pressing his arm into his body and bringing his foot up on the bench, he used his leg to keep the T-shirt in place. With his good hand he took his mobile phone out of his pocket and stared at it, wondering whether to phone an ambulance himself.

He decided not to. The ambulance service wouldn't take too kindly to being called out twice for the same incident.

CHAPTER ELEVEN

She made it across the old bridge, which had been built in 1611, and now was one way only but not, thank God, on foot. Looking frequently behind her, leaving bloody footprints, she slowed as she came to the end, looked all around, then quickly crossed the road to get out of the way of the street lights and sat down with her back against the wall in a dark corner.

Huddled in on herself she wondered again how she'd managed to escape, and prayed her luck hadn't run out. It had been luck that had made her lunge to the left, catching the smaller man unawares. In other circumstances she would have laughed at the girly scream that had come out of him when she'd bitten down hard.

She had to rest now. Her body could only take so much at a time, and she was burning up energy quickly, far too quickly. At this rate she wouldn't even get out into the fields.

Two cars came speeding across the bridge, their headlights cutting huge swathes of light in the dark. Pushing her body flat against the wall, she prayed that they couldn't see her.

Because of the angle of the jutting wall, the lights went up the outside of the wall and over her head. She remembered to breathe a few minutes later.

What a mess!

What a fucking mess!

She stared down at her bleeding feet and wanted to cry. She had never felt more alone in her whole life.

CHAPTER TWELVE

The hospital was relatively quiet, four or five sitting in the waiting area, with another three outside smoking their heads off under the No Smoking sign as the ambulance carrying Evan and Danny pulled up to the doors.

'I hate these places,' Danny muttered, jumping down from the ambulance as the paramedic helped Evan down and took them up to the reception. Giving what details he had to the receptionist, he left them to fill in the blanks as he hurried back to his waiting ambulance, which had already received another call.

As they sat down, Danny looked at the red-lit moving sign on the wall. 'Bloody hell, two hours waiting time... Shocking.'

Evan sighed. His arm was giving him pain and he felt totally exhausted, which he put down to blood loss. He could still feel it oozing out and running down his arm. 'Go home if you want,' he snapped, not meaning it to come out sounding the way it did, but Danny took no offence.

'Don't be bloody stupid, man, would you leave me?'

'Well, stop whining then.'

'Sorry.'

'We won't be that long anyhow. It's hardly bleeding at all now. Only a couple of stitches, the medic said.'

Danny grunted, then pulled his feet off the seat in front as a middle-aged woman and a younger one, obviously her daughter and sporting a spectacular black eye, sat down.

When they were settled, the younger one said, 'Mam, what am I doing here?'

'He hit you,' her mother stated with anger in her voice.

She took a moment to digest this, then went on, 'Who's got the kids?'

'Your brother's got them.'

This went on for more than an hour, the same two questions over and over. Everyone sitting there realised that the poor girl was suffering concussion, and her mind was on a loop. Finally, after what seemed the hundredth time, she got as far as. 'Mam...'

'He hit you, and your brother's got the kids,' Danny, unable to stand any more, said quickly.

There were sniggers from the waiting people, one or two belly laughs, plus a dig in the ribs from Evan.

The younger woman turned and gave him a soulful look, which made Danny feel about two feet tall, even though the mother's lips had twitched in a semblance of a smile.

Two and a half hours later, plus three stitches, they were climbing out of a taxi at Evan's flat. Danny fumbled for change as Evan, looking at the dark windows, said, 'Alicia must have gone to bed.'

'Can you blame her? It's bloody four o'clock in the morning, mate... Keep the change,' he nodded at the taxi driver.

'I'm not that friggin' hard up.' The man threw five pence at him then pulled away.

'Ungrateful sod.' Danny glared at the taxi.

Evan stared at his friend, and shook his head, 'Sometimes...'

'What?' Danny held his hands up, feigning amazement.

'Never mind. Are you coming up?'

'No, I'll see you in the morning.'

'It is the morning.'

'Yeah, see you later in the morning... Actually,' Danny yawned, 'it'll probably be tomorrow morning.' He walked away, and Evan went up to his flat.

Quietly Evan opened the door, not wanting to wake Alicia. They had decided not to worry her – after all, his injury was far from life-threatening. They just didn't hadn't thought it would take this long. He knew though that she would go spare when she woke up.

He slipped his jacket off and hung it over the side of the chair, sitting down to take his shoes off, easing his body back into the red settee that Alicia loved, and he hated with a vengeance. He sighed, and staring at the clock thought, Tonight I got off lightly.

71

Would I do it again?

Probably.

Shaking his head at his own stupidity he got up and tiptoed into the bedroom, because the floor was wood and creaked like an ancient door. Plus at four in the morning Alicia was never at her best. He reached the bed.

The empty bed!

'What?'

Dragging the quilt off to make sure, he stared open mouthed at the empty space.

CHAPTER THIRTEEN

Danny headed for home, his hands deep in his pockets, his mind on Shelly. Where the hell is she?

She wouldn't have gone home, she hates her brothers. All they ever do is boss her around all the time and treat her like a little kid.

They did, too. He'd seen it first hand. Got to admit that Liam's all right, and a good laugh at times but Gary, nothing but a pain in the arse.

The other two brothers were married with their own families now, but they all still did what Gary said. Danny knew that they had, in all fairness, brought her up when their parents died. Really they were just being overly protective, but Shelly couldn't see that. She would do her own thing, whatever the cost.

There was a wooden bench outside the flat.

Sitting down, he pulled out a crumpled packet of cigarettes, lit up, watched the blue-grey clouds swirl from the glowing tip in the breeze that had sprung up from nowhere. Then stared at the sky, which was becoming lighter by the second. Pretty soon the early morning workers would be heading off to their daily grind.

He silently thanked God that he and Evan had another three days' holiday left. The way he felt today, work would have been impossible.

He shook his head and puffed air out of his cheeks. They should have gone abroad. A few years ago they would have been on the plane and away.

Bloody women!

Complicate everything. 'Cos they couldn't all get their holidays at the same time, me and Evan are denied our annual trip abroad. No lying on the beach this year for us, slyly watching the topless babes.

Blackpool, Alicia had suggested. A weekend even, as a last resort, just for a break, she'd argued.

Last resort all right. Who the fuck wants to go to Blackpool? Full of rampant teenagers, screaming kids and the bloody blue rinse brigade.

Finishing the cigarette, he stamped it out and was about to get up when he was suddenly flooded with longing for Shelly. His body sagged. He flopped back on the bench, the longing becoming an actual pain.

I should have listened more, not been so bogged down by work. Gotta find her and tell her that I do love her.

A ring! That would make her really happy. Doesn't mean that we have to get married – well, not for a good long time anyway. A long engagement. Yeah, he nodded, smiling to himself. That would be good. As long as possible. Ten years? Maybes. I could live with that all right, lots of people have really long engagements these days.

'I do love you, Shelly,' he muttered to the newly emerging buttercups on the grass verge.

Should have been saying it more often!

Really should have.

Whatever we fell out over, it's all my fault.

Gotta be!

Slowly he nodded his head. He would look for her today, even if it meant going back to Durham and facing her brothers. But first he would try those flaming weirdo friends of hers. His eyelids began to droop. His last thought before falling into a deep sleep was, find those weirdoes.

PART TWO

CHAPTER FOURTEEN

DAY ONE

Danny was woken up a good hour and a half later by the milkman vigorously shaking his shoulder. 'Wh...?' he muttered, opening his eyes. The sun was just coming over the rooftops. He blinked, wondering where he was, and shivered.

'Somebody nick yer shirt, son?' the milkman asked, noticing the blood on Danny's jeans, but saying nothing.

He knew the young man well enough, having passed the time of day with him more than once, but in this day and age it paid to be careful. Far too many nutters around. He stepped away, closer to his cart, one leap away if needs be.

But he needn't have bothered. The guy was his usual amiable self. 'No, no, my friend got in some bother last night, you know how it is... Never mind, I'm going in... Bloody freezing.'

'Yeah, you do that before yer catch yer death, sunshine. It's a bit nippy this morning all right.'

Danny hurried up to the flat, his teeth chattering all the way. His mouth tasted like a dead rat had taken up residence in there, and he could murder a cup of coffee. He also needed about twenty-four hours or more sleep before he could even hope to feel like a human being again.

Opening the door quietly, he crept inside in

much the same way as Evan had done a couple of hours ago. Then he remembered there was no need, Shelly wasn't here.

'Unless,' he muttered, ever the optimist. With hope rising, he thought, she could have come home last night. Yeah, she might have. And at the end of the day I can't really remember what the hell she was gone for.

'Well, she could have,' he argued with himself, then quietly, full of hope, he opened the bedroom door, ready to jump on the bed.

'Oh, yes! Shelly babes,' he yelled, seeing a mass of black hair spread out on the pillow. 'Shelly, I'm sorry, it was all my fault. What ever it was, I didn't mean it. I'm sorry... I'm sorry, sorry, sorry... Here I come, babes.'

With a grin wide enough to split his face in half, he crossed the small space in four strides, cast off his shoes and yanked the quilt off, his grin by now even wider. 'Shelly, oh Shel–'

The quilt slid out of his suddenly slack hands and fell in a crumpled heap on the floor. Danny gasped. His jaw hung open; not believing what he saw, he blinked rapidly and started to tremble. His lips moved, no no, no, but there was no sound. His vocal cords were frozen in shock.

Shelly's naked body was covered in blood. Her hair was hanging over her face, partially obscuring it, and what could be seen was hardly recognisable. Every single inch of her was red, as if she'd been painted the colour of death. He looked at his hands, covered in blood from the quilt. Forgetting that he had no T-shirt on, his whole body shaking in horror, he wiped his hands across

78

his chest, leaving large red swathes.

'No,' he yelled loudly, finally finding his voice and backing away from the bed, then 'No,' again before turning and running out of the bedroom. Practically in free fall, he made it down the stairs. His hands still slippy with blood, he struggled a moment with the lock. Then he was outside.

He ran in a blind panic along Mary Street, bumping into early morning shoppers, scattering parcels of newspapers. A bakery delivery boy cursed him as a tray of pies hit the pavement, but Danny was oblivious to everything and everyone around him except the fact that Shelly was dead. He carried on shouting over and over, 'She's dead, she's dead.'

Fearing this half-naked, barefooted screaming madman careering along the street yelling his head off, people scattered out of his way. He saw none of them. His eyes were full of blood, his mind was full of blood.

CHAPTER FIFTEEN

She couldn't go on, no matter how terrified she was. She had to stop, or collapse in this field miles from anywhere, to be found God knows when, after dozens of crawly slimy creatures had feasted at her body. The mental picture of it stopped her in her tracks. She shuddered and felt sick. Gagging, she headed slowly towards a fallen tree.

79

Shaking with fatigue, she sat down and took her Nova pen out. After a moment staring at the pen she hated, but knew was much better than the needles she'd once used, she dialled five units less than usual, then injected the insulin into her stomach. Quickly she threw four fruit gums into her mouth, but almost at once she knew it wasn't enough. Sweating profusely, her hands shaking, she managed to get another three sweets into her mouth when she'd swallowed the first lot. Then to be on the safe side, she popped another two. She still had a long way to go, and eyed the half-packet that was left with dismay.

She knew she wouldn't make it without food.

She had walked most of the night. Kept to the fields as much as possible, ducking every time she saw the headlights of a car or lorry, fearing a heart attack at any moment the way it pounded in her ears each time she saw a light or heard something in the field.

'Oh God.' The information she carried in her head weighed heavily. She had to get to safety so that she could pass it on. Everyone should know about this, but until they did, nothing would be done, these people would go on forever.

She knew that she would have to be even more careful now that it was full light. She needed a phone box. There were two or three small villages within the next couple of miles. At least one of them should still have a working public phone. With a deep sigh, and dredging up a wealth of determination – a lot of people depended on her without them even knowing it yet – and keeping close to the hedgerows, she plodded on.

CHAPTER SIXTEEN

After jumping on the train at the last minute, disappointed that Smiler hadn't turned up to at least say goodbye, and having shown the train guard his badge and assured him that Tiny was a well-behaved police dog, Mike found a seat in economy.

Thank God, he thought, after pushing Tiny as far under his seat as he could get him, which wasn't very far – fully half of him was touching the facing seats. Three hours to Durham was a long time to stand in the corridor.

Shaking his newspaper out, he settled himself down for the journey, wishing that he'd driven down in the beginning. He hated long train journeys. He felt captive from getting on the train to getting off, and would much rather travel by car.

A few minutes later he decided to take his jacket off. Even though it was lightweight summer wear, he knew he would be more comfortable in his shirt sleeves.

At last the train pulled away and he scanned the rest of the carriage. Pretty full for this time of day, holiday season, families desperate to get out of the big city, see a bit of green. Although he had to admit London had surprised him in that respect, more grass around than he had ever thought. In more ways than one, of course. Apart from this three-month stint, the only other time he'd been to London had been a school trip.

A young mother with three kids under five, all, the mother included, dressed in yellow T-shirts, caught his eye. The kids were reasonably well behaved so far, occupied as they were with drawing paper and colouring pens. He wondered how far up the line they would get before pandemonium broke out. The mother had piqued his interest because she reminded him of Kristina Clancy, same short dark bob and large brown eyes. He'd worked with Kristina on a few cases. They'd even had something going once. It had petered out though, probably due to the pressures of the job. They were still friends, although she had moved further north and married someone called Timothy Mears, or Myers, he couldn't remember. He'd never met the bloke anyhow. The last he'd heard Kristina was somewhere on the edge of Scotland.

Relegating Kristina to the back of his mind he opened his newspaper. The first thing he saw was a full page advert for perfume, the girl with the red hair and red dress smiling out at him. He'd also noticed her on just about every billboard in the city on his way over to Kings Cross.

Well, that just about explains that, he thought with a slight smile. Of course, the other business, that was just Smiler's mind hyperacting again.

He knew he would miss the kid, and didn't even want to admit to himself how disappointed he was about Smiler not turning up at the station to see him off.

Although in all fairness he may not have got the

message, in which case he might phone. Though it had struck him at the time that Rita was so grateful, she would scour the earth to pass the message on. The main thing was that Smiler had promised that he would never again under any circumstances attempt to take his own life, and that drugs were a thing of the past. Whether these were promises he could keep or not remained to be seen, but Mike believed that Smiler would try. All he'd ever wanted or needed was someone to give him a chance. At least he'd managed to keep off the drugs for the longest time in nine years, the poor bugger had been smoking dope and dipping into his mother's other habits before he was even eight years old. Yesterday must just have been a flash back, and I certainly handled that all wrong.

He sighed inwardly. If there was some way that he could go back and find the creeps who had used Smiler, Mike would see that they would be behind bars for life, each one of them with a severe chronic complaint, after he'd dealt with them himself, of course. But with Smiler's mother dead there was no way of knowing who or where they were, nor even just how many of them there had been. No one to even ask, as most of those years were blocked to Smiler, his mind doing him a great kindness by closing over the worst of it. But sometimes, mostly when it was least expected, Smiler's eyes would cloud over. Mike would know that a breeze had lifted the curtain at the edges and Smiler was peering into the abyss.

Looking up as the train pulled into York, he heaved a sigh of relief. Good, not long for home now. He patted Tiny, whose behaviour had been brilliant. Obligingly, the big dog had let anyone who cared to pat him, and revelled in it.

The yellow T-shirt family got off the train, the two smallest having fallen asleep as they were closing in on Peterborough. Thank God, Mike had thought, as he'd watched their lids start to droop. Their chattering had begun to get on his nerves.

Out of habit he scanned the train again, his eyes flitting back to a passenger who had held the newspaper up to his or her face for the whole journey. Mike frowned as the train pulled away.

His curiosity piquing as they neared Darlington, Mike got up and headed for the toilet, his feet poised and his left hand clenched just in case an undesirable hid behind the print. He managed as he came next to the seat to take a look over the top of the newspaper.

'I knew it.' He yanked the paper out of Smiler's hands. 'What the hell do you think you're playing at?'

Smiler grinned at him. 'Time for a change?'

Hiding his pleasure at seeing him, Mike pointed back to his seat. 'Get over there.'

CHAPTER SEVENTEEN

Smiler did as Mike told him. Grabbing his newspaper, and the remains of the can of Diet Coke that he'd nursed for the whole journey, he moved to Mike's table. Hesitant at first when he saw the huge dog looking up at him, gently he patted the dog's head as he eased into the seat. Tiny rested his head on the seat next to Smiler and watched him.

'Shift,' Mike said when he came back. 'I can't bear to travel backwards. Bad for the sinuses.'

'Er, who told you that?'

'Move it.'

'OK, OK.' Smiler hastily changed seats. 'Is, er ... is he all right?' He jerked his head in the direction of Tiny, who had turned round and, still watching Smiler out of one eye, was resting his head on the other seat.

When Smiler was settled, Mike said, 'Actually, he'll have your hand off as soon as look at you. So don't give him an excuse.' Smiler recoiled, and the look on his face made Mike laugh.

'Just kidding, he's a great chap. Say hello to Tiny.'

'Tiny!!!' At the sound of his name, Tiny wagged his tail and snaked his tongue out to lick Smiler's hand. 'You never said you had a dog.'

'Never said I didn't... Anyhow, it's a long story. OK, so what do you have to say for yourself?'

For a moment Smiler just looked into Mike's eyes, then he blurted quickly, 'First off, Mike, I'm sorry.' Smiler nodded. 'I didn't think things through before I blew. I should never have...' His voice trailed off as he sighed.

'So you came all the way up here to say that?'

When Smiler didn't answer, Mike went on, 'Well, for what it's worth, so am I.' He touched the back of Smiler's hand, the only contact Smiler would allow from anyone. A nod and the

85

hint of a smile let Mike know that they were friends again.

'I'm not going to take the huff again, Mike, honest, I know you can't help but say whatever's on your mind like you always do.' Smiler shrugged. 'You're a good man Mike. I just wish... I wish I'd met you a few years ago.'

Mike swallowed the lump in his throat, knowing how hard it was for Smiler to talk about personal stuff, even though he could ramble on forever about anything else.

'I only did what anyone el–'

Smiler stretched his hand across the table, his fingertips just touching Mike's hand. Interrupting him he said, 'No, Mike, if you hadn't helped me I would be worm food by now.'

Mike sighed. He believed that everyone deserved a fair chance in this life. The trouble was, countless thousands, perhaps millions, never got it. 'All right, let's just let it drop now, eh, kid, and agree to disagree on the mumbo jumbo stuff.'

Smiler nodded, sighed his relief. 'Yeah, OK... By the way, I had a dream.'

'Oh, bloody hell.' Mike tutted, looked at the ceiling, then back at Smiler. 'Not the voices again.'

'No, listen, Mike. You're heading into danger, real, real danger, they told me. It was black, all black, hard to see at first. There's water though, I know that much... A lot of water!'

Mike frowned at him. 'Well, it would be wouldn't it?'

'Sorry?'

'Hard to bloody well see, if it was all black!

How many times have I told you, all this crap is just your imagination working overtime... That and the shit still rattling around in your brain... You should write flaming fiction. Look.' He opened his newspaper and pointed at the woman in red. 'She's all over the friggin' place. You couldn't help but see her... And the only water in Durham is the bloody River Wear, and I can't remember a time when it's burst its banks.'

Smiler looked at the advert and shrugged. He'd seen the poster all over the place this morning and had made the connection, thinking that the poster must have been easy to spot from the place where Mike had been in danger. It proved a point to him, but he knew Mike would see it differently.

Looking Mike in the eye, he went on adamantly, 'Pretty soon you will be involved with something way too dangerous. And it won't be in Durham... Oh, and the Wear did burst its banks, one night in November 1967. That was before you were born, though. It's all on record.'

'Well, I needed to know that.' Mike gritted his teeth. Sometimes he felt like strangling the kid. 'And in case you hadn't noticed, danger comes with the flaming job, Smiler, or haven't you realised yet I'm a fucking copper? Danger's the name of the game. It says so on the contract.'

Smiler's lip twitched, then he said, 'Duh... Of course I know that, but I couldn't let you go into this frightening business without knowing the danger.'

'Knowing what, for God's sake?' Mike demanded, going on without giving Smiler a chance to answer. 'You see, that's half the problem, you never seem to know what, do you? And guess bloody what else, Smiler, there's danger everywhere. You're in danger crossing the bloody roads, man.'

Smiler sat back and frowned. 'You saved my life Mike. In some cultures, that makes you responsible for it.'

'Yeah, does it now?'

Smiler nodded solemnly.

'OK, let's just make sure you don't let me down and turn into an axe murderer or worse, 'cos I'll have you.'

He was rewarded with a half-smile, before going on, 'And if it's my life that's in danger, kid, how the hell does that involve you and the half-dozen passengers you carry around in your head?'

'Cos I'll be with you.'

'No you won't, sunshine, trust me. You're on the next train back to London.'

Smiler crossed his arms. 'No way, mate. Too hairy down there now.'

'What do you mean?'

'You should know, Mike, there's some new shit just hit the streets.' Smiler looked at him in earnest, pleased that he had something concrete to tell him. 'Oh yeah, and it's coming from the north.'

This tied in with what Mike was working on. Frowning, he asked, 'So what do you know about this new gear?'

Briefly Smiler told Mike about his encounter with Snakes and the yellow tablets. 'And that's all really, I er ... I threw it at him and ran like hell.' Smiler put his head down, ashamed to admit that he'd run.

'No, no, Smiler. Trust me, you did the right thing.'

'No I didn't. I should have found out more.'

'You're too vulnerable at the moment, mate, to take risks like that. You really did do the right thing... I'm proud of you.'

Smiler lifted his head, his eyes shining. His words full of awe, he said, 'Honest, you really mean it? You're proud of me?'

Nodding, Mike said, 'I am, kid. It took some guts to walk away.'

They both became quiet as the train pulled into Durham and they were greeted with the magnificent sight of the castle and the cathedral.

'Wow,' Smiler said.

'Yeah, always gets me like that. You should see it on a night when it's lit up, from here the view is fantastic... I know I'm home when I see it.'

Spotting the trolley attendant making her way up the aisle, Mike asked, 'Want a fresh can?'

'Oh, yes please.' Smiler nodded vigorously.

'Crisps, choc bar?'

He nodded again.

A minute later, fresh can of pop in hand, and after a long thirsty swallow, he said. 'Did you know that the castle was begun in 1072 as a defence mound by William the Conqueror? Then various bishops over the years added to it. The cathedral was begun in 1093, took around forty years to build, and really was built as a shrine to St Cuthbert. It's also the best preserved Norman building, probably in the whole world.'

Mike continued to stare at the castle and

cathedral as they pulled away. What the hell can I say to that?

Plus Mike wasn't always sure if Smiler was spouting the facts to him, or trying to educate the passengers in his head. It was eerie the way Smiler spoke when he recounted anything he'd read.

The kid was always right, though. Never in his life had he known anybody soak up facts like Smiler. He'd used reading as a way to escape from the living hell he'd been born into, spending most of his time, when not earning on the streets, in the library. He'd devoured every single word he came across, and frequently spewed them right back out to anyone who cared to listen and just as frequently to those who didn't.

They were nearly at Newcastle when Mike's phone rang. 'Yes, this is Mike,' he said, then went quiet as his frown got deeper. 'OK,' he replied a few minutes later, 'I'll stay on till Berwick... Right, got it.' He snapped his phone shut and, still frowning, tapped his fingers on the table.

Getting Mike's attention by doing a little tapping of his own, Smiler raised his eyebrows in a question.

'OK, here's what we do. Instead of getting off at Newcastle, we're going on to Berwick on Tweed... It seems that a young woman's been found dead in the flat she shared with her boyfriend, in the middle of town.'

Smiler shivered, and said quickly, 'She's got black hair, Mike. I know she has... Bet you any- thing you want to bet. That her hair's black.'

'Stop it right now, Smiler. See, this is what I

90

mean, you go off half- cocked and there's what, a one in three or four chances that she's got black hair? Now if you said she has pink hair with tartan patches and silver trim on the ends, and it turns out she has, then I might start to believe.'

Smiler shrugged as Mike went on. 'I have an Aunt May, she lives on Holy Island and takes lodgers in. I often pop up for the odd weekend. It's where I grew up, with Aunt May. Sometime today we'll get you settled. That's if she's not full up with tourists. Until then you'll have to hang around outside the hospital, or wait in the car, whatever.'

'I can look after myself, you know,' Smiler mumbled, staring at the magnificent coastline as the train headed further north. 'Whatever you might think.'

Mike sighed. 'Smiler, it might not have sounded like it, but I really am happy to see you.'

This seemed to please Smiler. Although he brought his head to the front and kept it down, Mike could see the glimmer of a smile.

'Are you really?' Smiler asked quietly.

And the truth was, Mike really was glad to see him. Smiler had grown on him like a second skin, though, he thought, how the hell I'm going to explain him, God only knows.

He nodded, and relaxing, Smiler tore the wrapper off his chocolate bar and settled back in his seat.

'Oh, one more question,' Mike said, 'How did you know which train I would be on?'

'Rita.'

'Rita!' Mike laughed.

91

'Apparently she trawled the whole of London looking for me. She found me at five o'clock this morning.'

'Ha, well, it's true what they say then, isn't it... One good turn deserves another.'

'Oh yeah, you're definitely her hero.'

'Well, there you go. Us heroes can't be picky,' Mike replied, and laughed as he picked his newspaper up. As he turned to the page he had been reading, Smiler put his hand on the paper. 'One other thing, Mike.'

Mike frowned. He could tell by Smiler's tone of voice that he was not going to like what was coming next. 'Go on.'

'For the last few days there's been what I can only call a countdown number in my head.'

'A countdown number?'

'Yes... It started a few days ago, this huge burning number, number five. Then yesterday number four... And today it changed and jumped to number three.' He sighed. 'I think it's a countdown. I think it means you have three days left.'

'Three days left for what?' Mike couldn't help it – he shivered inside. Listening to Smiler was like listening to an age-old prophet of doom.

'To save a lot of people. Rita thinks the same.'

'What... Rita?'

Smiler nodded solemnly. 'Yeah, Rita. She sees things as well.'

Mike shook his head. 'God help us all.'

CHAPTER EIGHTEEN

Jill Patterson stood with her hands on her hips, her lips pursed and her brow furrowed. She was staring down at the body on her mortuary slab. She was puzzled, to say the least. Never before had she ever seen anything like this. Something was nagging at her though, right in the corner, scrunched up where she couldn't get hold of it, like someone's name you half-remember that keeps slipping away and disappearing back into the mist.

Recently moved from Birmingham to Holy Island, Jill was a thirty-five-year-old divorced mother of two girls. A petite natural redhead, with large green eyes that could wither any opponent who cared to take her on. Especially a man. She would go more than the extra mile to prove her point against a man.

Still not over her bitter divorce, it was rumoured she hated anything in trousers. She did, however, possess a sense of humour and had that rare ability to be able to laugh at herself – most of the time. Lately, even that seemed to have deserted her.

She heard the brief knock, then the door creaking open, and glanced round, annoyed that her concentration had been broken. She frowned at the tall, handsome, dark-haired man who walked in.

93

'Hello. Detective Inspector Mike Yorke,' Mike said, moving quickly forward with his hand stretched out to shake hers. 'You must be the lovely Jill Paterson I've heard so much about.'

Please, she thought, but said a confident, 'Yes,' as she held her gloved hand out, palm up.

She'd heard about Michael Yorke, and on first glance most of what she'd heard was true. He's certainly a looker, but is he the good, decent bloke they say he is? One thing for sure, he's certainly full of himself.

Anyhow, she strongly doubted that he was as good as people said. None of them ever are. Scratch the surface and men are all the same. Three meals a day, a shag when it suits them, and that's only if any of the rest aren't available.

When she'd found out that her ex-husband had a veritable harem, it had broken her. It had taken her cousin Billy to take control and pick up the pieces. He'd suggested the move north and so far she loved it. The island was fantastic, so much history, and the locals were all very friendly.

'Oh, right,' Mike said, taking in the gloves. He dropped his hand and moved to the far side of the table. Looking down at the body, he slowly shook his head. A pretty girl, her black hair resting on her shoulders emphasizing her paleness. He guessed early twenties, and wondered what her story was. Too young though, he thought, whatever it was, far too young. Dead before the poor soul's even had a chance to live.

'Can you tell me how?' he queried, looking for any marks, bruises, knife wounds, but could see nothing. Her throat was clear, so she definitely hadn't been strangled. In fact she looked nothing more than as if she was peacefully asleep, though her lips seemed to be stretched into a tight grimace. Puzzled, he swung his head to Jill.

She turned to a drawer in the long wall cupboard behind her and pulled out a pair of opaque rubber gloves. Handing them to Mike she said, 'Put them on, and help me turn her over.'

Doing as he was told, with a slight lift of his eyebrows, Mike put the gloves on, and together they turned the dead girl onto her stomach.

'You've done this before?' Jill asked, though it was more of a statement than a question. In her experience most of the coppers would look but didn't like to touch.

'Once or twice.' Mike replied, wondering why she was such a prickly pear. The gossip is that she's a man-hater. There has to be a reason, she's a damn good-looking woman.

He turned his attention to the corpse. 'Oh, Christ.'

'Hu, sort of.'

'What do you mean, sort of?' Mike practically whispered, unable to take his eyes off the horrendous mess in front of him. He had never in all his working life as a police officer seen anything like it. Bodies pulled out of the water after a week slow-waltzing with a dozen crabs didn't come close.

'The poor girl's been scourged.' Jill pointed to the bruised wrists. 'Some incredibly depraved, evil thug has hung her up by her wrists to a post or wall. Then whipped her from the top of her arms, down her shoulders and back.' Slowly

95

Mike's eyes followed the pointing finger. 'Across her buttocks, then down the back of her legs and calves and carried on all the way down to her heels.'

After a moment's silence contemplating what the poor young woman on the slab must have gone through, though he was hard pushed to even try to imagine it, he said, 'What are these?' Mike pointed to one of the many two-inch-long white ribbons of flesh hanging just about everywhere.

'Muscle.'

He'd half-guessed that's what they were, and had the crazy thought that no way could she be comfortable lying on that mess.

He looked up at Jill. 'What sort of madman would do such a thing? The agony she must have gone through... It's... It's so, so friggin' well unbelievable.' He shook his head in angry bewilderment, shuddering at the thought of the poor woman writhing in pain. Gritting his teeth, he silently vowed to drag whoever was responsible to the real justice he deserved, and not just a slap on the wrist, and a few years behind bars in a cushy jail.

'I don't think,' Jill said after a moment, 'that the scourging is what killed her. In fact she may have been – actually, the more I think about it, she probably was – dead after the first lash.'

Mike gave her a puzzled frown. 'So what?'

Jill looked steadily at him for a moment, took a deep breath, then went on. 'When the body first arrived here, her front was covered in blood, even though as you've seen, there's no wounds at all on the front of her body. If the blood flowed from the back of her, there would have been flow lines, but the blood was evenly spaced from her scalp down... It's my opinion that she bled out of her sweat glands.'

'What?' Mike looked at Jill with disbelief. 'Surely that's impossible.'

'No, it's called hemathidrosis. I was puzzled for a while until I remembered reading about it.'

'Hema what?'

'Hemathidrosis. There's only about a dozen recorded cases, and it's only seen in someone who has undergone absolute tremendous stress and agony. In hemathidrosis a person actually bleeds from every sweat gland in their body.'

Mike was quiet for a long moment, visualizing what must have happened. 'So what would you say she exactly died from – the scourging, or the hema-what's-it?'

'Fright. Pure utter fright.'

Mike digested this, vowing even harder to find the monster responsible for this atrocity. 'OK, then, is there anything else you've found out?'

'I'm not finished yet.' She looked at him, her green eyes unblinking, leaving it up to him when he wanted to come back.

'Tomorrow?' he questioned with a raised eyebrow. 'Will that be all right?'

She nodded, then turned to one of the drawers in her wall cupboards, dismissing him.

Mike raised his eyebrows, OK, it was her domain. He wanted to get started on the boyfriend as soon as possible anyhow. 'Oh, the girl's family are coming up to give a formal identification, some time this afternoon, if that's all right with you?' he asked, but thought, damn tough if it isn't.

She shrugged. Without turning round, she said, 'I'm not going anywhere.'

'Bye then.'

Covering the body up, she muttered something that could have been goodbye, or might just as easily have been, fuck off. Judging by her attitude, Mike wouldn't have been the least bit surprised if it was the latter.

He shrugged, and with a small smile turned and left her to her own devices.

CHAPTER NINETEEN

Outside, Mike found Smiler sitting on the wall, his hands under his thighs, and his legs swinging. Tiny's lead was hooked onto Smiler's right foot. Sitting down next to him, and ignoring the enquiring look from the WPC in the waiting patrol car, Mike waited for the inevitable question. He didn't have long to wait.

'She's got black hair, hasn't she?'

Staring at the police car, Mike sighed, then turned to Smiler. 'Yes, she's got black hair. But answer this one, if you're so clever – how did she die?'

'Judging by the amount of blood that I saw, she must have bled to death.' Smiler nodded his head with conviction, then looked grim-faced at Mike.

Mike was quiet for a moment, digesting what Smiler had said about the girl bleeding to death, which was in fact basically what had happened. Then he came back with, 'Well, there you go, then, Smiler. Most people who are murdered, unless poisoned or strangled, do bleed to bloody death.'

'So there was a lot of blood? More than normal, would you say, Mike?'

'I suppose so...' He glanced back at Smiler, sighed, then said, 'Give me one of your fags.' Mike smoked rarely, so rarely he never thought about buying any, just borrowed the odd one now and then. Smiler handed him a cigarette along with his lighter, and waited patiently until Mike said, after lighting up and taking a deep draw, 'The poor woman was scourged.'

Smiler looked at Mike with horror. For a while he just stared at him, then he said in a hushed voice, 'Do you know exactly what happens when someone is scourged? Do you, Mike? Do you really know?'

'Well, after the friggin' mess I've just seen, you can guarantee I have some idea. But I bet you can fill in the blanks.'

Taking that as an invitation, Smiler went on, 'Historically a scourging consists of thirty-nine lashes with a wooden-handled whip of about eighteen inches long, with nine leather thongs about six to seven feet long. At the end of each thong is a piece of lead shot, and attached to the lead shot are pieces of sheep or cattle bone. The idea behind this is that the lasher, snapping his wrist in a certain way, causes the weight of the lead shot to dig into the flesh, while the sheep bone digs in under the surface, and literally lifts small shards of skeletal muscle about two inches long.'

In his mind's eye, Mike saw the ribbons of white muscle hanging from the girl's body. 'Oh, my God.' He actually felt sick. He shook his head as he puffed air out of his cheeks.

'Well, yes, because in the Bible it states that Christ was scourged. Then he bled through his sweat glands as he carried his cross.'

'Hmm. That's what she meant.'

'What?'

'Never mind.' Mike looked at Smiler, at his under-developed body that had, in the last few months, definitely put some weight on. But he still had the body of a scrawny twelve-year-old, and Mike wondered just how much knowledge was in that head of his. Sometimes it was like listening to a college professor spouting off about his favourite subject. Smiler repeated word for word everything he'd read, and rarely in the voice of a seventeen-year-old street kid.

Smiler nodded solemnly at Mike.

After a moment, Mike said, 'You sure you're not a fifty-year-old dwarf?'

Smiler laughed, a rare event that brought a smile to Mike's face.

'Come on, sunshine. Let's get you sorted. You have yet to meet the great, the funny, the fantastic Aunt May.'

'Are you sure she knows I'm coming?' Smiler asked, the smile gone and a hint of nervousness in his voice. He was never keen to meet new

100

people. He could often see the horror on their faces when they looked at him.

'Told you, I phoned her. She's looking forward to meeting you. She'll be cooking something special. Not that everything isn't special, she's a great cook... And I think you'll love the island. Now come on. I've got stuff to be getting on with.'

They got into the car, unaware that they were being watched, although Smiler shivered and gave Mike an odd look that he missed entirely. He was too busy flirting with the blonde WPC.

CHAPTER TWENTY

About the time Mike and Smiler were heading towards Holy Island, a meeting was taking place in London. In a high-rise apartment on Canary Wharf, eight men sat around a table. Two European princes, an American military leader, a Russian billionaire – though they were all billionaires in their own right – a French count, a Swiss banker, an African leader and an English nobleman.

The apartment was luxurious in the extreme; dealing in flesh paid highly indeed. Cream carpets so thick that you sank into them with each step, cream walls hung with colourful paintings by old masters that most of the world didn't even know existed. It suited these men to carry on the rumour they had started many years ago, that the Vatican had it all.

Cut-glass ornaments in blood red were scattered around the room. Three Jacuzzis, two hot tubs on the verandas, stocked with everything a man could want. Here you were waited on by slaves, willing and unwilling – the unwilling beaten into submission, then plied with drugs to make them as complacent as the willing.

The apartment belonged to the English man, the earl. James Henry Simmonds was tall, slim, fair-haired and utterly charming when he needed to be. But tonight was not one of those occasions. Tonight he was with his own kind, brothers in spirit if not blood. He swallowed the remains of a rich old brandy, put the glass on the table, took a deep breath, and, interrupting everyone, said in a loud voice, 'He has to go, or he'll bring us all down. Can't you all see this?'

Getting the attention he wanted as everyone paused and looked at him, he went on. 'Times change, but some of us stubbornly refuse to adapt.' He glared vehemently at the Russian when he said this. 'We knew a long time ago that this day would come, and now that it has you all sit there like fucking old men dithering about what to do.'

Kirill Tarasov glared back, his thick lips curled into a snarl. 'When you decided to call an emergency meeting, I did not know it was to condemn one of our own.'

'I agree, though. He's lost it.' They all turned to look at the American, as he went on in his high-pitched voice, 'And we have to think of our own safety. Strange events, these. They may have been predicted, but none could see the true scope of things.' The American, a small, squat man with a

102

bald head and the innocent sounding name of Billy Slone, nodded slowly. As well as his military status, the Slone family looked after the pharmaceutical side, investing millions to make billions, legal drugs which cured one ailment but caused three others, which needed more medication and on and on. Their research had come up with the latest illegal drugs to hit the streets as well as being responsible for what was already out there.

'What to do about it, though.' He nodded at Kirill. 'Kirill's right, he is one of our own. We have never in God knows how many centuries turned on our own. It's an unwritten law.'

'Yes, we have,' Simmonds snapped. 'I checked with the historian. It's happened twice before. One of them was an ancestor of his. The stupid idiot thinks he's fucking Rasputin.'

'Hmm.' Prince Carl had been quiet up until now. 'So, seeing as our own scientists proved centuries ago that madness was mostly, unless self-inflicted by drug overuse, in the genes, how was his line allowed to breed?'

Rene Farquhar rose and moved to the window, where he turned his handsome face dark against the bright sunshine to look at them all. His English impeccable, he said, 'The same way as the homosexual gene has stayed with us. No matter how hard we tried to eradicate it, it still came through.'

'Yes,' Prince Carl agreed, 'but not in the families.'

'Does it fucking well matter?' Simmonds snapped. 'The man's completely lost the plot. He had his chance when we had to move out of France early last year. We should have got rid of him then. I did say, if you remember.' His petulant mouth took on a self-righteous pout. 'It's barely eighteen months, and he's up to his old tricks again. Prancing around Northumberland, proclaiming himself as the fucking Leader. Not caring one bit about what will happen if his true identity is found out. If something isn't done soon, we'll all suffer. Trust me, we can't take the risk... And I for one am not prepared to do so, not for that megalomaniac.'

'I still can't understand why his gene pool wasn't weeded out centuries ago, if it was proved that his branch was so damn susceptible to madness?' Prince Carl said.

'I already said, for fuck's sake.'

'We could always go back to Africa,' Tarasov put in, attempting to placate, seeing Prince Carl starting to take offence at Simmonds' tone. Picking up an apple from the fruit bowl, he brushed it on his cashmere jacket before taking a bite, looking warningly under his eyelids at Simmonds.

'What, because of one man?' Slone said, immediately making clear his alliance with Simmonds. 'And you all know white flesh brings in more capital these days, especially from the wealthy African and Arab states. The world has changed a lot this last century, no matter how hard we've tried to slow progress down.'

'Thank you,' Simmonds said, a look of satisfaction on his face. 'Oh, and when are we going to release the AIDS cure? You know, bring the price of black flesh back up? We all know that's the reason it's gone down, fear of the AIDS virus.'

104

'The meeting to discuss that is scheduled for six months' time, as you well know.' Prince Carl glared at Simmonds. 'Please stick to today's problem... How many know of the body?'

Simmonds sniffed, but answered the Prince. 'At the moment, a few of the Northumbria Police. Their best man arrived back there this morning. He's been in London for a few months, investigating missing kids and drug trafficking. We've managed to throw spanners in every direction he's turned until now, but I'm certain he suspects something.'

'Good, is he?' Prince Carl asked, refilling his whiskey glass from the sparkling decanter on the solid gold coffee table.

'From what I've been told, very good. He managed to escape a trap set for him last night, though God knows how.'

'Why hasn't he been recruited, then?'

Simmonds shook his head. 'He was deemed too high risk. A man of many morals, allegedly.' He laughed.

'Everyone has a price,' the American said.

Simmonds turned to him and sneered. 'Apparently not this man.'

'OK, I get the picture. So what do we do now?' Slone looked at all of them in turn. They were all silent, none of them wanting to be the one to put it into words.

The one in question was, after all, family.

The families had been around for more than fifty-one centuries, long before the birth and death of Jesus Christ. Started by thirteen ruthless men, down through the ages they had come, with

105

members in every secret organisation known to man and many that were not. Always keeping their own secret, their fingers on the pulse of the world they secretly ruled. And now the future they had delayed for all those centuries had arrived. In the age of the computer, with knowledge only a click away, the world their forefathers had known had shrunk to a fraction of its size.

Prince Carl lit a cigarette in the silence, blew smoke at the ceiling, admired the solid gold ceiling rose. Two unicorns back to back. He had the same rose in his French castle, as they all did in their various dwellings around the world. 'OK, the way I see it, it's time for his line to end. Madmen are too unpredictable. The last thing we need in this day and age is a loose cannon. Some of these conspiracy theorists are getting closer to the mark all the time.'

'Yeah.' Tarasov said. 'I actually read an article the other day that said the flat screen TV was around fifty years before we let it go on the market. Good job they don't know the half of it.'

'Where are they getting this from?' Simmonds threw his glass at the wall. It shattered on impact. A trail of golden whiskey ran down the wall and fell onto the sparkling broken crystal. Immediately a young, dark-skinned girl ran in and cleaned it up.

Tarasov shrugged. 'Don't know, but some of the peasants are getting pretty close. You would be amazed if you widened your scope and did a little reading.'

'I have people to do that for me,' Simmonds sniffed.

Farquhar said, 'Kirill's right, though, we are going to have to be more careful. The peasants have rights, you know. We can't go swashbuckling around the world like we used to do. Sometimes it amazes me how we've made it this far.' He laughed.

'You know why we've made it this far,' Slone snapped. 'Because of all the failsafes in place. They have been there for centuries, and so far they've worked.'

'So far,' Tarasov snorted.

'OK, enough. We have to make a decision now.' Simmonds was adamant. Grim-faced, he looked at each of them in turn.

'How many in his immediate family?' Prince Carl asked.

'Fifteen legals, God knows how many out-breeds. The legals are spread around the world, most of them doing good work for the families.'

'Any of them showing signs of madness?'

'Only one, but it's really more that she's hyperactive, and slightly eccentric.'

Prince Carl sighed. 'Makes no difference, they all have to go. It's the way. Ask the historian.'

'Why?' Farquhar asked. 'Surely we can keep them under surveillance? It's more risky killing a whole family these days than the last time we did some weeding. When was it, 1640? For all our sakes, we must be more careful now.' He looked at Simmonds as he went on, 'Not easy to go around chopping people's ears off now ... not en masse, anyhow.'

Simmonds curled his lip. 'Yeah, well, at least they still kept their heads. Not like the revolution that your ancestors stirred up a couple of hundred years later.'

Tarasov looked at Simmonds with delight on his face, 'So it was you behind that black man losing his ears a few months back. Thought at the time when I read about it that it might be... In the genes, is it?' He laughed.

'You read too much,' Simmonds snarled at him. 'And at least my family doesn't fucking well eat them!'

'Hmm.' Prince Carl looked over the rim of his whiskey glass at Simmonds.

'OK. I think we better move on,' Slone said, thinking about the time his grandfather had told him about when he'd been a young man, when four main leaders of the families had knives at each other's throats. And apparently that had not been the first time. Everything about the families was documented by the historian, and to be read only by the family leaders. What the head of each family chose to tell those not in the loop was up to him.

He looked at the three men who had yet to have any input. Their faces were unreadable. Then he glanced quickly at Simmonds and nodded for him to move on.

'So, that's it then. We are in agreement?' Simmonds looked at them all in turn.

'No,' Tarasov said. 'I vote he goes, but not the family. It's far too risky. He's in England, remember, not some third-rate country where we can buy silence... And, easy as it might be to wipe him out, fifteen others are all connected. Most of them in high profile jobs around the world.'

Shaking his head he went on, 'A lot of questions are going to be asked... Also, I do know her quite well, and before a vote is taken I would exercise my right to speak for her life.'

'I agree.' Slone said, and everyone nodded. 'We keep close tabs on them, especially the female. Just because she's hyperactive doesn't mean she's mad. If we'd gone after every rogue gene there wouldn't be any of us left, for Christ's sake.'

'I also know the woman in question,' the African leader said. 'She is more eccentric than anything else, but an excellent pathologist. It would be a shame to lose her genes. She is also in the loop, being one of the three closest relatives, and clever enough to suss out what may happen to her and the rest of her clan. I vote that one of us pay her a visit and explain the situation. She will understand the need for his execution. I do believe she is working in the north of England.'

They all raised their hands. 'Seeing as you know her so well, why don't you do the visiting?' Prince Carl said.

The African nodded.

Tarasov sighed. 'Once we were thirteen families.'

'And now we're nine,' Simmonds snapped, peeved that the Japanese silk baron, and the Swedish government minister still had not arrived, but thankful that the vote had been passed without them. It only needed one more than half of them to make a law, and now it was passed it could not be undone.

There was silence for a few seconds before Slone asked, 'And the English cop?'

'For the moment we keep an eye on him.' Prince Carl replied. 'Dead cops cause questions.'

'And those around him?' Simmonds said. 'He's got this kid in tow, used to be a druggie and as mad as a hatter.'

Prince Carl shrugged. 'People like that, not hard to get rid of. Accidents can easily be arranged if needs be.'

CHAPTER TWENTY-ONE

Mike dropped the WPC off at Berwick Police Station. Using the police car until he could pick his own up from Durham, where it was being held in a friend's lock-up, he drove Smiler and Tiny to his Aunt May's house on Holy Island.

When they arrived, she was waiting at the gate for them. Mike had explained all about Smiler over the phone, and about the scars on his arms and face, so as not to give her too much of a shock, though he strongly doubted if anything in this world could shock Aunt May. She had after all dealt with that kind of thing before. She smiled and nodded a welcome at Smiler, then froze rigid, her eyes wide with exaggerated fear, when Mike got Tiny out of the police car.

'And where, Michael Yorke, do you think that brute is going to live?' she demanded. 'You said nothing at all about bringing a monster home with you. Dear me, he's bigger than a bloody Shetland pony. Fairly outdone your bloody self

110

this time, haven't you! And a barn to keep the bloody brute in, we haven't got.' She folded her arms across her chest.

Mike grinned. 'Well, not quite, but he can always have my room. Anyhow, you know you love dogs, Aunt May... If I hadn't rescued him he probably would have starved to death by now, and I know you wouldn't like that to happen – a good honest, kind, loving and caring woman like yourself, Aunt May.'

'Oh yeah, got more bloody blarney than the Irish, you have.' She looked at Smiler. 'He's been picking up waifs and strays since he could get out on the street. You wouldn't believe me if I was to tell you what he's carted home.'

Smiler gave her a brief smile. He hoped she wasn't counting him as one of Mike's waifs and strays, though he knew deep down, really that's just what he was. He also knew enough about Aunt May from what Mike had told him to know that she would not have meant anything bad by the remark.

Mike put his arm around her shoulders, kissed her cheek then gave her a hug.

'Away with your charm, Michael Yorke.' She tutted. 'You've always been able to charm the birds right out of the trees. A wee dog I wouldn't have minded so much, for God's sake. But this ... this great big ugly brute...' She glared at Tiny, who wagged his tail. 'What's its name?'

'Tiny.'

'You're joking.' She threw Mike a look of comic amazement.

Mike shrugged. 'That's the name he came with,

Aunt May... Anyhow, it's only for a couple of days.'

'What is – his name, or how long he's staying?'

Mike grinned. 'As cute as ever, Aunt May.'

Shrugging, she turned her attention to Smiler. 'You'll be walking the bloody brute, I presume, and feeding it?'

Smiler nodded quickly.

'OK, but one hair, one whiff of a smell, and he's out. I mean it... It's a good job I'm not full up. More cancellations than enough with all the bloody rain we've had this year,' she grumbled, glaring at Tiny as if the weather and lack of bookings were his fault.

'Thanks Aunt May, you're a doll.' Mike bent and kissed her cheek again. 'Gotta go now, we'll talk when I get back.'

'Get away then, and don't forget to check the tide.' Grinning, she turned to Smiler. 'He got caught on the causeway one night and the helicopter had to come out and rescue him.' She rolled her eyes in mock horror. 'How bloody embarrassing is that?'

Not knowing if she really wanted an answer or not, Smiler nodded, and bit his lip to stop an actual laugh at the picture in his head of Mike standing on top of a car, the raging North Sea all around him and being rescued by a helicopter, as she went on, 'And him living on the island most of his growing years in short pants, he really should have known better, shouldn't he? No one, but no one, beats Mother Nature, certainly not bloody Michael Yorke. Mother Nature isn't that easily charmed.'

Mike laughed. 'Never gonna live that one down, am I? And your memory's fading, darling, I never wore shorts. They were a few generations before me. Don't know who you're thinking about there – some old sweetheart, perhaps?'

'Get away with you.' Laughing, she flapped her hands at him.

Mike's phone rang. Still smiling at Aunt May, he took it out of his pocket. 'Hello, this is Mike.' His smile faded as he listened intently to the voice at the other end. 'OK,' he said a moment later. 'I'm on my way.'

Slapping the phone shut, he said to Smiler and Aunt May, 'Gotta go, guys. See youse both tonight. And you be very good.' He patted Tiny's head, and received a wag from his tail, and a nudge on the knee from Tiny's nose.

As Mike headed back over the causeway, a picture of the murdered girl entered his mind. He couldn't begin to understand the pain she must have suffered at the hands of the depraved bastard who had murdered her. Thank God two suspects were being held at the station.

Though it seemed too easy. Far too easy!

Almost as if they had been handed to them on a plate. Which made Mike all the more suspicious. Nothing involving murder was ever that easy.

He drove over the causeway, reminding himself to pick up a timetable of the tides. He never wanted to go through the experience of being rescued from a car roof ever again.

113

CHAPTER TWENTY-TWO

As Mike pulled away, Smiler looked out of the corner of his eyes at Aunt May, thinking to himself, Ohh dear me, she's got to be the oldest chick in the world.

Even though it was a warm day, Aunt May, all four foot eleven of her, was swaddled in a thick brown cardigan that probably could go round her twice. Her short iron grey hair was permed to within an inch of its life, and she had wrinkles on top of wrinkles.

Then she smiled. Her blue eyes, far from faded and full of intelligence, laughed out at the world.

'Come in, come in,' she said, pointing back at the red door with her walking stick.

Smiler followed her. The path was bordered with red and blue petunias, the lawns on either side looking like they had been cut with a pair of manicure scissors. The window boxes were brimming with more petunias, and the doorframe was covered in a pale purple clematis. An overriding perfume came from the honeysuckle that climbed rampantly over the left side of the white-painted house.

'Nice flowers,' Smiler remarked. He felt obliged to make some sort of conversation, seeing as the woman was being good enough to put him up.

'Too leggy,' she replied. 'All the rain has made them twice as tall as they should be, so the

114

bloody flower heads suffer.'

'Oh, yes, it definitely spoils them.' Smiler had delved into many a gardening book.

Just before he stepped over the threshold, a shadow seemed to pass in front of him. Smiler shivered. He spun round, a prickly feeling dancing along the back of his neck. It was a sure sign that he was being watched. It brought on a fresh bout of shivering that he could not control. He began to rapidly count the fingers on his left hand with the forefinger of his right.

Noticing this, she said, 'Come in boy, come in. Don't be bloody sh...'

Aunt May looked over Smiler's shoulder. For a moment she froze. Then she seemed to shake herself, looked at Smiler, gave him a lopsided smile, and again told him to come in.

She showed him up to his room, a small but neat place, a piece of heaven to him after some of the doss houses he'd woken up in. The overriding colour was blue – pale blue walls, dark blue carpet, dark blue bedspread and curtains. Even the one picture on the wall was a field of blue-bells. He remembered a one-room apartment in London that was the size of this room, an apartment that six of them had shared. Those walls had been blue as well until the day Irish Jimmy lost it, and took a razor blade to his own throat, and changed the colour of the walls to red.

But that was cool. All that was in the past. He could live with blue.

Aunt May urged him to leave his unpacking until later, because tea was ready now.

Facing the window, he sighed, but it was a sigh

of contentment, the first such sigh he had ever experienced. He stared out at the sixteenth-century castle standing regal in the sunshine. Then he blinked rapidly, as dark thunder clouds began to rise above the parapet. He blinked again, and they were gone. Once more the land-scape was bathed in glorious gold.

His packing consisted of two T-shirts, both black, and an extra pair of jeans, which was a lot more than he'd had a few months ago or, as he secretly liked to call it, the dark years. Life before Mike.

He shook himself, not wanting to go down that dark road to the before place. From now on that place was to be avoided at all costs. He was wrapping all those terrible memories up. They were parked in a corner of his mind behind a very high wall. Just a few loose ones to catch that crept up on him now and then in the middle of the night, or at a lonely time.

He followed Aunt May down the stairs and into the floral living room, which was in direct com-petition with the garden. Flowers on the wallpaper of every shade imaginable, huge red flowers on the carpet and, not to be outdone, the settee and matching chairs looked like someone had scat-tered half a dozen packets of mixed flower seeds over them. Smiler much preferred his room's décor.

They walked through into the large kitchen diner that had three small tables, each with three chairs pushed in. All the tables were covered in sparkling white tablecloths and set for tea. The cream place mats had floral designs, and so did

116

the white teacups, a different flower on each one.

He guessed Aunt May was a flower nut. On the opposite side of the kitchen was a huge old-fashioned cooker. The sink was under the window, which had fancy cream nets up, and cream-painted cupboards ran round the walls.

'Sit here, dear,' Aunt May said, pointing to the first table as she walked over to the cooker.

Smiler sat down. When she opened the oven, his nostrils flared as the wonderful smell of home-made chicken casserole invaded the room. His mouth watered as his stomach rumbled. He hadn't realised how hungry he was. For years he'd eaten so little, most days getting by on handouts from a baker's wife round the corner from Cardboard City. She gave stuff away to the homeless, unbeknown to her husband, on a regular basis. His stomach was used to getting by on very little, and had been since forever. He could eat now though, since he'd met Mike, not huge amounts, but a hell of a lot better than he ever had before.

He had to stop Aunt May from filling his plate to overflowing, it would be bad manners if he couldn't eat it all. The lady was, after all, Mike's aunt, and deserved his respect.

'Aren't you hungry?' she asked, her nose shrinking into the middle of her face as she frowned at him.

'Yes, but I... Er... I can't eat a whole pile... Small stomach.' He patted his stomach and threw her a twitch of a smile.

She tutted, then said, 'OK, son, but in my opinion growing boys need a lot of bloody fuel.'

Smiler nodded as he looked at his plate.

CHAPTER TWENTY-THREE

Driving into Berwick, Mike decided to drop in at the murder scene before going to the station. A policeman was standing outside the door to the flat, in the process of chasing half a dozen nosy kids away as Mike pulled up.

'Hey, copper, is that right – the bloke who lives in there's a murderer?' shouted one of the boys, no more than eight years old with a shock of red hair.

'Has he chopped somebody to bits?' asked a wide-eyed blonde girl of the same age, her voice rising with fright.

'On yer bikes,' the policeman replied, his eyes on Mike as he got out of the car.

Mike showed his badge. The officer nodded as he stepped to one side to let Mike through.

'Hey, mister,' the redhead shouted.

'I'll not tell yer again,' the copper said, this time glaring at the boy. The kids scampered off, and Mike hid a smile as he opened the door. He noticed the bloody handprint on the door, plus two others along the hallway. The bedroom door was open and, as Mike stepped in to the bedroom, he bit down on a gasp. He found himself looking at a scene from a slaughterhouse.

The sheet had been taken away for DNA tests, but the blood had soaked through. Ninety per cent of the mattress was stained and still looked damp, showing just how much blood the victim had lost.

Mike stepped closer. The place smelled of blood and he wrinkled his nose.

'She's obviously been murdered here,' he muttered, walking round the bed to the wall and back again, studying the bed from every angle.

'The vicious bastard.' He turned his attention to the rest of the room. Next to the bed, where a lot of the blood was, small chunks of white clung to the wall. He shuddered, knowing it was flesh, seeing in his mind the whip falling on the girl, pulling back ready for the next lash, scattering blood and tiny pieces of flesh in its wake.

Taking a deep breath he continued his survey of the room. Nothing looked like it had been disturbed in any way. Standard white furniture, probably flat-pack. A double wardrobe, a night stand with an alarm clock, and a large set of drawers, with a smaller set underneath the window.

There were blood and specks of flesh on every item.

Mike frowned as he looked at the trail of bloody footprints that led outside. Probably the same person who the handprints belonged to. As if suddenly realising what he'd done, the bastard had panicked then turned and run, not caring what he touched or what sort of trail he left.

Leaving the house, Mike had a few words with the policeman outside before, grim-faced, he got into his car and headed for the police station.

CHAPTER TWENTY-FOUR

Smiler had been introduced to the two other guests, a pair of oldish ladies – one so fat she had three chins, dressed in a red jogging suit which only emphasised her many other rolls of flesh, the other in a blue suit, and thin enough to give Aunt May a run for her money. The pair of them giggled their way through tea like two excitable schoolgirls. They were on holiday together, and had so fallen in love with the island they were thinking of buying a house. Trouble was, they complained to Smiler, there were none for sale.

Smiler nodded his sympathy, and decided to look round the island for himself.

It was a place that had been on his 'must visit' list ever since he'd read about it. The stories surrounding the island had taken his mind away for a long time to that special place, leaving his body in limbo to deal with the day-to-day trauma of living.

Holy Island. Lindisfarne. Special names for a special place.

Tea over, he thanked Aunt May for the fantastic meal, said goodbye to the ladies, who were heading home that night at low tide, and went outside.

Deciding to walk along to the castle first, he rescued Tiny from the back garden and called into the village shop for cigarettes. He stepped over a placid-looking Golden Retriever to get into the shop, having tied Tiny up out of the way, not knowing how he behaved around other dogs. But there was nothing to worry about. The retriever lifted its head and yawned at him, then did the same to Tiny, who sat down and ignored it. Smiler laughed. He liked animals, especially dogs. Dogs could see things. They were in tune to the senses that most humans had lost long ago.

The shopkeeper, a small thickset man with a long nose, his wavy brown hair brushed over his head in thin strands to cover his baldness, served Smiler, suspiciously watching a group of youths at the back of the shop through his thick glasses, his mean eyes nasty slits.

'You with them?' he snarled, as he handed Smiler's change over.

Smiler shook his head. 'No. Why?'

'I've seen that sort of scam before. You keep me occupied while they do the nicking.'

'Well, you've got it wrong this time. Sorry.' Smiler pocketed his change. He stared for a moment at the shopkeeper's right hand, at the obvious bite mark in the soft flesh between thumb and forefinger. Looking up at the shop-keeper's face, he felt a familiar shiver inside.

'Dog bite,' the shopkeeper offered by way of explanation. Dismissing Smiler, he swung his attention back to the boys. 'Do you lot want any-thing?' he demanded as Smiler walked out.

Miserable git, Smiler thought. That bite's too small to be off the retriever and that's a fact.

He nearly tripped over Aunt May on the step.

'I see you've met our temporary shopkeeper,'

121

she whispered as, laughing and giggling, the boys tumbled out of the shop. 'He's from the mainland. The real shopkeeper's a very nice man. On his holidays. France, I think he said – or was that last year?'

'Oh, right,' Smiler said. Nodding to her, he took Tiny's lead and set off.

He crossed the road opposite the Lindisfarne Scriptorium and headed on past The Ship Inn. At the bottom of the street was Sandham Lane, with Aunt May's house at the far end. Sandham Lane was the only street that had a name plaque on it. This, Aunt May had told him, was so that the old dears off the bus trips would know where to meet up. She'd also told him he must never say P-I-G on the island. He spelt the word in his head. It was very unlucky to say it out loud. Being very superstitious, Smiler didn't even want to say it in his head. Bad luck was the last thing he needed, he certainly wasn't going to encourage it.

Passing Sandham Lane, he headed for the castle. The road was busy with tourists. To his right was an ice cream van that looked like it was doing a roaring trade, and next to it a fish and chip van, equally busy.

He carried on down towards the castle, one of many in the northeast of England. Being a sixteenth-century castle, this one was much younger than a lot of castles in the area. Lindisfarne's position in the North Sea had made it vulnerable to attacks not only from the Scots, but from the Vikings as well. The island had once been a very volatile area and had a fascinating history.

As he walked towards the castle, in his mind's

eye the tourists became Vikings on the rampage. He flinched as one huge warrior strode towards him. Keeping his eyes directly in front of him, Smiler kept on walking, telling himself over and over that Mike was right, it was all just his imagination.

The warrior, complete with horned headgear, holding a shield in one hand and a spear in the other, kept on coming. Behind him a huge band of warriors, all glaring ferociously at Smiler, kept pace with their leader.

Smiler stared in terror, then blinked rapidly when Tiny pulled on his lead. But the huge man kept on coming and remained a Viking – until he passed Smiler's peripheral vision, when he became a family man in blue T-shirt and jeans. Smiler turned his head quickly, and stared out at the empty sea. As a party of tourists passed behind him, he let out the breath he wasn't aware that he'd been holding, then shuddered. It seemed as if a cloud had suddenly covered the sun.

He reached the castle. To his immense relief, the Vikings had faded, and normal twenty-first century people walked back and forth. A group of about thirty people hung on to a tour guide's every word. Lovers walked past hand in hand, basking in the late afternoon sunshine. A couple of old men with walking sticks stepped out of the way of a party of pre-teen school children. None of them gave Smiler a second look, although Tiny drew admiring glances, and many pats – which, as usual, he accepted fawningly.

Smiler found the island fascinating, and much larger than he'd first thought. The air was bracing, and the sun shining. He actually felt more at home after only a few hours than he had anywhere in his life. Certainly Aunt May's cottage was really welcoming, much more than any place he'd ever lived with the woman he'd called mother.

He ran the fingers of his right hand down the scars of his left arm, paused a moment, each slash fresh in his mind, then reversed the process.

If only ... if only life had been different. He could still see his mother's face. Just over thirty she'd been when she'd died, and had looked sixty years old or more. She had never shown him any love that he could remember. The only touch his skin had felt from her hands had been a hard slap or a punch. He often wondered why she just hadn't aborted him. No life at all would have been better than the one she'd given him.

Why had she let those things happen to him?

Why hadn't she tried harder?

He tried to put her out of his mind. Every time he thought of her, he knew, he just got upset. He was starting a new life, another chance, thanks to Mike.

Hold onto that thought, he told himself, think of Mike, think of anything. Snakes raking in the gutter for his gear, his first proper Macky Dee's with Mike, Aunt May's leggy flowers. But he wasn't strong enough. He shuddered, and the sky began to darken. His breathing became harsh. A small doorway opened in his mind. He tried hard to close it, but the rift grew bigger, letting things slip through, things he didn't want to remember, things that should stay buried, things that crushed his soul.

A moment later they faded, and a girl with long dark hair lay huddled in a field, crying for help. She was weak, terrified and a long way from home. Her fear transferred to Smiler as he sank deeper and deeper into the abyss of his own mind.

CHAPTER TWENTY-FIVE

She sank into the grass. Thankfully, the driver of the car hadn't seen her. She'd panicked for nothing. When the car, lorry, whatever the damn thing had been, hadn't stopped, she'd walked for another three hours, and now she was totally exhausted. Looking down at her poor aching feet, she bit her lip. She'd used her lighter to burn the stitching round the sleeves of her short jacket, then, ripping the sleeves off, she had shoved her feet into them, doubling them over. To be able to walk she'd had to leave her toes exposed. Each one was cut and bleeding, and the sleeves were worse than useless now. Blood was seeping through the holes, mixing with the dry earth to make mud and infection.

She sighed, a pitiful lonely sound in the silence of the empty field. The last thing a diabetic needs is damaged feet. That bottle top she'd pulled out had hurt like hell, but she couldn't even remember standing on the damn thing.

Taking the remaining sweets out of her pocket, she stared at them for a moment. Knowing there was nothing else she could do, she put a handful in her mouth and started to chew.

Tears fell unchecked down her face. She had always found self-pity pathetic, but she had never been in a situation so frightening in her life. Looking around, she guessed that somehow she'd wandered inland, which was what she'd intended. She also figured that she was near the village of Fenwick, a small hamlet three or four miles from Holy Island. Her heart sank, even further than she thought was possible. This was a place she definitely didn't want to be, far too close to the brothers and him! She had planned on being much, much further inland than this.

She knew she couldn't walk any further, and that in a few more hours she would without doubt be in a coma. She'd tried to fight this damn disease, like she knew better than the doctors. It got her as it always would, and with a vengeance. If she'd been alone that night, six years ago, when she had stubbornly denied that there was anything wrong with her, and her sugar had dropped so low it hardly had a reading, she could have gone so far under that the way back would have been nigh on impossible.

Damn it... Why the hell did I have to be the one to get it? There are millions of other people in the world.

Why me?

If I didn't have diabetes, I could have gone on, escaped – but I'm fucking well cursed.

'Shit!!!' she screamed with frustration, startling a flock of seagulls that took flight, screeching their way into the air.

'And that's all I need, somebody wondering what the hell's frightened youse ugly lot. Ohh. Damn, damn, damn.'

The tears came again, thick and fast as she looked around her, wondering what to do. It gave her only small satisfaction to remember how hard she'd bitten down on that creepy bloke's hand, running away, screaming and spitting blood out of her mouth, a taste she had no fancy for. Really it had been nothing short of a miracle that she'd escaped at all.

Sighing, as a feeling of total, utter helplessness came over her, she folded in on herself and sank to the ground. Staring at sharp blades of grass, she cried some more. Then slowly a look of determination came over her face.

'Sod them,' she murmured, lifting her face to the sky and feeling the warm sun on her skin. 'Sod the fucking lot of them... Who the hell do they think they are, coming here with their freaky plans? Bunch of fucking creeps... Well, I'm not dead yet!'

Slowly, stubbornly, she struggled to her feet. The main problem, she figured, was finding somebody to trust, as well as finding somebody who would even believe her.

'One thing I know for sure.' She took a step, then another, stuck her chin out and muttered defiantly, 'I'm not dying in this fucking field.'

CHAPTER TWENTY-SIX

He doesn't look like a murderer. But then, really, not a lot of people do. OK, if you have any sense you can spot the nutters right off, but that doesn't necessarily make them all murderers. Mostly the real culprits wear a sane mask that can fool even the best of policemen, as well as judges, doctors and lawyers, Mike thought, as he watched the man through the two-way glass. This one had been picked up running amok, covered in blood, in the main street. But is it a sure-fire bet that he's guilty?

Mike was waiting for Detective Kristina Clancy. It had been a surprise to find her working in Berwick. A nice surprise, because she hadn't changed one little bit. She came thudding down the corridor, her brown eyes laughing. He was surprised to see she'd grown her hair, and now sported a saucy fringe.

Mike smiled. Late as usual.

As they sat down and Kristina switched the tape on, Danny Wilson looked up. Having been told in full detail how the girl had died, Kristina was finding it hard to hide her feelings. She threw Danny a look of undisguised disgust.

'OK. Care to tell us what happened?' Mike asked, his voice quiet but laced with steel.

'I don't know,' Danny sobbed, 'you've got to believe me, I don't know...'

He looked at them both in turn, his eyes wide with amazement, shocked to find himself in this predicament, before hurrying on. 'I was at the hospital all night, honest. Ask my mate Evan, he'll tell you. Then ... then I fell asleep on the bench outside... I went in a couple of hours later and ... and there she was... Oh,' his face lit up, 'the milkman, he'll tell you...Yes, the milkman ... he woke me up, he did, because I was asleep on the bench, he'll tell you.' Danny nodded his head adamantly, pleased that he'd remembered at least one person who had seen him.

'Name of the dairy?' Kristina asked.

'Don't know.' Danny kept hold of his hands to stop them from shaking.

'We'll find out.'

Danny tried a small smile, but it was rewarded by a frozen stare that made him even more nervous. He swung his face towards Mike. No joy there. The glaring look he received was worse than the one from the woman.

'So you truly expect us to believe that someone broke in and murdered your girlfriend while you slept outside?' Mike asked, with raised eyebrows.

'A likely story.' Kristina snorted. Without giving Danny a chance to say anything, she went on, 'Have yer seen what yer've done to her, you mad bastard?'

'I haven't done anything.' Danny's voice was rising higher by the second, panic obvious in every word he uttered as he stared at Kristina and Mike in turn. 'Honest, it wasn't me... It was not me... It was not me.'

'Where's the weapon?' Mike asked. 'Where did

you manage to hide it?'

'What weapon?' Danny frantically looked around. The room was small, bare cream walls, one desk, four chairs, one door. His eyes skittered back to the door. The surface was covered in scratches. His imagination went wild. He pictured people trying to claw their way out of here. His heart lurched, pounding in his ears. The walls, the doors, everything was closing in on him. There was no escape. How could he get out of here?

'Where is the weapon?' Mike demanded again, leaning forward over the desk.

Weapon? Danny's mind struggled to get round what they were saying. I wouldn't hurt her. I've never once lifted my hands to Shelly, never mind use a weapon!

What sort of a weapon?

A knife?

A gun?

Judging by the hate in the eyes of these two coppers, it has to have been a pretty nasty weapon.

Oh Jesus.

And the way the woman cop keeps looking at me as if I'm some sort of an animal is seriously freaking me out.

What am I supposed to have done?

'I love Shelly,' he blustered, glancing quickly from one to the other.

'Fine way of showing it,' Kristina said. 'Just admit it, tell us what happened and it'll all be over... Cuppa tea, nice long rest, maybes even a shower.' She smiled sweetly at him.

Danny looked at the woman in amazement. Is

she taking the piss?

Mike, his voice now soft and chatty, said, 'Did she annoy you, is that why you killed her? We both know how annoying women can be, don't we? Promise you the moon, then change their minds when you're up and ready for it.'

'Or,' Kristina suddenly snapped, 'find her in bed with one of your mates, eh? So yer thought yer would just kill her for having sex with someone else, even though you play those sort of games? That's it, isn't it? Male ego hurting, was it? So just kill her, eh? Restore the balance of power? Is that how it was?'

'No... What games? I don't know what you're talking about... I didn't kill Shelly, why would I? You've got it all wrong.' Danny jumped up, judging the distance to the door. He had to get out of this nightmare.

'Sit down,' Kristina said.

For a brief moment, Danny glanced down at her. Suddenly unable to control his fear and panic, he made a bid for the door, only to be blocked by Mike, who grabbed him from behind and forced him back into his seat.

'Try that again, and I'll fucking well see that you're incapable of even walking again, never mind running.' The words had been whispered in Danny's ear so that the tape wouldn't pick them up, as Kristina conveniently coughed as loud as she could.

'I want a solicitor.' Shaking, Danny slumped in his seat.

Mike nodded at Kristina to switch the tape off. Kristina spoke into the mike, ending the session, then turned it off.

'I just bet you want a solicitor. Realised what you've done now?' Mike slapped his palms hard on the desk, and Danny, his eyes bulging in fear, jumped.

'It wasn't me, honest.' He sobbed like a baby. 'Where's Evan? He ... he'll tell you it wasn't me. It couldn't be me, see, 'cos I told you where we were last night. Ask Evan.'

'Was he in on it an' all, eh?... Some sort of filthy disgusting perve ring yer've got going between yer's?' Kristina yelled. 'For God's sake, is she even the bloody first? Is she? Is she? How many others have yer disfigured in this way? Tell me, are we gonna find more bodies? More poor girls discarded like so much trash?' She leaned forward in her seat, her voice suddenly calm and controlled. 'How many more?'

Terrified, confused and utterly devastated at the thought of Shelly being dead, Danny could only gaze at the floor, tears running unchecked down his cheeks.

Disfigured? What do they mean, disfigured?

Oh God, what the hell has happened to her?

Why would anyone want to hurt her, disfigure her? His brain actually hurt trying to figure out the whys.

Shelly got on with everybody, and she could certainly stick up for herself if she had to. If he hadn't seen her blood-covered body himself, Danny would never have believed it.

In fact, he still didn't believe it. He was stuck in some sort of nightmare with these monster coppers, and he really couldn't tell which one was worse. He'd never been in a police station in his life before, never mind being interrogated by the coppers from Hell.

'Oh God,' he muttered.

'Pathetic,' Kristina said.

As Kristina glared at Danny, Mike opened the door and asked the officer outside to take Danny back to his cell until the duty solicitor could come in.

'And send Mr Miller in,' Mike said, as the officer escorted a sobbing Danny back to the holding cell.

CHAPTER TWENTY-SEVEN

Jill was just finishing her salad sandwich when there was a knock on the door. One of the porters popped his head round.

'The family's here now, Jill, two brothers.'

'OK, send them in.' Jill hastily shoved her tea into a drawer kept empty for that purpose. Relatives could turn up at any time, and the last thing they expected was the person dealing with their dearly beloved's body to be taking care of their own body's demands.

The two brothers walked into the morgue, their faces grim. With them was the blonde woman police officer that had picked Mike and Smiler up from the train station. The younger brother was dabbing at his eyes with a paper handkerchief. The older one's face was set in a stern mask.

Jill introduced herself, and found out that these two brothers were Gary and Liam. Gary's head was shaved bald, and he had the stance of a boxer. Liam was taller but much slimmer. Both of them wore dark suits with white open-necked shirts. Liam's suit looked like he had grown out of it, or borrowed the suit from a shorter friend. As Jill took the white sheet off the body, she heard Liam sob.

For a moment there was silence as all three of them stared down at the dead girl. Jill stepped back to leave the brothers alone with her. Sometimes, even though the family had been told more or less what to expect, they still couldn't believe that the lifeless body in front of them was the same person they had last seen laughing or crying, or in some cases arguing. Jill always felt sorry for the relative who had last seen their loved one alive after a vicious argument.

Liam's sob turned into a gasp as Gary said loudly, 'What the fuck?'

Jill frowned. 'Excuse me?'

Gary recoiled from the table, and spun round to stare at Jill. His face was covered in red blotches and she could feel the frustrated anger radiating off him. He swung his arm back and pointed at the dead girl. 'It's not her. That's not my sister. It's not our Shelly.'

'What?'

'It. Is. Not. Her. How many times, for God's sake?'

'But she was found in your sister's boyfriend's flat, in their bed to be precise. And she fits the description,' Jill said, her eyes flickering towards

134

the dead girl.

'Well I'm sorry, pet, we don't know who the poor bugger is, God bless her soul. But that sure as hell isn't our Shelly.'

'You're certain of that?' the policewoman asked. She stepped forward and looked from one brother to the other.

Liam nodded, staring in wide-eyed horror at the dead girl. 'She's got the same hair, definitely the same hair,' he managed a moment later. 'But that's it. Don't know about the eyes. Our Shelly...' He sobbed, looked at Gary and muttered, 'Sorry,' as he dashed tears from his eyes.

Jill was unsure whether they were tears of relief that it was not their sister, or tears of sadness for whoever this was.

CHAPTER TWENTY-EIGHT

Smiler found himself outside the priory with no recollection of how he had got there, only a sinking feeling deep in the pit of his stomach, and an overwhelming blackness in his head. He sat down on a seat near the entrance.

'Nice here,' he muttered.

'Yeah, great view.'

'See that tiny islet over to the right?'

'Yeah.'

'St Cuthbert used to live on there. Did you know that one day, when he was visiting the Queen in Carlisle – not the present Queen, of course – he knew by second sight that her husband, the King, had been slain by the Picts doing battle in Scotland.'

'Hmm.'

'Did you know he had the gift?'

'No... Going to be some more slaying. Because she got away.'

'Sorry?'

'The girl. The girl's in trouble.'

Tiny put his large head on Smiler's knee and whined, accompanied by the giggles of two small girls who were staring at Smiler.

Blinking rapidly, Smiler looked at the girls, who, still giggling, ran away.

He sighed, knowing he'd had an away moment, and patted Tiny's head. 'Come on, boy.'

He headed back to the village quite unable to shake off the feeling of dread that seemed to have been following him around for weeks.

CHAPTER TWENTY-NINE

Jill stared at the two brothers, their faces deathly pale. They were looking at the dead girl in fascination, relief clear in their eyes and the sudden relaxation of their bodies. But Jill could detect pity as well, at least from the taller brother, who was still staring in awe at the dead girl. The other one's face was changing rapidly from relief to anger and back again.

Not their sister, Jill thought, so what the hell

136

was this girl doing in their sister's bed?

Walking over to the bench, Jill pressed a button under the counter. The alarm would bring two burly porters, double-quick. People did strange things when confronted with the dead, especially if it was their first time. The rare shock of finding out, after you had prepared yourself for the worst, that it wasn't one of yours lying there on the cold steel slab, strangely sometimes did not bring the relief that one would expect.

As discreet as ever, the porters came in, gave Jill a brief nod before making themselves busy at the far bench, moving stuff around from one place to another. Keeping their backs to the brothers, they listened to every word that was said, ready to spring into action if one of them turned nasty.

'So what now?' Gary asked, tearing his gaze from the girl to stare at Jill.

Jill shrugged. 'Nothing. She's no kin to you, is she? All I can do is apologise for the mistake.'

'That's all right.' Liam beamed and nudged his brother. 'Don't you understand? It means our Shelly's still alive. She's still alive, we gotta tell the others.'

'Aye, but you're forgetting something, aren't you? Like, what the hell was this poor lass doing in her bed? Eh? Why would she be in our Shelly's bed? That's what I want to know... And just where the hell is our Shelly?'

Perplexed, Liam shook his head.

'Tell yer what,' Gary went on. 'Some bloody half-arsed idiot's got a hell of a lot of explaining to do... Come on, Liam, let's get the hell out of here, right now.' He turned abruptly and walked out, leaving Liam to say goodbye.

When they had gone, Larry, the taller of the two porters, turned to Jill. 'Wouldn't like to be the one he's looking for.'

'Me neither.' Sighing, she covered the girl up and pushed the slab into the freezer, confining the unknown girl to the cold and dark.

CHAPTER THIRTY

A few minutes later, Gary stormed into Berwick Police Station, demanding to know, before he'd even crossed the threshold, 'Who's the stupid jerk, who told us our sister Shelly was dead, when it wasn't even her? And what the hell is going on here? Is this place full of fucking morons or what?'

He banged his fists on the desk as he glared at the sergeant. 'I have just been to the morgue to identify a total stranger. Do yer have any idea what that's like? Do you?' Behind his back, a red-faced Liam was mouthing 'sorry' to the desk sergeant.

Sitting in the waiting room, Evan glanced quickly up. Have I heard right? Did Gary just say Shelly's not dead?

Shelly's not dead. No. Frowning, he shook his head. I must have heard wrong, it's the grief talking. Who else could it be, if it's not Shelly? I would know for sure if Danny was playing away. No way would he be able to keep something like that to himself. Not his style to mess about. Anyhow, Danny couldn't keep a secret if his life depended on it.

Just then, the officer who had taken Danny to the holding cell appeared, to collect Evan.

'Here, you,' Gary shouted, catching sight of the policeman, and storming up to him, 'What's going? You friggin' lot thick around here or what?'

The constable ignored him, and the desk sergeant came out to try to calm him down. Evan could still hear Gary shouting his mouth off as he and the officer walked down the corridor.

It was obvious Gary hadn't recognised him, and Evan was pleased. It was to be expected – he hadn't met up with them for years – but the very last thing he wanted was a run-in with Shelly's brothers. They had a reputation for looking after themselves. And it didn't look like Gary had calmed down any. He'd always had a big yap on him.

Walking into the interview room, Evan sat down on the chair indicated by the officer, who then left. The male copper was staring at the woman with an odd look on his face as he put the phone down.

'So, er, what's going on?' Evan asked, his nervousness obvious in the way he chewed his lip and fiddled with his hands. 'Nobody seems to know.'

Mike and Kristina stared at him. This made him even more nervous.

Evan tried again, beginning to feel really uncomfortable and actually guilty of something. He just wished he knew what. 'Where's Danny?'

Mike answered his question with one of his own. 'Where's your girlfriend Alicia?'

'Wh...?'

'She didn't come home last night did she?'

Evan shook his head.

'Please answer yes or no for the tape,' Kristina said.

Evan cleared his throat. It felt as if it was full of sand. 'No, she didn't. I've been wondering all day where she is.' He looked from one to the other with a sinking heart, wondering where the hell all of this was leading.

'Does Alicia have long black hair?' Mike asked. 'Is her hair very much the same as her friend Shelly's?'

Evan, his eyes full of a frightening suspicion, quickly said, 'Yes, yes she does... I... I was at the hospital, got in around four and she wasn't in... Why do you want to know what colour her hair is?'

'Is it usual for her to stay out all night?' Kristina asked, guessing rightly where Mike was leading with his questions.

'No, not really. Actually, not at all, not without letting me know about it... No, she never stops out.'

'Was she very good friends with Shelly?'

Evan's heart was flipping over in his chest, wondering where all this was going to end up.

'What do you mean, was she?'

'How close were the four of you, eh? Share a lot, did you?' Mike glared at him.

Evan did not like the way these questions were going. Even less did he like this officer's use of

140

past tense.

'Nothing like what you are suggesting, officer,' Evan replied stiffly.

Mike studied him for a moment. Was Evan visibly shaking? Without taking his eyes off Evan's face, Mike said, 'The young woman found in your friend's flat, in your friend's bed, is not who we first thought. She's not Shelly.'

Evan was quiet for a moment, digesting what had been said. For God's sake, it makes even less sense now. Why would someone else be in Danny's flat, in Danny's bed?

'Not Shelly? So that's what her brother was yelling about... So, er ... who is it?' If Evan thought his heart was roller-coasting before, it was definitely on the ghost train ride now. He kept seeing Alicia's long, silken black hair. Seeing her from the back, walking arm in arm with Shelly the day after they had both dyed their hair. He and Danny had been taking the piss out of them, laughing and joking at the Terrible Twins.

Mike opened the door and gestured for the constable to come in. 'Put him in a cell, please.'

A cell? The words screamed in Evan's head. 'Why?' he demanded as he rose unsteadily from the chair. 'I haven't done anything... You can't put me in a cell.' He stared at Mike. 'I haven't done anything wrong.'

'Yes, we can. We need to sort a few things out,' Mike said grimly. 'Take him.'

The officer took hold of Evan's arm above the elbow. Silently, in shock, Evan allowed himself to be led away. When the door closed behind him, Mike said, 'I reckon it might be him.'

'Why?' Kristina was looking at him with that quizzical look he'd always loved. He mentally shook himself. She's married, that means there's a huge 'Don't Touch' sign hanging around her neck... Behave yourself. He gave himself a mental kick.

'Do you know something, I think perhaps, Kristina, that we might be right in thinking it's a love triangle thing.'

'There's four of them. In case you don't know, Mr Yorke, a triangle has only three sides.' She held three fingers up, as she repeated with a sarcastic twitch to her lip, 'Three sides.'

'Don't be picky.'

She laughed. 'OK, so what do you reckon?'

'Remember – although nobody has legally declared it, we still have one girl missing. What if one of them found out that the other one was having an affair with his girlfriend? That would be a motive as old as time.'

'Enough to warrant?'

'Wouldn't be the first time.' Mike rested the palms of his hand on the desk, and chewed his lip as he looked down at her.

'I don't buy it.' She shook her head.

'Why?'

'Because the way I see it, it would have to be Evan, but I know you're betting on it being Danny.'

'Why Evan?'

'Because he could have done it while Danny was asleep on the bench.'

'Or,' Mike rubbed at the small mole on the side of his neck, just above his collar line, 'Danny

142

could have pretended to have slept for an hour or two on the bench. Now that would give him plenty of time. He'll have a good idea what time the milkman comes. He could have slipped out five minutes before the milkman was due, and pretended to be asleep.'

Kristina tapped her teeth with her fingernail. 'Not sure if any of it holds water.'

'Hmm. Actually, I'm not sure any more either. For a fact, they were seen together too much last night. But I've a strong hunch who the dead girl really is.' He strode to the door. 'Reagan,' he shouted, 'bring Miller back in.'

Two minutes later, Evan was standing in front of Kristina and Mike.

'Would you care to take a ride with us, Mr Miller?' Mike asked.

Evan had a feeling that it wasn't a request. Trembling, he nodded.

CHAPTER THIRTY-ONE

'Idiots!!!'

Dressed in brown monks' robes, tied in the middle with thick string which was fraying at the ends, their hair shaved in the middle into a perfect round spot, the two men kept their heads down and stared at the floor, cringing as The Leader berated them over and over. The tongue lashing had gone on all day, every time something reminded him of the one who had escaped

– and he had been reminded often in the last twenty-four hours.

'Do you realise what could go wrong if word gets out? Do you? Do you?' he yelled. 'It won't just be me, they'll come after all of us. All of us.'

They kept silent, having answered this question too many times to count. Neither of them had a clue who would come after them. As far as they knew, the man in front of them was The Leader. Everything they did was under his orders. If they thought him mad, they kept quiet out of fear. They had seen too much not to be afraid. They had followed him from France – not that they'd had a choice, they did what they were told, and unless there was trouble, like now, life was good. Very good.

Shaking his head, The Leader began pacing the floor. 'How the hell can she have disappeared?'

Knowing this question wasn't meant for them, and that the Leader was just sounding off, they still held their silence.

'Impossible.'

He stopped pacing and turned to them. Silently they waited their fate. The Leader did everything on a whim. If he wanted them dead, there was nothing they could do about it. Fighting would be futile, because everyone in his service would turn against them. They had done the same to others.

Just as he opened his mouth, his mobile phone rang. Frowning, he pulled it out, looked at the caller id, and smiled, his thick lips stretching across his fat face.

'Pray these have had more success,' he said quietly, as he pressed the answer button.

He listened for a few minutes. His face, already angry, grew even more so. Eyes bulging, he threw the phone across the room and, hands clasped behind his back, began pacing back and forth.

Stopping suddenly in the middle of the floor, he glared at them. 'Impossible. She's only a woman! A slip of a girl. No peasant girl can outwit me. Impossible.'

They kept their heads down. A moment later they heard the door slam, then the key turn in the lock. Quickly they glanced at each other, their fear jumping the space between them. Finding out at first hand what it was like to be on the other end of the treatment they had been dishing out for years, the brother on the left felt his heart swell and burst with fear. As he collapsed in a heap, the other, a lapsed Catholic, fell to his knees, imploring the God he had neglected for years to save him.

CHAPTER THIRTY-TWO

Tarasov and Prince Carl shared a taxi to the airport. Prince Carl was bumming a lift home from Tarasov. His own private jet was in use by his family, who were looking at property on Bali. They joked about it as they watched the English countryside flash past them.

'So both daughters are finally leaving the nest?' Tarasov asked, a smile in his voice.

'Yes, and friends at last. Thought it was never

going to happen. Although Sabrina is the first-born, Aimee is her equal in everything, actually surpassing her in some things. I'm pleased they've finally buried the hatchet. The last thing I want is a family war. Both girls have quite a following.'

'Your Sabrina will be the first woman leader for nearly fifty-seven years, is that right? When her turn comes, of course. And that, we both know, won't be for a long time yet... Hopefully.'

Prince Carl sighed. 'That has been a bone of contention between them for years, ever since they were brought into the loop – when my brother and his oldest son were lost to us in that plane crash.' He shuddered. 'The only thing we can't account for – genuine accidents...' He paused for a moment, then, shrugging the past away, went on, 'When Aimee found out that her sister would be the family head when I pass on...' He shook his head, remembering just how very badly she'd freaked out. 'Any problems like that with your children?'

'No,' Tarasov said simply, but thinking, not with my children. The three of them inherited their mother's weak genes, all of them too easygoing for their own good. None of them will be a force in the families, though a couple of the grand-daughters are looking good. The shame of it all, though, one of the peasant bastards I fathered thirty years ago is a real mover and shaker. He will rise, but can't ever be in the loop. He will never be recognised as one of mine. Even if I pointed him out, family shoulders will only shrug. So what? It happens all the time. We all have a peasant or two like him.

Tarasov had murdered his older brother when he'd been admitted to the loop – pushed him off a mountain when they had been skiing. Suspicions had been aroused, but no one had come right out and said anything. It happened, had been happening for centuries. It was the way of the families. The leaders had to be the strongest. It was the way, had been since the beginning. Sometimes the true leader was not always the first-born.

He turned to Prince Carl, and broke a cardinal rule. He spoke about family business away from the meeting. 'Tell me, do you think that Simmonds is overreacting? We all know how excitable he can get, sometimes over the smallest little thing. How he doesn't blow a gasket when he gets het up, I'll never know.'

He watched as the blood flushed Prince Carl's face and neck. Prince Carl looked at the driver, noticed the wires coming from his ears. Obviously a music freak. Safe though, they had used him often enough. Turned his face to Tarasov, he studied him for a moment before saying, 'No, I don't think he is for once. These are trying times. A loose cannon is the last thing we need.'

'Yes. I suppose the fool in Northumbria will only end up attracting attention to himself.'

Prince Carl nodded his agreement. 'I'm afraid we made a mistake in not clamping down on free speech a long time ago. In my opinion, we have always been too lenient with the peasants. They should have found out long ago who the real masters of the world order were. I have always thought it a mistake that would one day rear up

147

and bite us when we least expected it to.'

'Ahh, but think about it, Carl, we have. You can still lose your head in a lot of countries for having a loose tongue. Disappearances can still very easily be arranged.' He took out his gold cigarette case and offered Prince Carl a cigarette.

'No thanks. Not keen on those Turkish ones.'

Tarasov shrugged, took one out for himself, and when he'd lit it went on, 'And the British and Americans are well on their way to losing what they see as a constitutional right. The do-gooders are curbing free speech on a daily basis. It makes me smile when I read of some of the silly things they come up with, and the government backs them! Running scared in case they upset this minority, or that minority. Playing right into our hands.' He rubbed his hands together to emphasis the fact. 'Yes, give credit where it's due, Slone worked well on introducing that ploy.'

Prince Carl laughed. 'Yes, he did. Who would have thought the peasants would fall for that one? Especially as he had the gall to call it 'political correctness.' And Simmonds, you've got to give him credit for taking the competitiveness out of English school sport. Now that was a stroke of genius. Really, the silly misguided fools are doing our work for us. And Christmas, what about that?'

Tarasov sniggered. 'They won't be celebrating that much longer. Each year puts another nail in the Christmas coffin... Best thing we ever did, though, was when we gave them religion, now that was a master stroke. They've never stopped fighting with each other since. Must have taken a hell of a lot of planning back then.'

'Ahh, but remember – the Historian still insists that it had nothing to do with us, that all those things in the Bible really happened.'

'Come on – all those things?'

Prince Carl shrugged.

'You're a believer, aren't you?' Tarasov said, looking at Prince Carl with amused disbelief.

'Does it bother you?'

'Hell, no... It's made us all a lot of money.'

'It still does!'

When they reached the airport, the car drove them right to the door of the private plane. As soon as they got out of the car, the driver took off without a backward glance. They boarded, and were soon on their way, heading through the clouds over the rich blue and green world that they owned, and would go to any lengths imaginable to keep that way.

CHAPTER THIRTY-THREE

Jill glanced at her watch. Five minutes later than the last time she'd looked. 'Where the hell is he?'

She shrugged, muttered, 'Men!' under her breath, and glanced at the tide chart on the wall next to the small window. The causeway from the mainland to the island wouldn't be crossable till nearly seven o'clock. So why am I being so impatient? Billy will have made their tea. He always does when the causeway's closed at this time of day. Why am I stressing so much?

The girls knew what time she'd be picking them up from her cousin Billy's house, though sixteen-year-old Jayne kept insisting she was too old to be babysat. 'The days the crossing is open after school I could quite easily make my own way home. And why the hell shouldn't I!'

Jayne repeated this mantra on a daily basis, as if it was pre-recorded and all she had to do was press a button for the words to spew forth. Perhaps she was right. But Jill wanted them where she knew they were safe.

Am I being the control freak that Jayne constantly accuses me of being?

She shook her head in denial. No, Jayne is nothing but a miserable twisty little cow most of the time, with a sense of humour that went into serious decline a good few years ago. A teenage whirlwind, who thinks the world revolves around her and no one else. Her attitude alone causes more friction than enough in the flaming house.

Daily Jill thanked God for thirteen-year old Cassie, a sweetheart. She smiled at the thought of Cassie. Though to be truthful, not so long ago, Jayne had also been a sweet even-tempered child. Jill sighed. Hormones! Who the hell invented them?

A knock on the door disturbed her thoughts, and she got up. 'Come in.'

Mike put his head round the door. 'All ready for us?'

'Sure.' About time, too. She opened the drawer and pressed the button that would automatically push out the panel bearing the dead girl, and

150

watched as a man and a woman PC followed Mike Yorke into the room.

The man was visibly trembling, his eyes darting here and there around the room, anywhere but at the table. Finally they found a spot in the region of his shoes.

'Evan Miller, meet Jill Patterson, our very own pathologist,' Mike said.

Definitely don't like the twinkle in his eye. And it is a twinkle, however clichéd it sounds. The man's a menace, Jill thought, and the silly police-woman's falling all over him already.

'Huh,' she said, not meaning for it to come out loud, as she held out her hand to Evan.

'Sorry?' Mike looked at her.

'Nothing,' Jill said quickly, giving Mike a look as if he was hearing things.

Withdrawing his gaze from his shoes, fully aware of the undercurrent between the two of them, but wanting to get this over and done with, Evan said, 'Pleased to meet you – but can we get it over with, please?'

He swallowed hard past the lump in his throat as, with a small smile, Jill nodded, and stepped closer to the table. She lifted the sheet and neatly folded it over, exposing the pale face of the unknown girl.

Evan gasped.

For a moment he was stunned. Nothing had prepared him for this. Even though, deep down, he'd half-expected it, on the way here neither of the coppers had mentioned that it could be Alicia. Even though he had a feeling, he had been too frightened to ask outright.

'It's her,' he whispered, then louder as he knuckled tears from his eyes, 'It... It's Alicia... Ohh, my God, Alicia. No, no,' he wailed. He felt his legs give way as the blood drained from his face. The next moment he was being helped from the floor by Mike's strong arms, his hands under Evan's armpits. He was led to a chair in the corner and handed a drink of water by the police-woman. 'Sip it slowly,' she cautioned.

Evan nodded automatically, before taking a sip then handing the plastic cup back to her.

Mike stared at him, almost convinced that Evan was innocent. Either that, or a fantastic actor and liar. He saw no reason to show him the state of the girl's back. If this man's innocent, then to see what's been done to the woman he loved would be sadistic torture. If he's guilty, well, then the bastard already knows what state he's left her in.

Mike had already tossed around the idea with Kristina that Danny and Evan could be in it together, but he wasn't sure about that any more either. He needed a motive and, although he'd slacked off on the idea that it was Evan and Danny, they still weren't in the clear. Jealousy was one of the main reasons in the world for murder, right up there with greed. If the four of them were bed-hopping then that could have triggered the murder.

He put a hand on Evan's shoulder. 'When you're ready, we'll go back to the station.'

Evan nodded, staring at the table. A small sigh, when Jill covered the body and pressed the button to take Alicia back into the dark, turned into a large sob.

CHAPTER THIRTY-FOUR

Danny lay on the bunk, his hands behind his head, staring at the ceiling. Shelly, dead. No way, man!

It's all a dream. No. It's not a dream, it's a fucking nightmare!

Everything seemed surreal. This wasn't happening to him. He shook his head in denial. He'd never in his whole life been in a cell. No way could he ever let his mother know. The shame would kill her. But it looked like some of these guys had been here more than once. Dates and names, scrawled and scratched all over the walls. One enterprising idiot had even managed to leave his signature on the ceiling.

'Must have been a bloody giant,' he muttered.

Robbie Magee, whoever he was, had at least four entries. A frequent visitor then, just pipping Allan Johnson whose signature was scrawled in three-inch high italics.

Shelly's not dead. She's not. No way.

She can't be. He shook his head adamantly.

So who the hell is that lying in my bed, pretending to be Shelly?

He saw the long black hair, so much like Shelly's, and his mind shied away from the only other possibility he could think of.

No way, man.

The hatch opened, and a tray, containing what

looked like a bowl of soup, two slices of bread and a cup of tea, was pushed through. 'Dinner,' said a disembodied voice on the other side of the door.

'Thank you,' Danny whispered, not wanting to upset the guard in case he put him in a cell with a mass-murderer, or worse, a rapist with a liking for men.

You see things like that all the time on the telly.

The hatch slammed shut with a loud clang and Danny jumped, banging his elbow on the wall. Wincing and rubbing the offended joint, he got up and went to the door. It smells all right, he thought, looking at the tomato soup.

'Hope there's no basil in it,' he murmured. Danny hated his food interfered with, as he kept reminding Evan and the girls. Lifting the tray, he took it over to the bunk. Hungry, he sat down and was about to put a spoonful in his mouth when he thought, Oh my God ... they might have spit in it. Slowly, he stirred the soup around in the bowl.

It looked all right, and I'm friggin' starving, shit, I gotta eat. He put a spoonful in his mouth.

'Bastard!' he yelped, as he burned his mouth. Staring at the hatch, he quickly slapped his hand over his mouth. Visions of a huge hairy prisoner, with a dick swinging down to his knees, being thrust into his cell by the guard, pushed all thoughts of Shelly out of his mind.

After taking deep breaths to calm down, and sitting with his eyes shut for a moment, he opened them and looked around.

Still here!

He sighed, and it welled up from deep inside. The tiny cramped cell had not miraculously changed into his kitchen, his table, his soup bowl, filled with the wonderful ham broth his mother made every Monday night through the winter.

No such fucking luck.

But thank God there's no huge hairy inmate sitting next to me either.

He tried the soup again. Still hot, but he could sip. He dunked one of the slices of bread and found that easier. He was famished, and spooned the rest in as if it were his last meal.

Dinner over he put the tray on the floor and lay on the bunk with his hands behind his head.

How long can they hold me here without charging me?

Was it twenty-four hours, on 'The Bill'?'

Or was that how long you had to be missing, before...? God, my head hurts.

Shelly's the soap fan, she would know.

Shelly's dead!

'She's not, she's not.' He rolled onto his stomach. Tears streaming down his face, he began punching the mattress, yelling over and over, 'She's not dead... Shelly is not dead. No way.'

Suddenly he yelped, as someone touched his shoulder. He had been making so much noise he hadn't heard the guard come in.

'Splash some water over yer face, young 'un, and follow me.' The guard, an Asian with long Elvis Presley sideburns, spoke gruffly, but not unkindly.

'Where, where to?' Wide-eyed, Danny stared at the man, his mind assaulted with horrors. God, I

155

could end up anywhere. Never to be seen again.

'Back to the interview room, where the hell do you think? Some time today, OK?'

Danny got off the bunk, washed his face, and hurried after the guard. It was the same room, with the same damp spot on the far wall, and the same two coppers. Only these two didn't play good cop, bad cop. They were both bloody nightmares.

Barely waiting until Danny had sat down, Mike said 'You'll be pleased to know that the lady in your bed was not your girlfriend Shelly An–'

'What?' Danny interrupted, his mouth hanging open.

'The body isn't Shelley's.'

'Not Shelly?' He jumped up. 'You mean, it's not her? Not my Shelly?'

'That's what I said.' Mike couldn't keep the amusement out of his voice.

'Yes!' Danny yelled. He punched the sky, went to sit down, missed the seat and fell on the floor.

Grinning like a fool, he scrambled back onto the seat. 'Not Shelly,' he repeated, looking at Kristina as if she was a long-lost friend, and not the monster he'd thought she was.

Shaking his head, he kept muttering, 'Not Shelly.' After a moment, he looked up at Mike, who was standing beside the window. The fear back in his eyes, he asked, 'So, er, so who is it?'

'I'm sorry to have to tell you this, but it's your mate Evan's girlfriend. Alicia.'

'Oh, God no.' Deflated, Danny fell back in his chair. Alicia, he thought, poor, poor Alicia... Poor Evan. He looked up at Mike. 'Where's Evan?'

'In a room down the hall, waiting for you. The time of death has been established, and you're in the clear. You were both at the hospital.'

'Does that mean...'

'Yes,' Kristina put in, 'you're both free to go.'

'Don't disappear, though,' Mike said as he opened the door. 'We still need to know what the dead woman was doing in your bed. Leave information about where you'll be staying at the desk. For obvious reasons, you can't go home.'

Danny shuddered. 'I'll be with Evan. I'll have to stay with him, can't leave him on his own.'

'Thought so.' Mike nodded, and patted Danny's back as he passed him.

He closed the door and looked at Kristina, his face grim. 'OK. We have to get to work. We have a mutilated body with no motive and no suspects.'

Kristina nodded. 'You're adamant it's neither of those two now?'

'Pretty much so at the moment.'

'Yeah, me too.' She took the photographs of the dead girl and pinned them all on the board, stepped back and stared at them. A moment later she puffed out her cheeks and said, 'We've got to get this one, Mike. What's happened here has not been a moment of sudden rage, jealousy or greed, not even downright caveman, spoilt brat, temper. Believe me, the bastard's enjoyed this. Boy, has he... He'll strike again. I wouldn't be surprised if she's not the first. Looks like a disciplinary action gone wrong. Or some sort of crazy sex game.'

'Where, though?' Mike shook his head. 'You say it's happened before, but we have no precedent for this at all. I've never come across the likes of this in my life. Someone so terrified that they basically bleed out of their skin?'

Still staring at the photographs, Kristina sighed. 'It's a power thing, gotta be.'

'I'm more inclined to agree there. A sex game wouldn't go this far. Deaths have occurred when someone got over-excited, but they've mostly been accidental. To me, this was intended to cause death... It's a punishment for something.' Mike nodded at the photographs. 'Definitely.'

'But why put her in Danny's bed?'

Mike shook his head. 'Pass.'

'Do you think maybes Danny could have pissed someone off? Or maybes she has.'

'But why Alicia and not Shelly? None of it makes any sense.'

'And where does Evan fit in?'

'Jesus Christ. A riddle within a riddle.' Mike patted his pockets. 'Got a fag?'

Kristina walked back to the desk, opened her bag and gave him a packet of Regal King-Size.

'Light?' he asked, grinning, as he took a cigarette and put it between his lips.

'God!' Kristina snapped, 'no change here, is there? Don't you know where the shops are?'

Mike smiled. 'Here, love.' He handed the lighter and cigarettes back, then went over to the window, opened it wide, had a look round and stuck his head out.

Kristina shook her head as Mike blew smoke rings into the sky. Like Mike, she'd seen enough human depravity, things that never left the police station, the kind of stuff that you never took home

158

with you, or it would shadow your life forever.

Walking over to stand beside him, she squeezed his arm. 'Don't worry, Mike. We'll get him,' she said quietly.

CHAPTER THIRTY-FIVE

Having hidden at the back of the garden for over an hour, knowing there was someone inside, Shelly watched a man and a woman leave the cottage and drive off. She waited a further five minutes, just in case they forgot something and came back, before creeping up to the window and looking in.

The cottage was at the edge of the village, its nearest neighbour an easy fifty yards away, with the back garden leading onto the field. The window Shelly was looking into gave her a view of a small, but very neat kitchen.

'So where's the key?' she muttered.

Having never broken into anywhere before, she didn't have a clue where to start. But she had to get in. Her need for food was building rapidly, and she desperately needed some footwear. She started to shake. The day was certainly warm, but the heat she was feeling belonged somewhere in the tropics.

She tried the plant pot outside the door. No joy there. It had been a long shot anyhow. Likewise, the dustbin held nothing underneath but a half a dozen snails.

159

She would have to break in – and the place was covered with burglar alarms.

Must be guarding the crown jewels, she thought. Looking around, she spotted a half-brick lying on the grass near the shed. Picking it up, she weighed it in her hand as she studied the shed for a moment. She decided to try the door. It was open.

Cautiously she peeked inside. The usual garden shed implements covered the walls. There was a bench running along the window wall that looked out onto a garden planted with neat rows of carrots, potatoes and leeks. She'd eat the carrots raw if she had to but balked at the leeks. She nearly missed the envelope, but her eyes skittered back to it.

Still being very cautious, her senses tuned for the slightest noise, her body poised and ready for flight, she stepped into the dark interior and walked over to the bench. For Katie, it said on the envelope. Who the hell Katie was didn't matter to her. Shelly's need at this moment was greater than any Katie could have. Ignoring the shaking, which had suddenly become a lot worse, she quickly tore the envelope open. If she thought there might have been some nourishment in it, she would gladly have swallowed it whole.

'Please, God... Please, God,' she whispered. Then, a moment later, joyously, 'Thank you... Thank you!' as a large key fell from the envelope into her hand.

'It's gotta be for the back door,' she muttered, overjoyed at her find, the only good thing to have happened in the last twenty-odd hours. The very worst hours of her whole life. Guess good things have gotta happen some of the time.

'Thank you.' She kissed the key.

'Whoa,' she said a moment later, heading out the door, as she wobbled and hit her shoulder on the frame. Knowing that her sugar levels were dropping rapidly, and that she was well on her way to a bad hypo or worse, she tried to hurry. But her legs were dragging, each step slower than the one before, as she rocked from side to side like someone on the outside of more than one bottle of wine.

It felt as if she was plodding through treacle. Pretty soon she just wouldn't care any more.

She might have a few minutes, or the next step could find her on the ground.

CHAPTER THIRTY-SIX

Evan and Danny stepped out of the police station. Silently lost in their own thoughts, they headed towards Evan's flat. Neither noticed the two men emerge from the dark side street, and follow them down the road.

Still without saying anything, Evan because he had nothing to say, and Danny because he didn't know what to say without putting his foot in it, they reached the door to Evan's flat. Evan put his key in the lock, turned it, and was suddenly pushed from behind. Losing his footing, he landed inside on his hands and knees.

'What the hell are you doing, Danny, you bloody idiot?' He turned as he got up, the angry expression on his face changing to one of puzzlement when he saw Danny struggling to pull Liam's large hand off his mouth. He found himself standing eye to eye with Gary.

'What?' he asked flatly.

'Inside.'

Liam dragged a struggling Danny through the door, kicked it shut behind him, and followed Gary, as Evan backed down the hallway.

'Sit,' Gary snarled, when they were all in the sitting room. Evan sat down quickly, while Liam pushed Danny down onto the settee.

'Fuck off, yer ugly prick,' Danny shouted, when Liam finally let go of his face. 'Who do you think you are? Acting like a pair of friggin' thugs, you ... you...'

'Shut it,' Gary hissed.

'No, I won't shut it. His fucking hands stink of garlic. Have you never heard of soap and water?' Danny spat the taste of garlic out of his mouth and, lifting up a corner of his T-shirt, rubbed his lips. Glaring at Liam, he muttered, 'Scruffy bastard.'

Liam shrugged and sat on the chair facing them, as usual leaving what was to be said to Gary.

'Right, yer stupid twat, where the fuck is she?' Gary's question was directed at Danny, while Evan looked on, totally out of synch, feeling as if he was on the inside of a fish tank receiving the world five seconds after everyone else. All he could see was Alicia's pale face. Right now it was all he wanted to see. He couldn't have cared less what was going on around him.

'I don't know,' Danny yelled back. 'Do you think for one minute I'd be sitting here if I did? Anyhow, how did you know that ... that me and Shelly were, er...' Deliberately, they had not told Shelly's brothers that they were together, because she was adamant that she had to prove herself without them. She had big plans, had Shelly. Sometimes, when she was in full flow, Danny wondered if he was part of these future plans.

'Living together,' Gary put in. 'What do yer think we are? Like we're gonna let our little sis go walkabouts? Like we didn't know she was shacked up with you? We knew from the beginning... She seemed happy, it's what she wanted.' He shrugged. 'OK, it hurt when she turned her back on us, but we gave her the space she wanted... And look what the fuck happens.'

Danny recoiled, his head pressed back on the settee to escape Gary's face, which was now only four inches from his.

'She, she went out two days ago, and that's the last I saw of her. I was gonna start looking today, honest. Then the next thing I find,' he glanced quickly at Evan, 'well, you know.'

'Know what?'

Danny swallowed hard. He practically whispered, 'The dead girl.' He looked out the corner of his eye at Evan, but it seemed Evan was totally unaware of his surroundings. 'It, it's Alicia, Evan's girlfriend.'

'Ohh.' Gary swung his head towards Evan. 'Sorry for yer loss, mate. Truly we are. If there's anything we can do, yer've just gotta ask... But yer gotta understand here, mate, because of her condition, we've gotta find our Shelly.'

Evan went right on staring at the fireplace, his expression a total blank. Everything Gary had said had gone straight over the top of his head. Gary turned back to Danny. He glared at him for a minute that seemed to stretch to ten. When Danny began to fidget, Gary said at last, 'She's a fucking diabetic, yer stupid prick. She can't just go walkabout, no way. And she wouldn't anyhow, not unless she was terrified of something. And you'll know as well as we do, our Shelly isn't easily frightened... So what the fuck's been going on? You beating her up, eh? Are you? 'Cos if you are...' He lifted his fist. 'I swear I'll fucking well kill you.'

'No, no,' Danny protested, horrified that anyone could even think that he would hit a woman. 'I wouldn't...' He sighed. His eyes full of tears, he repeated, 'I wouldn't. Honest to God.'

'OK.' Gary stepped back, letting his hand, still clenched in a fist, fall to his side. 'Let's say I believe yer, just for the time being. OK... So who's her best mate up here? You know, the one she hangs out with the most?'

Danny looked at Evan again. 'Al... Alicia.'

'Thought as much.' Gary stopped himself just in time from saying, And look what happened to her. 'There must be others?' He frowned at Danny.

'Yeah, a couple, I was going to look them up today.' He nodded, eager for Gary to think he was on the case.

'Right. We'll go and grab something to eat, then we'll come back for you, OK... So don't do any sort of disappearing act. 'Cos we'll find you. And God help yer when we do.'

Eyes wide, Danny nodded again, wanting rid of them for Evan's sake, but pleased in a way that he had them onside in his coming search for Shelly. Some of the creeps he had to visit, he'd rather have a bit of muscle with him. Plus he needed some time to come to terms with what had happened to Alicia. He couldn't shake off the black thought that Shelly might have suffered the same fate. But if she has, where the hell is she?

Is she lying in some godforsaken hovel, like a piece of discarded rubbish?

Please God, don't let her be lying somewhere all alone, not that, please not all by herself, he begged.

Sighing deeply, he got up to see them out. He had only taken a few steps when there was a sudden pounding on the door. Passing Gary and Liam, he hurried down the hallway. Opening the door, he found Alicia's family standing outside. Her mother, grandfather and two uncles, the only family she possessed, apart from three small cousins. Danny ushered them in.

'I better put the kettle on,' he whispered to Gary and Liam. They nodded, and made their way to the door. 'See you in a bit,' Danny said, closing the door just as Alicia's mother started crying. With a heavy heart, he went back into the sitting room.

CHAPTER THIRTY-SEVEN

Mike spun the pen through his fingers like a majorette's baton. After it had clattered on the floor for the fourth time, Kristina said loudly, 'For Christ's sake, Michael.'

'Oh, oh, I'm in trouble... Michael!'

Kristina, like Aunt May and a few good friends, only ever used his full name when they were annoyed with him.

'I'm trying to concentrate here.' She scowled, and he smiled at her. Ignoring his attempt to charm her, she turned back to her computer. 'Go and find someone to arrest.'

'Now, that's a good idea. Any suggestions?'

She narrowed her eyes, and he knew he was heading into deep water. 'OK, sorry. Fancy a drink?'

'A coffee would be good.'

Pulling a sour face, he said, 'Yeah, OK. Though why you still drink that poison...' He waved as he headed out of the office. Only then did Kristina allow herself a smile.

She'd loved Mike once, probably still did a little. Who wouldn't love a man who took time out of his busy life to help train a bunch of football-mad kids, visit his maiden aunt as often as he could, call in at the RSPCA at least once a month with a tray of dog food? It was only because he spent so much time away that he didn't have half a dozen mangy mutts of his own.

But, boy, could he be as pig-headed as he was charming.

Sighing, she shook her head. And now, from what he'd told her, he had another couple of lost souls under his wing.

She pressed a few more keys, then sat back in amazement. Quickly she read down the page.

'Mike!'

CHAPTER THIRTY-EIGHT

Shelly knew she had to reach the fridge, but the reason why was fading fast. Drink? Eat? Drink? The fridge seemed a thousand miles away and travelling, as, wobbling from side to side, she slowly crossed the kitchen floor. 'Gotta get there,' she muttered, 'just gotta get there.'

She stared at the tiled floor for a moment; red and white tiles. OK, take one at a time.

'Why?'

Sugar, I need sugar, that's why. I have to have it. Have to or die.

Reach the fridge, gotta reach the fridge. She stared at the large white door. There'll be food inside.

'Why bother?' she muttered, her foot hovering over a red square. ''Cos, 'cos them bastards will, will, win if, if I don't get there, there.'

Putting her right foot down, she dragged the left foot forward. Slowly, one step at a time, her mouth set in a stubborn line, she reached the fridge. All she wanted to do was rest, but something was driving her on. She knew deep inside that to stop now would be fatal, but her reason for crossing what had become an immense space was fading fast.

She stared at a fridge magnet of the Tower of London as her hand scrabbled weakly at the fridge door. Her fingers might as well have been feathers for all the good they were. Her heart was pounding so hard and fast now, it seemed as if it would burst.

Rapidly she blinked. Her eyes were full of glittering shards. She shook her head to dispel them as her fingers finally settled on the handle. She pulled at the door, but it seemed to be stuck tight.

'Open, damn it.' Her words were slurred. She wanted to sit down, anywhere would do, she really couldn't care less now.

With a sigh, she gave up and slowly started to slide down the side of the door.

CHAPTER THIRTY-NINE

'What?' Mike frowned, putting his head round the door. 'A mouse in the house?'

Kristina tutted. 'As if... No, look.' She pointed urgently at the screen of her PC.

Mike moved into the room. A moment later, he said, 'Well, that was kept quiet. How the hell has this not been heard of before now? Jesus Christ...

Come on, Kristina, it's just about one of the nastiest things we've ever seen.'

'A need-to-know basis perhaps?'

'Get me that guy on the phone.' He moved to the world map that took up half the office wall, and concentrated on a small town in France.

When the call came, it was from a Detective Benoit Moreau, whose English was impeccable. More than can be said for my French, Mike thought, as he said, 'Hello, this is Mike.'

'Hello, hello,' Moreau replied. 'You are enquiring about a body of a young man found in a bed early last year, yes? A body that had been scourged.'

Mike winced, seeing the girl's back all over again. 'Yeah. Sickening, isn't it.'

'I had nightmares for months,' Moreau said. 'He reminded me so much of my son. Same age, same colouring.'

'Is there anything you can tell me about the case? Did you arrest the murderer?'

'No ... it was, as you say, a one-off. No leads, nothing. When his partner committed suicide, the case was closed.'

'She committed suicide?' Mike frowned at Kristina.

'It was not a she.'

'What... Oh, so they were gay?'

'Such a silly word for homosexuals, but yes, they were gay. The case was closed.'

'And you were happy with that?' Mike sensed a note of discontent in Detective Moreau's voice.

'I had no choice. The orders came from way above me. I was ordered to let it go. But Detective

169

Yorke, I had ... have a feeling that it was a warning.'

'A warning?'

'Yes.'

Mike felt as if he was trying to pull teeth. Moreau wanted to talk, but there was something holding him back, and he was choosing his words very carefully. 'You mean it wasn't the partner?'

'No. The partner's alibi was sound. He was on stage, three hundred miles away, at the time of death.'

'Hmm. Famous, was he?'

'On the brink of international fame. According to my son, that is. He would travel all over France to the concerts.'

'So how did he die?'

'He killed himself two days later, a drug overdose. He was found in his hotel room.'

'OK, so who do you think the warning was for?'

'I have no idea ... I really must go now. I hope I have been of some help... If you find whoever did this, please be so courteous as to let me know.'

'Of course. One other thing, did, er ... did any of the bodies suffer from hemathidrosis?'

'No, definitely not.'

Mike was disappointed, 'So you know what it means.'

'Of course.'

'Oh, well. Bye then.'

'Goodbye.'

Mike put the phone down and looked ruefully at Kristina, who was frowning at him. What she asked next made him feel much better.

'What's hemathidrosis?'

CHAPTER FORTY

'Bloody idiot,' Mike yelled, as the small yellow car cut him off on the turn towards the island. 'Stupid yellow bloody idiot. Hours yet before the tide comes in.'

He followed the car through Beal, over the train crossing, down the long windy road and onto the causeway, and saw that the water was actually lapping at the edges. 'Must have read the table wrong,' he muttered.

Further along he realised that he hadn't got it wrong. The tide was going out and the causeway must have only been open half an hour or so. 'So what's the rush, little yellow bird?'

The car started to slow down. At the same time, Mike saw Smiler sitting on a large boulder at the end of the causeway. He had Tiny with him. A young girl with long black hair was sitting next to him and stroking Tiny who of course was revelling in her attention.

The yellow car stopped alongside them and, to Mike's surprise, Jill Patterson jumped out. Running round the car, she grabbed hold of the girl's arm. Mike pulled up behind them, and got out of his car in time to hear Jill shouting at the girl, who was desperately trying to pull away from her.

'What do you think you're doing? You scared me half to death when you weren't there. You know you have to wait. Don't you? Don't you?'

The girl scowled as she yelled back, 'Why should I? You think I'm still a baby, don't you? Well, I'm fed up with it.' She tried to pull her arm away, but Jill's grip was stronger than hers. 'I'm quite capable of getting the bus home, you know that, instead of waiting three hours for you with boring Uncle Bill. Listening to him rabbiting on about absolutely nothing.'

'You know the rules.'

'Rules, rules, rules.' The girl stamped her foot. 'I'm sick of you and your rules. That's all you're about since we moved to this stink pit. Rules, rules, rules.'

'What have you done to your hair?' Jill shouted, even louder, as if she had just noticed it. Then she looked at Smiler. 'And what are you doing with him?'

By now Mike realised that the girl must be Jill's older daughter. Yes, he thought, on first sight Smiler can be a bit of a shock, but it takes two to tango and she's not going to vent her anger on him. Mike stepped forward. 'All right, Smiler?'

Before Smiler could answer, Tiny growled. Taking his lead from Smiler, Mike pulled the dog to the far side of the rock.

'You! If that dog attacks me...' Jill glared at Mike.

'Calm down, and he won't.' Mike stroked the back of Tiny's ear and felt the dog's hackles begin to flatten. 'Good boy.' Handing the lead back to Smiler, he said, 'Head for Aunt May's.'

Nodding, Smiler jumped off the rock. 'OK.' He turned to the girl. 'See you.'

'Sure,' she smiled. Rolling her eyes in the direction of her mother, she grimaced.

'Get in the car.' The girl finally managed to pull her arm away and, glowering at her mother, stormed to the car. Getting in, she slammed the door behind her hard enough for the window to shake.

'Got your hands full there,' Mike said. 'She, er ... she looks a lot like you. Apart from the...' He moved his hand over his hair. 'You know.'

'It's none of your business.'

Mike held his hands up in mock surrender. 'Sorry.'

'Huh.' Turning, she got back in the car. Without giving them a second look, she drove off.

'Wow, talk about getting burned.' Mike shook his head, got into his own car and followed her into the village. With a sinking feeling, he muttered, 'Jesus,' when she stopped in the street only four houses along from Aunt May's.

He watched as the girl got out of the car and ran to the house, followed by a younger girl. Then Jill got out and went round to the boot. She took a couple of carrier bags out, slammed the boot shut and, scowling, followed the girls into the house. Not once did she look up the street at him.

He was brought out of his reverie by Smiler tapping on the window. 'Gonna sit there all night?'

Shrugging, Mike got out of the car. 'I guess that's her daughters?'

'Yeah, of course. When she called her Mum, it was a dead giveaway, Detective.'

'Very funny... What's she like?'

'Who, the daughter or the mum?'

'Smiler,' Mike growled.

Smiler shrugged. 'She's nice. Apparently her hair was the same colour as her Mum's when she left the house this morning. She says a few of her friends have dyed their hair this week. They're talking about getting face studs now.'

'Can't see her mother liking that, can you?' Mike opened the door, and Smiler and Tiny followed him through the hallway and into the kitchen.

Aunt May frowned at Tiny. She pointed to a blanket in the corner. 'Bed, now.'

Tiny obeyed immediately, and was rewarded by finding a bone hidden in the blanket. Thumping his tail, he sat down, lay down, got up again and turned around a few times before finally settling down, watched by a still frowning Aunt May.

Mike sat on a kitchen chair, stretched his legs out, and winked at Smiler as he sat down in the opposite chair.

'Well,' Aunt May said, looking at them. 'I thought it best if he had something to chew on instead of the furniture.'

'Tell the truth, Aunt May, you love him already.'

'Hmm. That huge ugly beast? I don't think so... Anyhow, I'm off down to see Sally-Anne, it's cards night. But I'll probably pop in and see Jill for a mo first.'

Mike's ears pricked up. 'Would that be Jill Patterson, four doors down?'

'Oh, I wondered when you would meet her.'

'I met her today, actually. She's the pathologist

174

on the case I'm working on now.' He shrugged. 'She doesn't like me very much, I'm afraid.'

Aunt May tutted. 'Well, that'll be a first. Met your match at last, eh? An actual bloody female who can resist your charms. Poor you...Anyhow, she's a very nice lady. And she has her hands full with that oldest girl of hers.' Aunt May looked at him, one eyebrow raised as if daring him to say otherwise.

Mike shrugged again. Smiling at him, Aunt May slipped out the back door.

Suddenly becoming aware that Smiler was staring at him, Mike said, 'What?'

'You're not gonna like it.'

'Spit it out.'

'They killed the wrong girl.'

Mike sat up. 'What are you talking about?'

'They killed the wrong girl,' he repeated. 'The other one's hiding, but she's very, very poorly, close to the vale.'

'What fucking vale?' Mike asked, exasperated. It had been a long day, and he was tired. All he really wanted now was a shower, a couple of cans, and an early night.

'You know what I mean. Close to the other side.'

'Smiler, I really haven't got time for this. Go and watch some telly, eh? I need a shower and a rest.' Mike rose and went upstairs, leaving Smiler to his own devices.

CHAPTER FORTY-ONE

Shelly hit her head on the bottom corner of the fridge, and moaned as her head fell forward. The force pushed the door open. Blinking, she saw a carton of orange juice. Inch by inch, and not even sure why now, she reached for it. Slowly, her fingers wrapped around the carton. Then they slipped and her hand hit the floor.

After a moment she tried again. This time she managed to pull it out, but forgot what to do with it. Her hand, weaker than the wing of a dying bird, flopped and hit the floor again. The carton hit the side of her face, and the loose top came off. Orange juice trickled into her mouth, slowly at first, then more. She swallowed, using her last reserve of energy. And reaching deep within her, she found the strength to grasp the carton, tilt it further up until she was gulping.

She drank nearly half the contents before dropping the carton. She watched, not really caring as the juice ran across the floor and pooled in the corner beside the back door. Slowly, over the next five minutes she began to sit up. Realising her predicament, that she was far from stable yet, she rested her back against the cupboard and, leaning forward, peered into the fridge.

Ham. No good.

Potato salad. Ugh.

'Please don't let them be diet freaks... Ahh,

thank God.' She reached out, her hands still shaking, for the chocolate cake, and brought it to her mouth, practically drowning herself in the cream filling as she stuffed it in as quickly as she could.

Ten minutes later, her sugar levels climbing but still feeling shaky, she got up from the floor and made her way upstairs. Three rooms, two facing each other, the other one facing her. Opening the door on her right she found a small boy's room, untidy with clothes, empty pop cans and chocolate bar wrappers scattered about the place.

Judging by the amount of toy trains and the pictures on the walls, she thought, the little scruff is obviously a train freak.

Nothing there for me.

She crossed the landing. The next bedroom had to be the boy's parents, a double bed with white and lemon bedspread and matching curtains. Noticing the nearly full ashtray on the bedside table, she sniffed. Disgusting, smoking in bedrooms. She never allowed Danny to do that. Apart from the smell, she had a phobia about fire. Moving over to the white painted wardrobe, she flung the door open.

'Yes!' She pulled out a pair of pale blue jeans. They looked a size too big, but they would do. A pink blouse that would fit nicely. Obviously whoever the clothes belonged to was pear-shaped.

Quickly, she took the clothes into the bathroom. There was no time to shower, she had to get out of there as soon as she could. Her poor feet she would definitely have to bathe. She looked down at them and winced. Sore and bleeding, they seemed to hurt more the longer she looked at them. 'Shit.' She would have to shower. It would be quicker anyhow.

No one likes confrontation, especially when they're naked and wet, but she was nearly past caring and figured she would be a match for Katie, whoever she was.

'Bring it on, Katie!' she muttered, as she stripped and jumped under the shower.

Ten minutes later, dressed and feeling so much better, she ran a brush through her hair. Looking in the mirror, she wondered where she'd got that bruise on her temple. Gently she touched it, and winced.

'Where the hell?'

No matter how hard she tried to remember, there was no recollection. Shrugging, she threw the brush on the bed, left the bedroom and hurried down the stairs. Crossing the sitting room, she picked the phone up. She tried Alicia's mobile number first, tutted when there was no answer, and decided to ring their flat. She would leave a message for Evan – if she phoned Danny, she would never get away. He would want the full story now, and there was no time.

What do I say? She paused, the phone halfway to her ear. It will have to be something only Danny would understand. But what?

Sighing, she muttered, 'I love him to bits, but sometimes he's such a damn thicko.'

Making her mind up, she rang Evan. Disappointed that there was no answer, she left a one word message. Danny should know what that means, she thought, hanging the phone up.

Her clothes stuffed into a plastic carrier bag, and pleased for the strong pair of black court shoes she'd found that, thank God, actually fit, she stood up to go. She lifted her head and glanced out of the window. Her blood froze. Her heart hammered in her ears. A face was pressed against the glass, staring in at her.

CHAPTER FORTY-TWO

A few hours later, Mike came downstairs to find Smiler fast asleep in front of the TV. He heard a scratching at the kitchen door, and hurried along the passage. Tiny greeted him with a frantic tail wag, and a friendly whine.

'Need to go out, boy?' Mike smiled as he clipped the dog's lead onto his collar. 'Come on, we'll leave Sleeping Beauty to his dreams. God knows what he'll have imagined when he wakes up. Probably half the village will be full of zombies and vampires.'

They walked up to St Mary's Church, through the churchyard, passing headstones so old that the weather had removed all trace of whoever they'd been dedicated to, out of the gate at the far end and down to the rocky beach.

Mike let Tiny off to roam around, and, pleased that the tide was out, he walked across to the tiny islet where St Cuthbert had spent years of solitude.

Sitting down on a boulder, his back to the large

cross, he stared out at the Farne Islands. Every now and again he turned his head and looked over at the magnificent Bamburgh Castle.

He loved it here, loved the peace it gave him after days, or weeks, dealing with the human depravity that seemed to be getting worse on a daily basis. This was where he'd played as a boy, with his friends who were like brothers, but more than brothers. Tony Driver and Dave Brooks.

Strange how things work out, he thought, as Tiny came up and shoved his head under Mike's hand to be patted. Cops and robbers, that's what we played, just about every day. Me and Tony, the good guys, and Dave always the bad guy. He followed through at school an' all, forever getting flung out of lessons with his big mouth. Trouble was never very far away from Dave. But look where we are now – me and Tony still the good guys, and Dave... He sighed. Dave's gone one better, a real good guy. He only went and joined the monastery on the mainland and became one of the brothers. Who would ever have believed that was gonna happen?

'Amazing,' he muttered.

A breeze sprang up, bringing the smell of the sea with it. Mike breathed deeply. He could taste the salt on his lips as he pictured them running around. Some days they played at pirates, or space ships, but they always went back to cops and robbers. Three boys, one whose parents had died in a car crash, one whose teenage mother hadn't wanted him, and the other used and abused and failed by the system. All three had washed up on Aunt May's shores. She'd taken them in, left her job in Social Services and become a safe harbour for all three. It must be nearly a year since I've seen Dave, and I'm overdue a letter from him. Frowning, he made a mental note to visit the monastery when this case was over, before he went back to Durham. Time... It just runs away with you.

'I thought that was you,' a voice said behind him. Pulled abruptly out of his thoughts, Mike swung round to find Jill Patterson standing next to him.

'Well, hello,' he smiled.

She gave a quick twitch of her lips that Mike figured was an attempt at a smile.

'I saw you from back there. Er ... I owe you an apology. And him. I thought I'd best get it over with sooner rather than later.' Tiny wagged his tail as he sniffed around her feet. She gave him a soft smile and patted his head, adding, 'Actually, it may not have seemed like it earlier, but I really do like dogs.'

'Accepted,' Mike said at once, his smile stretching to a grin. 'On behalf of Tiny as well.'

She gave a faint smile, 'Sorry I was angry, I never should have snapped at you.'

'Kids, eh.'

'Hmm. It was a shock to see what she'd done to her hair. It was the last thing I'd expected.'

Mike remembered the face studs. If Jill thinks her daughter's hair was a shock, wait till the kid turns up tomorrow with face studs. She'll probably have a heart attack.

'She was supposed to wait at my cousin's. Of course, with Billy being in a wheelchair, he

181

couldn't really stop her from leaving. The little bitch hadn't even been to school. She'd been at a friend's. Apparently both of them spent the day dyeing their hair. Then she turned up at Billy's when she was supposed to, as if he wouldn't guess what she'd been up to. He played war with her, she stormed out in a strop and headed for home.'

Mike couldn't mention the face studs without dropping Smiler in it. Instead, he said, 'Perhaps you should check her friends out? They may not be...' He shrugged. 'Desirable?'

Jill sat down on a rock next to Mike. She was quiet for a moment, staring out to sea. Then, sighing, she shook her head. 'Jayne never brings them to the house, and she won't tell me who they are. I've thought of following her.' She looked under her lids at Mike, then swung her head back to face the sea. 'It may come to that yet. Short of chaining her up... She's sixteen. What the hell can I do?'

Mike was at a loss. There wasn't a lot he knew about sixteen-year-old girls. Except that they could cause some mighty big trouble if they took it into their heads to do so.

'I'm sure you put the right groundwork in...'

'Well, I thought I had. She's never been any bother at all until lately. Of course, the divorce...' She hesitated. 'Jayne adores her father...'

Suddenly she jumped up, her face bright red. 'Sorry, I really shouldn't be bothering you with all this. It's not your problem.' Her tone had suddenly turned frosty.

'Really, it's no bother.' Mike patted the rock

she'd been sitting on. 'I was gonna ask you a few things about the case. Why don't you sit back down?'

'You know my working hours, and where my office is. Good night.' Turning quickly, she walked away, leaving Mike watching her and wondering just what the hell her husband had done to make her the way she was. 'Jesus,' he muttered, for a few minutes there she'd nearly been human.

With a sigh, his reminiscing mood shattered, Mike stood up and headed back to Aunt May's.

CHAPTER FORTY-THREE

Mike found Smiler sitting hugging himself, rocking back and forth in the chair. His eyes were tightly closed, and he was muttering to himself in double-quick time.

'Smiler,' Mike said gently, touching Smiler's shoulder.

Smiler's eyes shot open and he stared right through him. Mike, who was not easily frightened by regular everyday things, nevertheless felt a chill that went right into his bones.

'What's the matter, Smiler?' Mike wanted to shake him, but knew that Smiler wouldn't like it. Gently, even though his heart skipped a beat, Mike said his name again. 'Smiler. Talk to me.'

Smiler blinked, then looked at Mike. This time Mike heaved a silent sigh of relief. He knew Smiler was really seeing him.

'What the hell... Are you all right, kid?'

He kept right on staring at Mike, until Mike was about to speak again. Then Smiler suddenly said, as rapidly as gunfire, 'They know they've murdered the wrong girl. They know they've murdered the wrong girl. They know they...'

'Smiler. Smiler, it's all right. Calm down. Chill, OK? You must have had a nightmare.'

Smiler looked vague for a moment, then started violently popping his knuckles, muttering so fast it was impossible to understand what he was saying.

Mike sighed, wondering if the island was the right place for Smiler. He seemed much worse then he'd ever been in London. I think the noise in the big city drowned everything out. Here, though, once the tourists have gone home, there's nothing but peace and quiet.

'I like your Aunt May.'

Smiler's normal voice came so suddenly that for a moment Mike just stared at him, even though, after all this time, he was used to Smiler's dips in and out of reality.

'Sorry, what?'

'Your Aunt May ... I like her.'

Hiding his relief, Mike said, as if nothing had happened, 'Yeah, she's a funny one all right, isn't she? What the oldies used to call the salt of the earth. She's lived on the island all of her life. Born and bred here. Guess she wouldn't live anywhere else... I spent a lot of my growing years here as well.'

'Sounds like you had a good childhood.'

Mike hesitated for a long moment before saying, 'Eventually... I'm going up to bed now.

184

See you in the morning, then.'

Smiler nodded, watching Mike leave the room, wondering what he meant by eventually.

CHAPTER FORTY-FOUR

Heart pounding, Shelly grabbed everything and ran. As she was climbing over the fence into the field, she heard a man shouting, 'Hey, you! Come back here!'

'Like that's gonna happen,' she muttered, as she landed in the field. 'No way!'

'Come back here!' the voice bellowed behind her.

Ignoring him, she ran to the corner of the field and scrambled through the hedge onto the road. Brushing twigs, leaves and grass out of her hair, she tidied herself up behind a large oak tree. Hearing no sounds of pursuit behind her, she waited until the road was empty and headed back the way she'd first come.

Searching her memory, she was pretty sure she'd never seen that face before. Someone as ugly as that you definitely don't forget. Even being pressed up against the window couldn't account for it. He certainly couldn't be Katie. But she knew that just because she didn't recognise him, it meant nothing. The brothers had many foot-soldiers, and she didn't know them all.

Again she cursed herself for having become involved. She'd seen a story, a story the whole world needed to know. She should have found help.

This is way too big for me to handle.

But who to trust?

Who to believe?

Already she knew of a certain high court judge, a police officer and a vicar. And these are supposed to be good people, for fuck's sake, she thought, quickening her pace as she pictured their faces.

If you can't trust them, who the hell can you trust? She knew their names, where they lived and even had photographic evidence. Still hidden, she hoped.

Evidence she would destroy as soon as she got the chance. She wanted none of this. God knows what they'll do when they found out just how much I really know.

But they obviously already have. The thought struck her as she carried on against the wind. For a moment it stopped her in her tracks.

Of course they already have. I wouldn't be here in the state I'm in if they hadn't.

'Fool,' she muttered. Cursing herself, she battled on against the strong wind that seemed to have sprung from nowhere in the last few minutes.

About a mile down the lane was a crossroads, which would take her to the place she wanted. If Danny had the sense to work out what she meant from the message she'd left, he would be there as soon as he understood it.

Which doesn't necessarily mean the same day, she thought ruefully, as she headed on up the road.

CHAPTER FORTY-FIVE

Danny had spent most of the evening with Shelly's brothers, visiting her friends. None had seen or heard from her for a couple of days at least. Now they were trying the last one that he knew of for the second time, hoping that she was now at home.

Gary leaned on the doorbell, still unconvinced that Danny knew nothing about why his sister was missing. He glared at him. 'She better be in, mate, for your sake.'

'Well, if she's not in,' Liam gestured with his hand towards Danny, 'we can't really blame him, can we? It's not his fault. I mean, he can't really be blamed if she's not in.'

Ignoring Liam's attempt at peacemaking, and fed up with people thinking he was a murderer, girlfriend-beater, kidnapper or whatever else, Danny snapped back, as usual without thinking it through, 'Look, I'm as sick of the whole flaming business as you are, OK? Got that?' He glared at Gary.

'Yeah...' Fist clenched, Gary moved forward, his face two inches from Danny's. Whatever he was going to say next was cut short by the door opening.

A pretty blue-eyed girl looked enquiringly at them. She had long black hair, nose studs, eyebrow studs and at least three in her top lip.

'What do you want?' she snarled. They could all smell the alcohol on her breath.

For God's sake, nobody light a fag up, please, or we'll all end up in Kingdom come, Danny thought, but said, 'It's me, Maria, love. Danny ... er, Shelly's boyfriend.' He stepped in front of Gary. 'We, er, these are Shelly's brothers, Gary and Liam. You might have heard her mention them.'

'Get on with it,' Gary growled at his side.

'I am! I am!' Danny snapped back, gritting his teeth.

Talk about attitude!

'We ... we're looking for Shelly. Could you please tell us when was the last time you spoke to her, or saw her? Has she phoned you? Or maybes she might even be here with you now?' He raised his eyebrows hopefully.

In his pocket, Danny tightly crossed his fingers. Ever since he and Evan had left the police station, he'd been skirting around the fact that Shelly might be lying dead somewhere, murdered by the same crazy bastard who had done for Alicia. Or, if she'd been there when it happened, had she managed to escape, and was now lying in a doorway somewhere, looking like a hopeless drunk and ignored by everyone who hurried past her? He knew she always carried emergency sweets in her pocket, he'd seen her through a couple of hypos. He knew they weren't pleasant, and what the outcome could be.

His hopes of her being with Maria were dashed a moment later, when Maria shook her head and tried to close the door in their faces. But Gary had been ready for this, and already had his foot firmly planted.

'Have yer seen her?' he practically shouted into Maria's startled face, as he towered above her.

'No! Now go away, before I call the police.' She pushed as hard as she could on the door, but she was no match for Gary.

'We just want to know if you've seen her in the last few days, that's all.' He punched the side of the door and growled his frustration. 'We need to know, for God's sake. Do you understand?'

'No.' Fear in her eyes, her whole body starting to tremble, she kept on struggling with the door.

Liam put his hand on Gary's shoulder. Understanding why, Gary restrained himself, knowing he wouldn't get anything out of her if he frightened her too much. With a supreme effort, he said calmly, 'Look, we don't mean yer any harm here, pet. We're just worried about our sister, that's all. We need to know where she is. If you're her friend, you'll know why we need to make sure she's safe. Time is important, she could be anywhere and be needing help.'

Maria sighed, and stopped trying to close the door. Her efforts had been fruitless, anyhow. 'The last time I saw her, she was in the nightclub. I went to the bar, and when I came back with the drinks, she'd gone. I asked around, and no one had seen her go. I've phoned her mobile a few times, but either there's no reception or it's dead. And that's everything I know.'

The three men stared at her. 'Look, honestly, that's all I know,' she repeated, staring back at them. 'Now, if you don't mind...' She made to

189

close the door again. This time it was the palm of Gary's hand that stopped her.

'If you do hear from her, tell her to get in touch. Right?'

'Yes. Now, please just go.' He took his palm off the door and it slammed shut.

Bending down, Gary opened the letterbox. 'I'm going to push my number through. If you hear from her, phone me, OK?'

Listening, he heard a faint 'Yes' from somewhere in the bowels of the house.

Hastily, he wrote his number down and posted it, as Liam said, 'Do yer think she's telling the truth, Gary? Only she seemed a bit nervous to me, like.'

'Yeah, she was a bit off for my liking, an' all. I wouldn't be surprised if she's hiding something... We'll be back though, we're not giving up until we find our Shelly.' He turned to Danny. 'We'll drop you at home and we'll be back in the morning.'

They went back to the car. 'I can walk from here, you know. It's not that far,' Danny said.

Gary started the car. 'Get in.'

Danny quickly obliged. When they reached Evan's flat, he said, 'Er ... do you think I should report Shelly missing? It's been forty-eight hours now.'

Gary glared at Danny in disbelief. 'What? You mean to tell me that yer haven't reported her missing yet?'

Danny licked his dry lips. 'The coppers know all about her. Didn't they think it was her who was dead?'

'It's gotta be official, yer stupid dickhead. Don't yer know it's all form-filling these days?'

'Oh right, I'll get straight onto it, then.' Danny quickly nodded his head.

'You do that. We'll be back in the morning.' It was the look in his eyes, and what Gary didn't say, that made Danny shudder.

He got out of the car and went up to Evan's flat, finding the sitting room and small kitchen empty. Pleased to see that Alicia's folks had gone, he tapped on Evan's bedroom door. 'You in there, Evan?'

'Yes,' came a flat reply.

'You all right?'

Evan didn't answer.

Shit. Of course he's not all right. What the hell do I say? Sighing, he came up with the only thing he could think of. 'Want a cuppa and something to eat, Evan? Toast? Sandwich? I think there's some corned beef in the fridge... How about a can of lager? Or I could go down to the chippy. A nice fish, eh? Some chips and mushy peas?'

He patted his back pocket. Shit, no cash.

'No.'

Relieved that Evan hadn't wanted anything from the fish shop, Danny said. 'All right, then... Do you want to talk?' Waiting for Evan to answer, he fidgeted with his belt loops, not knowing what else to say or do. Should I go in, maybes give him a man hug?

But Evan's answer was a final, flat, 'No.'

'OK. OK.' Danny backed away from the bedroom door. There was nothing else he could do. He had never had anyone close to him die before,

191

and was lost as to how to help Evan. He wandered around aimlessly for a few minutes, switched the kettle on, then switched it off, slouched back into the sitting room and flicked the telly on. Nothing on there again, he thought, staring at the blonde woman announcer. Something about floods further down the country. He stared at the terrible mess of people's homes, not really taking it on board. The trouble was, everywhere he looked, all he could see was Alicia's dead body.

It was on his third visit back from the kitchen, with a piece of cold, soggy pizza in his hand, when he noticed the red blinking light on the telephone.

'It'll just be someone wanting to tell Evan how sorry they are,' he murmured. 'People are kind like that.' Nodding to himself, he sat down opposite the TV.

He tried to concentrate again, this time on some sort of murder mystery. But he couldn't figure out what it was about, or what the hell the bad guy had done, or even if the bad guy was a guy. The repetitive blinking light that he could see out of the corner of his eye kept distracting him. Laying his head back, he sighed deeply. His heart weighed heavy inside him for Alicia, for Evan, and for Shelly. He looked up at the ceiling.

Where is she?

Where the hell is she?

Why don't you phone, Shelly? For God's sake, just phone me. You know I'll be worried.

He stared at the blinking light again. 'Should I?' he murmured.

CHAPTER FORTY-SIX

Aunt May let herself in through the back door. The first thing she spotted was Tiny. The first thing she heard was Tiny snoring his huge head off.

'Dear God,' she muttered, then shouted through into the sitting room, 'Hello? Has the Monster from the Black Lagoon been out tonight?'

'Do you mean Mike or Tiny, Aunt May?' Smiler shot back.

Not being aware of having given Smiler permission to call her Aunt May she nevertheless smiled. He seemed a canny enough kid, and God only knew what he'd been through. No doubt, in time, if Smiler didn't tell her all about it, then Mike would. He did seem terribly busy at the moment, with one thing and another.

She walked to the connecting doorway between the two rooms, and said with a laugh, 'It's hard to tell one from the other, but if they've both been out, I'll be happy.'

'Job done.'

'Well done, son. Fancy a chicken sandwich?'

Tiny snorted loudly, and raised his head. 'Not bloody you!' Aunt May curled her lip at him. 'Been all the same if I was a burglar. I could have been in and out with half the house by the time you woke up, stupid bloody mutt.'

Tiny wagged his tail at her, just as Smiler came

into the kitchen. 'Let me make us the sand-wiches, Aunt May.'

'Hmm, why not. Be a change to put me feet up. Two sugars, there's a good lad.'

'Count me in,' Mike said from behind Smiler. 'I'm starving.' He came into the kitchen, headed for the fridge, and took out a can of lager. Looking at Smiler pointedly, he went on, 'No tea for me thanks, got my own liquid refreshment.' He winked as, smiling, he passed them both, went back into the sitting room, and claimed the seat by the log fire which, although set and waiting only for a match, it was far too warm a night to light.

Ten minutes later, they were all seated and tucking into roast chicken sandwiches. Aunt May looked approvingly at the triangular, crustless sandwiches, while they all pretended not to see Tiny slowly wending his way in from the kitchen.

Mike hid a smile. Everything was working out the way he'd hoped. Aunt May seemed to have taken a shine to Smiler, and Tiny was working on her. Mike worried about her being on her own in the winter months, and these two seemed the perfect solution.

'I've been thinking,' Aunt May said, interrupting his chain of thought.

'Hope it didn't hurt too much,' Mike put in, before she could say any more.

Pursing her lips, she looked at Smiler. 'See what I have to put up with from the cheeky monkey?'

Smiler nodded solemnly. He was experiencing something he'd never had, a sort of family camaraderie that gave him a warm feeling inside.

And he was basking in it.

Mike laughed. 'OK, spill it. What have you been thinking about, Aunt May?'

'Well, I'm not sure if I want to go on this walk thing.'

'What walk thing?'

'I told you all about it,' she tutted. 'These bloody people, them strangers, they turned up a while ago and started getting everyone riled up about the Lindisfarne Gospels, saying they should be back on the island where they belong. But I don't like them... I did tell you about it, Mike, I'm bloody sure I did.'

Mike looked perplexed. He was convinced it was the first he'd heard, but he played along. 'OK, tell me again.'

'I just did.'

'Right. Why don't you like them?'

'Well,' she sniffed, 'a couple of them are foreigners.'

'That's no reason not to like them!'

'I know that, silly. I have met some nice foreigners, you know. That Greek couple who come every year, they send cards at Christmas. Then there's that other couple from France, they bring their three kids with them. Very well behaved they are, as well. And a very nice pair of young men from Florida, who come every spring. Actually,' her voice fell to a whisper, 'I think they're gay.'

Mike laughed. 'They can't hear you, darling. Florida's a long way from here.'

Smiler tried to hide a grin as Aunt May went on, 'I know that, clever bugger. But those up at the castle aren't nice men like the Florida guys. They rent some rooms up there at the castle, and look down their noses at the locals, and they order the staff around as if they were nothing but bloody slaves. Sally-Anne told me, she's worked there for years, and says she's never seen the like. Strut around like they own the bloody place. And they wander around with those metal detector things... Sally-Anne swears she saw them tapping walls in the castle. Actually, when I think about it, it must have been Tony I told, 'cos he asked me all sorts of questions about them when he phoned the other week.'

Mike frowned. He was about to speak when Aunt May screamed. Tiny had put his cold nose on the back of her neck and was now trying to lick it.

'Get back, you bloody great filthy beast!' She pushed him, but gently, and couldn't help but chuckle as Mike and Smiler erupted in gales of laughter.

CHAPTER FORTY-SEVEN

Further down the street was a far less cosy scene, as Jill Patterson and her daughter Jayne were at each other's throats yet again.

'But I can't see why you won't let me sleep at Uncle Billy's, on nights when the tide's in. I'm like a prisoner here. I hate it. You know I hate it.' She stamped her foot, which only made Jill all the more angry. 'It's your fault we live on a stupid island, of all places.' Jayne waved her arms around in frustration. 'I mean, Mother, get real. Who wants to live on an island? Not cool!'

'Yes, we live on an island and you were mad keen to come here at first. Why change your mind now? And really, you know fine well you can change everything to suit the tide. It's hardly that bloody damn restricting.'

Jayne stamped her foot again as she shouted, 'Isn't it? You don't get it, do you! We could just move to Berwick. At least there's more life there. I hate this place.'

Jill retorted, just as loudly, 'No, we can't just flaming well move to Berwick. When you are eighteen, then you can stop out on tide nights, and not until. I don't want to hear another word on the subject right?' She slammed a plate of spaghetti Bolognese in front of her. 'And you can get that muck washed out of your hair tonight, it's a right mess.'

Jayne jumped up. 'No, it's not and it won't wash out, see? It's a dye, not a rinse... And I'm not hungry. And I hate spaghetti Bolognese. That's why you made it, isn't it? 'Cos you know I hate it. And ... and I hate you as well. No wonder Dad left, I don't blame him. You eat this pile of shit.'

She pushed her plate across the table. Jill caught it just in time as it wobbled on the edge. Knowing she'd stepped way over the line, Jayne turned and ran from the room, leaving Jill staring angrily at the plate of food.

'She didn't mean it, Mum.' Cassie got up from the chair where she'd been sitting, with her hands over her ears hoping to block the row out, though with little success. She put her arm around her mother's waist, and laid her head on her chest. 'I love it here, Mum. It's much better than where we used to live.'

Staring at the door, Jill muttered 'But she loves spaghetti Bolognese. That's why I made it, you know she does.'

Jill was hiding the real reason why she was so upset. Her daughter telling her that she was to blame for her marriage break-up had really stung. *It's so unfair, but how do I explain it all without coming across as the bad guy in the whole sordid mess?*

Blinking rapidly to get rid of the tears in her eyes, she squeezed Cassie. 'You really do like it here, don't you, love? I know you're bound to miss your old friends, but you've made some new ones... Maybe that's what's wrong with Jayne, she's missing her friends. Speaking of which,' she held Cassie at arm's length, 'have you met any of her new friends yet?'

'Well...'

'Well, what?' Jill looked suspiciously at her daughter.

'There's this girl called Maria, I don't like her very much.' She looked up at the ceiling, as if to check that her sister wasn't spying on her, then whispered, 'She has loads of rings in her face, and I think she's drunk most of the time.'

'Most of the time!' Jill was shocked. 'How many times have you seen her?'

Cassie started to squirm, torn between loyalty to her mother and her sister. 'A ... a few times...

198

She waits outside of school some days. Her and Jayne walk in front of me, and they whisper all the time. She's got hair like our Jayne has now, long and black. I think it's her who made our Jayne dye hers.'

'Made?'

Cassie shrugged. 'You know what I mean.'

'No ... what do you mean? Did she force her?' Jill was frowning at Cassie. 'Did she force your sister to dye her hair? Tell me the truth, Cassie.'

Squirming, Cassie said. 'Not like, she held a gun, sort of forcing. She's been pestering her for weeks, though.'

'Is there anything else I should know?'

Cassie shook her head, trying to look away from her mother's piercing stare. 'Don't know what you mean,' she mumbled.

'Anything, Cassie. Like, have you seen our Jayne drink with this Maria person? Does Maria hand the bottle over to Jayne? I need to know, Cassie.'

'No. Maria does keeps handing her the bottle, but Jayne refuses... They keep whispering about the brothers, but I can't make out what they say because they hurry up and leave me behind. I think they must be Maria's brothers.'

Jill and Cassie fell silent at the mention of brothers, remembering a five-year-old brother and son, dead because a father and husband decided he had to see one of his harem on the way back from picking him up from school. A case of the wrong place at the wrong time. A drunken driver who served a mere year before he was back out on the streets, armed and ready to kill again.

Jill shuddered and held Cassie closer. Thank God for Cassie, she thought, looking up at the ceiling in much the same way as Cassie had done a few minutes ago.

CHAPTER FORTY-EIGHT

Danny stared at the blinking light. It was starting to drive him crazy now. Should I check it?

It could be important.

'No, better not,' he muttered, shaking his head, 'it's probably none of my business. It'll be some friends wanting to know about Alicia, and how Evan is, and I really don't think I can face them myself, never mind poor Evan.'

He went into the kitchen, and opened the fridge. 'I could murder a can, though.' Realising what he'd said, he shuddered and swung his head to the door, praying Evan hadn't heard.

'No joy', he sighed a moment later, looking at bottles of mineral water, and a couple of bottles of wine, which he'd never developed a taste for. Picking a glass up from the drainer, he filled it with water and wandered aimlessly back into the sitting room. The damn light was still blinking at him.

'Shit.' He put his glass on the coffee table then, remembering that Alicia had a thing about glass marks, hastily picked it back up and placed it on a red coaster on the hearth.

200

A moment later, he realised what he'd done. Alicia wasn't here any more to care about glass marks, or anything else, for that matter. She wouldn't ever be here again. He swallowed past the lump in his throat as he pictured her laughing. She'd always had an easy way about her. No way did she have Shelly's stubborn streak, nor her temper. If her family, friends and Evan were happy, then Alicia was happy.

'Don't think Evan's ever gonna get over this.' He frowned, wondering again, who and why?

'Alicia never hurt a soul in her life.'

There had to be a reason, and why in my bed? He shuddered, remembering how he'd thought it was Shelly. He knew he would never be able to get rid of the picture in his head of Alicia lying there so pale on the cold slab.

Is somebody trying to frighten me, or what?

But why?

He sighed. It was all pretty much beyond him. And the flicking phone is still blinking. 'Damn it. Can't stand this any friggin' more.' Picking it up, he pressed the message button. He froze in shock when he heard Shelly's voice, so much that he took none of the message on board.

'Friggin' hell.' Quickly he stabbed the button to replay the message, then again, four more times.

'Etal,' he finally murmured. 'What the hell does she mean by Etal?'

He flopped down onto the settee. Etal, Etal... 'Oh God.' He clasped his hands together to stop them shaking with excitement as a thought occurred to him. 'She's still alive... She is still alive... Thank you, God.'

He stared at the phone, then got up and pressed it again just to hear her voice. He listened to it again and again. Yes, she definitely said Etal.

Sitting down again, he put his elbows on his knees and rested his chin in his hands, running the word 'Etal' over and over in his head. Etal what?

It just doesn't make sense! Why the hell hadn't she said more on the phone? Unless she was in a hurry 'cos someone was after her?

Chewing his thumbnail and totally perplexed, he sank back into the cushions.

What the hell's going on? The frown line between his eyes grew deeper. What if it's the nutter who murdered Alicia? What if he's chasing Shelly?

He took a drink of water. 'Unless...' The next moment, he sat bolt upright in the seat, spilling most of the water over his jeans. Ignoring the cold wet patch, he yelled, 'Yes. Yes. That's got to be it. Etal Castle.' Satisfied with himself that he'd remembered the first time he'd told Shelly that he loved her, and she had told him back, was in the grounds of the ruined castle. He snapped his fingers. 'Gotta be Etal Castle.' He punched the air with his fist. 'Yes!'

Jumping up, he ran to Evan's bedroom door. His fist, ready to knock, hovered in the air for a moment before falling to his side. 'No,' he whispered, 'Evan's not gonna appreciate a trip out to Etal Castle at this time of night. No way, man.'

Turning, he went to the hall closet and picked Evan's black leather jacket off the peg. Shrugging it on, he searched for Evan's car keys. 'Damn it,

202

where the hell are they?' he muttered, after searching all round the sitting room for the third time, looking under cushions, under the coffee table, even tipping the chair up. Scratching his head, he looked around again. 'For fuck's sake!'

Exasperated, and impatient to be away, he went into the kitchen on the off-chance they were somewhere stupid, like in the sink. He'd found his own house keys there more than once. He spotted them immediately, hanging on the key rack. Tutting, he reached for them. 'Might have bloody well known.'

He stopped for a moment outside Evan's door, chewing his lip. He really didn't want to leave him, but Shelly needed him more. He had to go. He left in a hurry and headed into the street. Evan's car, a black Audi, his pride and joy, was parked at the curb. Danny got in, started the car, and, excited that he would soon be with Shelly, headed across the bridge where Shelly had fled a night ago. He failed to see the car, nor the men sitting in it, waiting across the road. Slowly they pulled out behind him and started to follow.

CHAPTER FORTY-NINE

Shelly sat with her back to the ruined inner wall of the castle. She'd managed, more by luck than any planning, to catch a bus that dropped her at Etal, knowing that she would never have been able to make it on foot. Her feet were really killing her now, even though the shoes were pretty comfortable. Her feet felt damp, and she knew they were probably still bleeding. A hospital was needed, far away from here, and as soon as possible.

She sighed, cursing herself again for having become involved. Yeah, it was a great story. Secret families running the world since God knows when. How the hell did I think I could take them on single-handed, when they had their fingers in every flaming pie imaginable?

Who would believe me anyhow? It would just get put down as another stupid conspiracy theory, if that, seeing as they control the newspapers, and the fucking Internet. We're all just a herd of cows to them, that's all we've ever been. Nothing more than cash cows to the bastards!

When she'd first found out about the whole business of the families, it had had a devastating effect on her. She realised now that it would probably have the same effect on everyone, everyone on the planet.

Would it be kinder to keep what I know to myself?

She tutted, thinking, quite a lot of people may even commit suicide if the truth ever comes out. The knowledge would be catastrophic. Suddenly finding out that we are nothing more than puppets. Used and abused by a bunch of fucking creeps.

But should they be allowed to get away with it? Can I let them get away with it? She clenched her fists in angry frustration.

Can I live with myself if I do?

For fuck's sake... They have cures for just about every illness in the world, and they just sit on them.

Damn it, they have got away with it for centuries. My parents died, and they could have been saved... Along with how many others?

It all boiled down to the same question. Who can I trust?

She looked up at the crumbling walls of the old castle and sighed. She loved it here. She and Danny visited often, and after a bit of a panic attack when she got here a few hours ago, she'd even managed to grab a cup of tea and a sandwich at the Lavender Teahouse set in the village post office, before it closed for the day, without actually drawing too much attention to herself.

Using the toilet, she'd taken her insulin, and collected enough food from the shop to see her through a small war. Now she was seriously wondering if she was going to have to spend the night here alone.

'Where the hell is he?' she muttered, staring up at the full moon.

She figured it was around eleven o'clock. Surely he's got the message by now, the stupid idiot? She fumed as she wrapped her arms around herself. A chill seemed to have set in, and she was starting to feel cold. She transferred her gaze from the moon to the stars as a tiny drop of rain tickled her cheek.

'That's all I bloody well need,' she said to the rabbits. She could only just see them as they hopped around the well-mown grass. At the sound of her voice they froze, then slowly one by one they started to disappear.

'Where are you?' She wanted to stamp her feet in frustration, but, knowing the pain it would bring, she kept it in check.

Really, I should have phoned Alicia. But the last thing Shelly wanted was to get Alicia into the same sort of trouble that she was in. Alicia would have insisted on coming to help her.

I will when I'm safe. Have to send her a warning, tell her to back off, keep away.

Alicia didn't know the half of it, and she sincerely wished that she didn't either. But it's done now.

She knew that Danny would help her, give her money so that she could go far away, if there was any place far enough away.

She sighed, her heart feeling a loneliness she never thought possible, and a fear of equal proportions.

A moment later her spirit lifted as the headlights of a car pierced the darkness in front of her. The remaining rabbits froze again, caught in the car's twin beams.

It's got to be him, she thought, jumping up. She had forgotten her earlier resolution to keep off her feet, crying out as pain shot up her legs from her injured soles. She moaned. Slowly lifting one foot at a time and carefully placing it down in front of her, she made her way to the corner of the wall.

She peeped round, her heart somersaulting. It could be them. I know they won't stop looking for me, not until they see me dead. She saw the car, but it was hard to tell what make it was in the dark. She figured it was black because there was no reflection coming off it. Then she recognised Evan's number plate.

'Yes!' She jumped from behind the wall, so excited to see Danny. She felt no pain until she was halfway to the car then, wincing, she dragged herself the rest of the way.

The driver's door started to open, and Shelly held her arms out. 'Danny, oh Danny.' Sobbing with relief, she reached the car.

CHAPTER FIFTY

Danny jumped out of the car, ran to Shelly and grabbed her tightly. In a state of near-collapse, thanking God that Danny had understood the message, Shelly rested her head on his shoulder and cried. Her sobs tore at Danny's heart. He found himself crying along with her.

After a moment, he held her at arm's length. 'What's all this about then, Shelly? Everyone's been worried sick, love. No one knew where you were.' Then, before she had a chance to answer, a sudden thought struck him. He gasped. Does Shelly know about Alicia?

Thinking he was shocked by the mess she was in, she said frantically, 'I ... I'm in trouble, Danny... Really bad trouble.' She put her face in her hands and sobbed. 'You've got to help me. Please say you'll help me.'

He put the thought of Alicia to the side for the

moment, waiting for a better time. 'Of course I'll help you, silly, you don't have to ask... But what do you mean, you're in trouble? Is that why you've been hiding, eh? Is someone after you?'

Sighing, she shook her head. 'I can't tell you. If you find out what I know, and they know that you do, they'll come looking for you and ... and... Ohh.'

'Who will?'

'Can't say... But we have to get as far away as we can now. Were you ... did anybody follow you?' She looked nervously over his shoulder.

Spooked, Danny looked behind him. 'No, don't think so.' He'd never thought to check, but *why would I?*

Because of Alicia, he answered himself. *Because some freaked-out headcase has murdered a wonderful person, and it's looking more and more as if Shelly may be involved.*

'Has this got anything to do with Alicia?' he asked, frowning at her.

Shelly hung her head for a moment, then looked up. 'Not really. Well, perhaps a little bit... Is she all right?'

Oh dear God, what do I say? 'Er... We best get into the car, Shelly. We'll talk inside. OK?'

But Shelly refused to move. 'No. Tell me now, is she all right?' she demanded, panic making her voice rise with every word. 'Tell me!' Grabbing hold of his jacket, she shook it as hard as she could. 'Tell me now, Danny!' Fear stared out of her eyes as she shook him again.

Danny sighed. He could tell by her voice that she'd guessed something was up or, rather, that

208

she knew for certain something was up. 'Please get in the car, Shelly. I'll tell you everything if you just get in the car.'

'No, damn it, I want to know now! What the hell's going on with you? I'm not stupid, Danny, you're an open book, always have been, now friggin' well tell me!'

He had no choice. He knew that Shelly never did what anyone told her, even if it was for her own good.

How to tell her?

How to say it?

Shit!!!

In the end, he did it the only way he could. Taking a deep breath, he said quietly, 'Alicia's dead, Shelly. She was murdered in our bed. I'm sorry... But no one knew if you knew about it. I thought that's why you might have run away... If you knew, that is. But you...'

'What!' Shelly's eyes widened in shock. She slumped against Danny and slid down his body, sobbing hysterically. Danny pulled her up. Half carrying and half dragging her, he managed to get her into the car and in the seat, belted her in then quickly ran round to the driver's side.

Slamming the door behind him, he reached over and cuddled Shelly to his chest. Her sobs were tearing at him, and tears filled his eyes. After a few minutes he lifted her face, wiped her eyes with his fingers, and said slowly, 'You've got to tell me what the hell's going on, Shelly. You know I love you to bits, and I'll help no matter what sort of trouble you're in. But unless I know what we're up against, I can't help, can I?'

'No,' she sobbed. 'Please, Danny, I can't tell you. Because if you know what I do, then they'll do to you what they did to Alicia. I couldn't cope with that. I can hardly bear this. Oh God, I can't believe it. Not Alicia.'

'Just tell me. We'll sort everything else out later.'

'How did they... How was she...' Shelly gulped, then sniffed before going on. 'How ... how was she murdered?'

'I don't know. All I know is, there was blood all over the friggin' place. I've never seen so much of it.'

'But...'

'That's all I know, right?' Danny snapped, sick of her trying to wriggle her way out of letting him know what he wanted. 'Now, for fuck's sake, tell me what the hell's going on.'

She sighed, and stared out of the window for a moment, before saying, 'OK. I'll tell you. But will you get my bag first, please? It's behind the wall.'

'You've got your bag.' Danny frowned.

'No, no, there's another one, a blue carrier bag. It's got food in it, a couple of chocolate bars, other stuff.'

'Oh Shelly, love. Sorry. Do you need something now?'

She nodded. 'I will do shortly.' Sighing again, she leaned her head against the headrest.

God, she looks so pale, Danny thought as he jumped out of the car. 'I'll be right back, love.'

He ran to the wall, looked round and spotted the bag at once. 'Got it,' he yelled, as he went to pick it up. His voice was drowned out by the car starting and the sound of spitting gravel.

'Shit!' Danny yelled, as he appeared from behind the wall. 'Shelly, what the hell are you doing?'

He ran after the car, but Shelly made it to the exit. Suddenly the full beams of two cars blocked the way out, lighting everything up nearly as bright as day.

'What the...?' Danny stopped dead a moment later, as he felt what he imagined to be a gun sticking in his back.

'Put your hands behind your neck,' a deep, guttural voice with an American twang said in his ear.

Danny froze, though his heart was doing double-quick time, 'Is ... is that a gun?'

'What do you think, dipstick?' Danny felt the gun grind deeper into his spine. 'Hands.'

Slowly, heart pounding, Danny put his trembling hands behind his neck.

'Now move towards the first car.' He did as he was bid. 'Not your car, stupid.' The American dug the gun into Danny's neck. Feeling the cold steel, Danny shook with fear. Wondering who the hell are these people? And what on earth can Shelly have done to upset them?, he reluctantly moved on to the first car.

Two other men got out of the second car, and between them pulled a screaming Shelly out of Evan's car. Yelling and kicking, she fought them every inch of the way. 'Get off me you slimy bastards,' she spat, her fingers clawing at anything she made contact with. 'Get off me, now. Go on, fuck off. Danny, help!' she screamed, trying her hardest to break free. But in her weakened state, she was no match for the men.

Danny was in no state to help himself, but struggling, he yelled, 'Leave her alone!' as one of them punched Shelly in the side of her head – only to receive the same treatment himself, from the man with the gun, a moment later.

'Bastard,' he muttered, dying to take his hands off his neck to rub his head. 'Bastard,' he repeated. Defiantly glaring at the gunman, he took his hand down and rubbed his head.

'Clever shit.' He raised his fist to punch Danny again. 'Put them on your head, and get in the car... Move.' The gunman shoved Danny so hard he nearly fell. Recovering his balance, Danny got in the car and watched, fists clenched, Shelly being pushed into the other car. The man with the gun jumped in beside him. He waved the gun in Danny's face. 'One word, one fucking word and you won't see past midnight. Got it?'

Staring at the man in horror, Danny nodded. *Just what the hell has Shelly got herself into? Are these men the reason Alicia is dead?*

DAY TWO

CHAPTER FIFTY-ONE

Danny stared out of the car window, his heart hammering. Although it was dark, he guessed it was probably about two or maybe three in the morning. But he didn't have a clue as to where they were heading, north, south, east or west. The fact that they hadn't blindfolded him was also more than worrying, his imagination running riot. He guessed that if he saw them, it meant that they weren't bothered, because he wasn't coming back.

Oh Shelly, what the fuck is all this about?

There were three men in the car with him. Big buggers, an' all, Danny thought, looking at the one by his side. He was staring straight ahead, as if it were a foregone conclusion that Danny would behave himself.

OK. So what would Evan do?

We have three heavies. He was staring at the bull neck of the one in front. Good God, a bloody mell hammer wouldn't take that fat sod down.

What would Evan do? Danny sighed, getting a threatening look from the man at his side.

Fuck you, an' all, Danny thought, turning back to look at Bull Neck.

Really, the question should be, what the fuck could anybody do?

Goosed, that's what we are!

The car started to slow down, and Danny

cocked his head to the side to look over the driver's head. The man beside him snorted as they stopped outside of a pair of heavy wrought-iron gates, as much as to say, Look all you want – you ain't coming back out.

Danny curled his lip at him, and the man snorted again.

The men in the front turned to look at them. 'Right cocky little twat we've got here, guys,' the man beside him said. The other two shrugged, showing complete uninterest as the gates started to open.

Slowly the car drove up a long, gravelled drive. Halfway there, Danny turned to the man at his side, and was about to open his mouth when the man drew his finger across his throat. 'Keep it shut.'

That did it. 'You fucking well keep it shut!' Danny yelled in the man's face, as he brought his head back and nutted him. The sound of the man's nose snapping was loud in the confines of the car.

He soon found out what a major mistake that had been. A moment later, he was dragged from the car and repeatedly kicked and punched by the three of them. The man with the broken nose seemed determined to kick him to death.

Danny thought he could hear Shelly screaming, as he rolled into a ball to protect himself. Soon, as blow after vicious blow rained down on him, everything started to go dim. A final hefty kick behind his ear dripped more blood onto the gravel and sent him spiralling helplessly into the dark.

CHAPTER FIFTY-TWO

'Danny. Danny.' Shelly's voice echoed in his head, as his eyelids flickered and he swam back up to the reality of his world.

Groaning loudly, he sat up and clutched his right side. 'Ow! The bastards, I think one of my ribs is broken.' He groaned again. 'Maybes all of them.'

'Careful,' Shelly urged, trying to get him to lie back down.

But Danny stubbornly refused. Resting his back against the wall, he looked around. 'Jesus Christ almighty, we're in a bloody cell... What the hell?'

Shelly nodded. 'We're at the monastery near Holy Island.'

She looked at his face and could see the pain he was going through, the struggle to understand what was happening. She'd bathed his head with a small towel beside the equally small sink in the corner, but there was still blood trickling from behind his ear. She guessed that he should have a couple of stitches in there. Most of the other cuts were superficial. She thought, he might be right about the broken ribs, the way the frenzied bastards went at him.

She wasn't prepared when he grabbed her wrist and squeezed tightly. 'What's going on, Shelly? And I want the truth. Are these swine likely to kill us?'

'Let go, Danny, that hurts.'

But Danny had crossed the line hours ago. This was the second cell he'd been in, in the last twenty-four hours. He had been interrogated by a duo of cops from Hell. A very good friend had been murdered, a murder that he'd practically been accused of. He'd been threatened by Shelly's brothers with a fate worse than death if any harm had come to her, whether he was responsible or not. And now he'd had the shit kicked out of him by a bunch of bastard morons, and he had a very strong hunch that he might well not get out of here alive. Enough is enough.

'Not until you tell me exactly what's going on. And I mean it, Shelly.' He glared at her.

'OK. All right.' She tried to pull her wrist back. Reluctantly Danny let go, but instead of speaking, she stared at the stone floor.

'Shelly,' he urged.

Finally she looked at him, deciding to tell him half the truth, because all of it, she knew, he wouldn't be able to cope with. Taking a deep breath, she said, 'This place is used as a storage place for kids. Mostly teenagers who are gathered from cities and towns up and down the A1 and sold world-wide. That is, the ones who are deemed good-looking enough. The rest are kept here to work the drug farms.'

'What?' Danny's jaw hung open for a moment, before he blurted, 'How the hell did you find that out?'

'You know I've always wanted to be an investigative journalist?'

'Friggin' well get on with it.'

218

'I am.' She narrowed her eyes. 'Just listen, will you?'

Danny stared stubbornly at the far wall, wondering what web of lies she'd concocted for this escapade.

'Well, I heard a story so crazy...' She shook her head. 'Didn't believe it at first. Anyhow, with Alicia's help, well, we did what you might call a little digging.'

'So these people, and your meddling, are the reason Alicia is dead?' Danny interrupted.

Tears filled her eyes as she nodded. 'I didn't know, honest, Danny. I heard they were after me. That's why I ran. I never dreamed Alicia was in any danger.'

'So you think they might have made a mistake...' He snapped his fingers. 'That's why she was found in my bed, isn't it? You do look a little like each other, especially since you both dyed your hair black. So what's the story?' He winced and gently massaged his right side, muttering, 'Fucking murdering bastards.'

Shelly wiped her eyes. She didn't think she'd ever get over Alicia's death. She shuddered as a sob escaped. 'I'm sorry, Danny. I'm so sorry.'

Gently Danny patted her arm. 'Just tell me what it's all about, and just what the hell we're up against here.' He touched her hair. 'And why? I loved your hair the way it was.'

'That's part of it. He likes long black hair. He ... he entices young girls, tells them he'll make them famous, star of their own show, all that crap. Only he doesn't tell them it's a pornographic show. Then when he gets them here he

219

changes, dresses like a monk.'

'Christ, what sort of creep is he? Dressing like a monk? Some sort of perve, eh?'

She gave a small hollow laugh. 'There's more Danny... A whole lot more. He–'

'Hang on,' Danny interrupted her. 'Why did you have to dye your hair? Why did Alicia? No.' He pushed her away. Suspicion in his eyes, he went on, 'Don't tell me you slept with him... Please don't tell me that, just for a fucking newspaper story. No way.'

Unable to meet his eyes, Shelly hung her head.

'You did, didn't you!' Danny shouted. Ignoring the pain in his ribs, he laid his left hand on her shoulder and lifted her chin up with his right hand.

She kept her eyes closed and gave a barely perceptible nod. 'Sorry,' she whispered.

'Sorry?' he yelled, pushing her away. 'Sorry doesn't cut it. Alicia died because of you and these fucking creeps... What about Evan, eh? What do you think this'll do to him when he finds out?'

Shaking her head, she begged, 'Please don't tell him Alicia was involved. It'll kill him.'

'You bet it will.' He was quiet for a moment, watching her, his mind in a whirl. 'I won't tell him,' he finally said, to Shelly's immense relief. 'He'll ask, I know he will, but I'll say that she wasn't involved and it was a case of mistaken identity. That's if we ever get out of here alive.'

She hung her head. 'I'm sorry, Danny, I ... I needed the story. It was the only way.'

She reached for him, but Danny pushed her

away. 'You fucking selfish cow... Tell you what, kiddo, it's over.' He shook his head in disgust.

'Please, Danny, I'm sorry. Please don't say it's over. Please,' Shelly begged, reaching for him again.

Danny stood up. Listing to one side and holding his ribs, he moved as far away from her as he could. With his back against the wall, his voice barely above a whisper as he tried to control his emotions, he stared at the woman he had one day hoped to marry. 'You said there was more?'

'Yes...'

The door banged open. Two of the men from the car came in and made a beeline for Danny. He pressed his back against the wall. Yet again there was nowhere to run.

CHAPTER FIFTY-THREE

An hour later, Brother Josh looked over the rim of his glasses at Brother David. Slowly he gave a barely noticeable shake of his head. Seeing this negative, Brother David's lips set in a firm line.

'Brother Josh,' he hissed over the body of the young man, 'if you won't help me, I'll do it myself. Can't you see it has to stop now? We can't go on any longer. This might be the only chance we'll ever get. At the very least...' Pausing for a moment, he looked down at the body. He sighed. Covering his mouth with his hand, he looked at Brother Josh, his blue eyes brimming with tears.

'I can't go on any longer. We have to help ourselves. The outside world will never find out what's happening unless we do something now, before we have to bury any more of the young.'

'If we take action now, and they find out about it, how many will they kill, eh, Brother David? Think about it. The Leader has no conscience at all. He cares about no one. And certainly not his own soul.'

'How many will they kill if we don't?' Brother David leaned on his shovel and wiped the sweat from his brow. He looked across the graveyard. In the last year there had been eighteen deaths, seven brothers and eleven teenagers. Two of the brothers had been murdered. The rest had committed suicide, unable to live with the hurt and destruction they had to deal out every day. Of the eleven teenagers, three had been flogged to death, five had died from drug abuse, a couple from sheer exhaustion, and one had managed an ingenious suicide by climbing to the roof and throwing herself off.

The graveyard was lit by the light coming from the two drug sheds which were joined to the great hall, where children as young as twelve were still working at this late hour. They would work until they dropped. Then a brother would pick them up and carry them to a corner, and wake one of the others to take his or her place. The manufacturing process never stopped.

Brother David couldn't work out if these were the lucky ones or not. Those who were considered pretty enough, boys as well as girls, were shipped out to God knows where. He'd overheard one of the Leader's men saying that the next shipment bound for Africa must have only blue-eyed blondes. His heart ached for them, an actual physical pain. It had lodged there the night The Leader had arrived and murdered two brothers by his own hand. He shuddered at the thought of where these children were going, and what sort of life they were destined for.

There were only six true brothers left. The rest were The Leader's men, a dozen, sometimes more. These masqueraded as brothers, and saw to the daily running of the place. They dealt with the odd necessary visits from the outside world with alarming skill, which led Brother David to assume they had done this kind of thing before.

'It's got to be now, tonight. Who knows what might happen tomorrow? You or I could be dead on a whim of that madman, then there will be no one to warn the outside world. It will go on and on with no end.'

Brother Josh sighed. Resigned to the fact that Brother David would go ahead without him, and with the knowledge that it would be impossible for one man to carry out the plan, he nodded.

Slowly, grim-faced, Brother David prised open the dead man's hand. He tucked the folded piece of paper inside and gently, as if the dead man could feel, closed his fingers around it.

'Are you sure he'll understand it?' Brother Josh watched the dead man's fingers being curled around the note. 'It just looks like a load of gibberish to me.'

Brother David nodded. 'He'll understand. He'll come.'

Moving to the man's shoulders, he lifted them as Brother Josh lifted the feet. Together they carried the body over to the wall, and hid it amongst the thick ivy that climbed up and over, tumbling to the grass verge on the other side.

They hurried back to the shallow grave and began to fill it in, shoring up the inside with rocks to make it look like someone was buried in there, and covering the top with soil. After they were finished, they carried the spades into the garden shed. They waited for a while until one of the many clouds passed over the full moon, then, leaving the shed, they crept silently back to the body. They picked him up, Brother Josh in the lead, with the man's legs round his waist, and Brother David bringing up the rear, again carrying the dead youth's shoulders. Reaching a gate in the wall, hidden by the years of thick overgrown ivy, they passed through, pausing only to rearrange the ivy behind them.

They had a good few miles to carry the body. Walking on the road would be no good. Even at this hour there would be cars passing. They'd thought of putting the body over a bike, but dismissed the idea. Pushing a heavy-laden bike through field after field would be practically impossible. They would have to do it the hard way, and carry him.

Brother David was still young and strong, but Brother Josh knew he was way out of condition, too many pies and far too much mead. They managed, with frequent stops, to pass over three large fields. When they laid the body down for the fourth time, Brother Josh, after stretching and getting the kinks out of his neck, caught a breath and said. 'It's no good, Brother David. We aren't going to make it back before someone realises we're missing.'

'Of course we are, Brother Josh. Take heart in the fact that we are crossing the very ground that St Cuthbert walked on, from Lindisfarne to Durham. The very cave he rested in isn't so far from here. Remember the monks who, two hundred years later, carried his body over the same ground. For seven years, they wandered. We don't even have to carry this poor young man for seven hours.'

Brother Josh hung his head. 'You're right, brother. I'm sorry, it ... it's just that...'

Brother David rested his hand on Brother Josh's shoulder. 'You're weary, Brother Josh. It's to be expected, after all that has happened. Not many would have the strength to go on... But we must see this through, too many young lives depend on us.'

'You're right, as usual. But if we don't make it back, the madman will flog the children as a lesson to the others. In fact, if he thinks he may be in danger, he'll probably kill them all.'

'We'll make it.'

Brother David looked so confident that it gave Brother Josh new heart and the strength to carry on. 'So ... you're absolutely sure the message will be understood by him only?'

'Certain. The man it's intended for is a very good man, with a strong heart, and an even stronger back. He will understand that everything has to be kept quiet. He'll come, I swear he will.

And he'll bring help. Then all this will be over. I promise you, by everything I believe in. He won't let us down.'

Brother Josh smiled as he bent to the task. 'What are we waiting for?'

CHAPTER FIFTY-FOUR

The Patterson household were up early. Mike noticed the lights, upstairs and in the kitchen, as he passed the house with Tiny. He thought of Jill as he and the dog walked along the beach. She certainly was a good-looking woman, but it seemed as if she hated him. Of course, this made him all the more determined to make her like him.

'But how?' he muttered, throwing a stick for Tiny. The dog caught it just before it entered the water. Bringing it back, he dropped the stick at Mike's feet. This went on for a good five minutes, until the last time Tiny dropped the stick, Mike didn't pick it up. Tiny waited, wagging his tail, then gave a bark to remind Mike that the stick was there. Mike, though, was busy, his hand up to shade his eyes from the rising sun. He was watching a helicopter coming into land.

'Now that doesn't look good,' he muttered, as the helicopter headed towards the field between Aunt May's house and the castle. 'Come on, boy. Home.'

Quickly he strode off. He was nearly there

when the helicopter landed. He watched as Jill Patterson ran out of her house, making a straight line for the helicopter. A policeman he recognised jumped out of the helicopter. Passing Jill, he gave her a brief nod, and headed towards Aunt May's.

'Oh-oh.' Mike broke into a run. 'I'm here, Jim,' he shouted, just as the policeman raised his fist to bang on the back door. Hearing him, the policeman dropped his fist and waited, grim-faced, until Mike reached him.

'What's up?' Mike asked, his eyes on Jill, who obviously knew what was going on by the way she quickly scrambled up the helicopter ladder. Then he realised he'd left the house without his mobile.

'There's been another body found, same state as the last one, Mike,' Jim said. He was deeply tanned from his holidays. Mike remembered him saying he and the wife were taking their first trip abroad.

'What, another scourging?'

'Yup... Only this time, he has a note in his hand.'

'Male!'

The officer nodded. 'Aye, and the note's addressed to you.'

'Me?' Mike felt a shiver rush up his spine. 'What does it say?'

'Nobody can understand it.'

'OK, give me a minute.' As the officer nodded, Mike quickly went into the house. It looked like Aunt May and Smiler were still in bed. Mike hurried up the stairs, struggled out of his joggers

227

and T-shirt at the door, and threw them into the laundry basket so as not to incur Aunt May's wrath if she saw them on the floor. He was never so tidy at home.

After splashing water over his face, he dressed in a dark suit and white shirt, grabbed his mobile off the dresser, slipped it in his pocket, put on his watch – a present from Aunt May that he was never without – and ran back downstairs. Hastily he got pen and paper from the sideboard, and left a letter propped up on the mantelpiece telling them he'd left early. Locking the door behind him, he hurried to the helicopter.

He sat next to Jill, who gave him the briefest of smiles. Even that seemed an effort Mike thought. He could smell her perfume, tried guessing which one it was for future reference. Women like it if you give them a bottle of their favourite. But he couldn't quite place it. If needed, he would ask Aunt May.

He liked the way she had her hair done in a French plait, which suited her. He noticed that tiny hairs on the back of her neck were still damp from the shower.

She must have felt his eyes on her. Turning to look at him, she said, 'What?'

'Nothing,' Mike replied innocently. 'Just looking at the view over your shoulder.'

'Huh,' she said, facing away from him.

'So, what's all this about then?'

'You know as much as I do. The body of a young man has been found in the back yard of the police station.'

Hmm, Mike thought, that's more than I know.

228

'So, it's been dumped overnight?'

'I guess so.'

He sat back, 'Has anyone read the note?'

'Aye,' Jim said from the front seat. 'But like I told you, nobody can make any sense of it at all.'

CHAPTER FIFTY-FIVE

Smiler sat at the table, a knife in one fist and a fork in the other. His hands rested on either side of a plate of bacon and eggs. He stared forlornly at the wall in front of him.

'Eat up, sunshine,' Aunt May said. 'They'll get cold. And there's nothing more disgusting than a bloody cold fried egg.'

Smiler turned his blank expression towards Aunt May. She hesitated on her way to the table, carrying her own plate of bacon and eggs in one hand and a teapot in the other. She'd seen the same expression many a time when she'd nursed during the Falklands War, dealing with shell-shocked soldiers and sailors, and then later, when she'd dealt with abused children. She knew that it didn't always need a loud bomb to shellshock the human spirit, be it young or old.

She put everything on the table and said gently, 'What's up, son? You look like you've seen a bloody ghost.'

Smiler's expression changed to one of total panic as he blurted quickly, 'She can't go.'

'Who can't?'

'She can't go.' Agitatedly, he began popping his knuckles over and over, so fast that his hands couldn't deal with the speed at which his brain was working. Out of synch, they dropped to his side as he repeated, 'She can't go. It ... it's day two.'

'Who can't? And what do you mean, it's day two? Do you mean you've been here two days? Smiler, you aren't making much sense this morning, love. Eat up, eh.'

But Smiler stood up and pushed the plate away from him. 'I have to warn her.'

'No, Smiler.' Aunt May was as adamant as he was. 'Breakfast first, then we'll talk. OK?'

'But–'

'No buts.' She pushed his plate towards him.

Obediently, Smiler started to eat. When he had cleaned the plate, he looked at Aunt May.

'OK,' she said, 'spill the beans, sunshine. Tell Aunt May your problem.'

'I...' He swallowed hard. How was she going to take this? Would she throw him out? After barely two days living here in a proper home, the last thing he wanted was to be back on the streets. Dare he tell her the truth? He hesitated a moment longer, then blurted out quickly, 'I see things.'

She leaned close and said with great interest, her head cocked on one side like a nosy little sparrow, 'You mean, like psychic visions sort of "see things"?'

He bit his lip. 'Yeah.'

She laughed, and Smiler's heart sank. But only for a moment, as she said, clapping her hands,

'Great, tell me more.'

'You mean that you believe?' Smiler asked in amazement.

'Why wouldn't I? I've lived long enough to see many a strange thing with no logical explanation. And you aren't the only one who sees things, Smiler. Rest assured, son, you aren't alone... I used to know someone who swore she saw the Virgin Mary on a regular basis.'

'Did you?' Smiler leaned forward eagerly.

'Yeah. She ended up in the nuthouse, though.'

Smiler's face fell. Aunt May reached out and patted his hand. 'Just kidding, son. Actually, to tell you the truth I don't bloody well know what actually happened to Edna Byers. I think she married and moved away... Anyhow, always keep an open mind, that's what I say, and that's what I kept telling my boys. Bet Mike doesn't believe, though.'

Smiler shook his head ruefully.

'Don't worry, it's his policeman's mind. He likes cold hard facts. So tell me, what have you seen?'

Smiler sighed, and did his best to explain. At first he found it hard, and stumbled awkwardly trying to find the right words. But gradually some of his life story began to emerge.

CHAPTER FIFTY-SIX

Cassie walked along the street towards the school. The bus had dropped her off earlier, but she'd backtracked to look in the shops. She'd caught the earlier bus to do just that, leaving Jayne to get the regular one. It was her mother's birthday in two days time, and everyone seemed to have forgotten. Even Mum.

She smiled, thinking of her mum. It had been exciting watching her go up in a helicopter this morning, and, knowing that she was nervous of flying, Cassie had been proud of her.

She looked at her reflection in a jewellery shop window. Everyone said she looked just like Dad, and Jayne looked like Mum. That's true, she supposed. I've got Dad's dark hair and eyes while Jayne has Mum's red hair. Well, she had Mum's hair yesterday morning before she dyed it. Which really was a pretty stupid thing to do, Jayne's hair is gorgeous. I always wish mine was that colour, instead of black.

She spotted a pretty red flower brooch surrounded by sparkling stones, and looked closer. She gasped when she saw the price. 'One hundred and fifty-five quid?' she muttered. 'No chance.'

She sighed, knowing her Mum would love it. Will Uncle Billy be able to lend me the money?

She doubted it. Uncle Billy was kind, but he she knew he didn't have that sort of money to spare. Anyhow, I've got no way to pay it back, and Dad certainly won't cough that much up, not if he thinks it's for Mum. Moving on, deep in thought, oblivious to the traffic around her, she didn't see the car coming her way do a swift turn and pull up slightly in front of her.

She recognised the voice though, a moment later, when she heard, 'Come on, kid, jump in.'

Cassie leaned forward, as Maria opened the door and poked her head out. 'Did you hear me? You're gonna be late. Might as well grab a lift to the school gates when it's offered. Come on, kid – don't just stand there, get in.'

Cassie hesitated. She glanced at her watch, and got a shock. Two minutes to go! Must have been daydreaming.

Still she hesitated. She knew enough not to get in a stranger's car, but Maria wasn't really a stranger – she was Jayne's best friend. Even if I don't really like her, I know who she is.

'You coming, or what?' Maria urged.

Making her mind up, Cassie moved towards the car. The school was only along the road, but the car would be quicker. And she hated being late. Everyone stares at you as if you're some sort of freak. 'Thank you,' she said as she got in.

CHAPTER FIFTY-SEVEN

Mike took Jill's coat and hung it in the closet before they entered the morgue.

'Thanks,' she muttered, walking over to the body, which was laid out with a white sheet covering it.

Mike stood close as she slowly folded the sheet away. The body was lying face down. His back, from his neck to his heels, was in the same condition as the previous one. Both Mike and Jill shook their heads at the sheer depravity of it all.

'Help me turn him over.' Jill handed Mike a pair of gloves. Silently he moved round to the other side, slipping the gloves on as he went.

As they were about to turn him, Kristina walked in. 'Jesus, not again,' she gasped. 'All I was told was to get myself over here, there was a body that might need fingerprinting – not that the poor sod was like this. Oh, dear God... It's so much worse in the flesh.' She grimaced as Jill and Mike looked at her. 'You know what I mean.'

'Afraid so,' Mike said, as he and Jill carefully turned the body. Mike winced, thinking the same as he had when he'd first seen Alicia. No way could anyone be comfortable lying on that horrendous mess. It was one of those ludicrous thoughts that were impossible to shake off.

For a few moments, all three of them stared at the dead young man. Finally, Kristina said,

'Anyone know who he is?'

'Never seen him around before,' Mike replied, as Jill shook her head. 'Er, he hasn't got hemathidrosis, has he?'

'No,' Jill replied, still staring down at the body.

'OK. Guess I'd better fingerprint him, then.' Kristina took her kit out of her bag and got on with the job, while Mike and Jill stepped back to give her room.

'Ohh,' Kristina said a moment later, quickly dropping the man's hand.

'Rat bites,' Jill said.

'Jesus... There'll be no fingerprints off that hand, then.' Pulling a disgusted face, Kristina walked round to the other side.

'Where's the piece of paper that was found in his hand?' Mike asked.

'In the office,' Kristina replied. 'Though it doesn't make a lot of sense. A few wiggly lines and circles.'

Mike frowned. 'Haven't got a clue.'

Twenty minutes later, Kristina waited until a large truck passed before pulling out onto the main road. Mike was in the passenger seat, staring at pictures of the dead man.

This close, he could smell Kristina's perfume. It was different from the one Jill wore, more flowery. He knew the name of this one. He'd bought it for her a few times. For a moment, it took him back four years to another hot sultry summer. Then he wondered why she never mentioned her husband.

A moment later, a loud bang on the windscreen, and Kristina's sudden harsh braking, caused his seat belt to nearly throttle him. 'What the..?' he yelped, looking around him.

'A kamikaze pheasant!' Kristina breathed deeply.

'That'll do it every time.' Mike looked over the car bonnet. There were a few wing feathers captured in the window wipers, but no sign of anything else. 'Looks like you've been lucky,' he observed, easing the seat belt away from his shoulder.

'Yeah, well, he hasn't,' Kristina said, staring at the dead bird through her rear view mirror. 'Bloody damn good job there was no one behind me.'

'Poor thing.'

'It was him or us,' Kristina said frostily, giving Mike a scathing glance.

'Yeah, OK.' Mike nodded his agreement as Kristina set off again. She was right, no argument there, but he still felt sorry for the poor bird. He was looking at it out of the side mirror and didn't see Kristina smile and shake her head.

A few minutes later they reached the station. Kristina got quickly out of the car, slamming the door behind her, and with Mike's help, gave the bonnet a thorough examination.

Mike was pleased they didn't find any damage. He knew, if even one of the avian kind had marked her beloved car, Kristina was quite capable of conducting a personal vendetta against anything with feathers.

He followed her into the station where they were met by chaos.

Mike recognised Shelly's brothers. The shorter

one, Gary, he thought, looked about ready to strangle the desk sergeant. Glancing up, the sergeant heaved a sigh of relief when he spotted Mike. 'See, here he is,' he said, pointing at Mike. 'Told you.' Transferring his gaze to Mike, the sergeant added, 'He didn't believe me when I said you weren't in.'

Gary spun round. 'You, at last! What the hell's going on here? My sister is still missing and so is that fucking prick of a boyfriend of hers. And you lot are doing sweet fuck-all about it.'

'If you would like to come through,' Kristina said placatingly, putting herself between Mike and Gary as she led the way through the double doors.

When they were seated in the interview room, Kristina said, 'I would like to assure you that we are doing everything we can to locate your sister.'

'Yeah, well, it ain't fucking well enough,' Gary interrupted.

'Excuse me,' Mike snapped. 'I'm the complaints department round here. Raise your voice once more, or use any more fucking foul language, and I'll toss you out on your ear. And that ain't a threat.' Mike had spoken quietly, but the menace in his voice was very clear.

Looking at Mike, Gary saw a man whose build was nearly equal to his own. Although he knew the man in front of him was a good few inches taller, it was the way he was staring at him that made Gary back off. There was no fear in those dark eyes, just a blank statement. Don't mess with me.

'OK,' he said after a moment. 'I apologise. I may be overreacting, but can't you see we're worried sick about her? She happens to be a diabetic, and time is important. She could be anywhere, needing help. That prick of a boyfriend of hers told us last night that he hadn't even reported her properly as missing, and now he goes AWOL.'

'Danny's missing now?' Mike frowned. 'Since when?'

'Well, his mate Evan, poor sod, says he's never seen him since last night, and his f... his car's gone as well. Evan's car, not Danny's. Didn't think he had enough common sense to drive.'

'How well do you know your sister?' Mike asked.

Gary frowned. 'What sort of question's that?'

'A simple enough one.'

'I...' He gestured towards his brother Liam. 'Me and my brothers, we brought her up after our parents died. She was only five years old. I think I know her pretty well.'

'Would she get involved with anything shady?'

'No.' The answer was sharp, indignant even. Gary glared at Mike.

'OK.' Mike stood up. 'If you've nothing further to tell us, leave your mobile number at the desk and I'll get back to you as soon as we hear anything.'

'Is that it, then?' Gary frowned.

Kristina threw him a warning glance. Reluctantly Gary stood up, pushing his chair out as he did so. It made an irritating scraping sound. Liam did likewise. Mike winced. At the door, Gary turned to face him.

Before he could say anything, Mike said, 'Trust me. Your sister will be top priority.'

For a moment their eyes locked. Then Gary nodded, trusting his instincts that this man would do his best to find Shelly, pleased that something was at last going to be done. Leaving the door to Liam, he turned and walked away. Liam gave them both a brief smile, then headed after his brother.

CHAPTER FIFTY-EIGHT

Simmonds' knuckles turned white as he squeezed the phone. 'I want you up there by tomorrow at the latest. I need someone on hand to make sure the job is done properly. Those fucking morons will go in half-cocked and kill the wrong man. The smooth bastard can easily persuade one of his followers to take his place. I know how he works... What?'

Simmonds frowned as he waved a young, beautiful, scantily-clad black girl out of the room. His frown deepened. She seemed to hover a lot, this one. Better keep an eye on her. Plus she wasn't that good a pet, she still had a spark in her, although he had to admit it did make things interesting now and then.

'What?' he asked again, his concentration having wavered for a moment.

After listening for a few minutes, he snapped, 'You're frightened you'll blow your cover? Who gives a shit! Get in there, and kill the fucking lot of them if you have to, then get back out. Simple.

OK... Early train. Got it?'

He put the phone down without waiting for an answer. Rising, he walked over to the window. From this high he could see most of London – or rather his part, the money part, the part that mattered. All else was superficial.

Power and money, that's all that counts, it's all that ever counts. And those peasant ants running around down there exist only to serve.

But Simmonds was worried, even if he wouldn't fully admit it to himself. For the first time in his life, as he surveyed his kingdom, he felt a twinge of fear – fear that the madman in Northumberland could bring everything they had built over the centuries crashing down around them.

CHAPTER FIFTY-NINE

Brother David lifted the young man's head up and gently fed him water, admonishing him to take only a sip at a time. When he'd judged the man had drunk enough, he laid his head back down on the pillow.

The man's eyes flickered open. 'Thank you,' he said quietly. 'Where am I?'

'The monastery.'

'Safe?' His eyes begged Brother David to say yes.

'Sorry. None of us are safe here. Our lives are held in the grip of a madman... What is your name?'

'Danny. My ... my girlfriend, Shelly... Is she all right?'

Brother David frowned. 'She is with the man who calls himself The Leader.'

Danny struggled to sit up, helped by brother David who put cushions behind him. 'I fucking hope not, I've heard enough of that bastard... Sorry, Father. How the he ... how was this allowed to happen, what's the coppers doing?' Danny shook his head and regretted every movement, as pain shot like a buzz-saw along his scalp. He didn't know what hurt the most, his head or his ribs.

'They came in the middle of the night over a year ago, he and his henchmen. They murdered three of our brothers and herded the rest of us into the Great Hall. This place is now the main drug factory for the whole of the UK and God knows where else. Also, he deals in flesh, either working the kids to death or selling them. That is the only reason you are alive, to work. Because the work force has dwindled over the last week.'

Clutching his side, Danny swung his legs off the bed, 'How the hell do I get out of this fucking nightmare? Sorry, Father.'

'You can walk out the gate, but you wouldn't get far. They would shoot you, and one other.'

'What?'

'That is how he keeps us here. Any attempts at escape and he not only kills the escapee, he kills others. No one wants the death of a child on their conscience. Some have committed suicide to be free, but now even that brings death to others.'

'The ba... So what happens now?'

241

'Now, seeing as you can stand up, you go to work.'

'No way.'

Brother David sighed. 'I'm sorry, but if you don't work, then trust me, you will be flogged.'

'Flogged? Where am I, Hell? We gotta get outta here, man ... like right now.'

'Have you not heard a word I said?'

Danny sat back down on the bed. 'This isn't real. I'm in some sort of nightmare. Some nasty bastard must have spiked my drink. That's it, that's what's the matter, I'm tripping off somewhere, aren't I? You're not real, are you?' He gave a nervous laugh, while Brother David looked sadly at him.

'Cos you see, everything just keeps on getting worse. When you think it's all over, everything takes another fucking dip ... sorry ... so it can't be real, can it?' He shook his head, felt the pain again, winced, and answered himself. 'No, it's just a nightmare. I'll wake up, and the last few days won't even have happened. Alicia will still be alive, and Shelly... Shelly...' He grabbed hold of Brother David's wrist. 'It is real, isn't it?'

Brother David sighed, as he nodded. 'Come with me. And keep quiet. The less attention you draw to yourself the better.' He'd thought about telling Danny that help might just be on its way, but the young man seemed rather hyper and could possibly blurt things out. No, best to keep quiet for all our sakes.

Frowning, Danny got off the bed and followed Brother David. They walked down a long panelled hallway, with at least a dozen doors leading off to

242

each side. As they closed in on the end door that faced them, Danny could hear a low murmuring. Brother David opened the door, and Danny gasped. The smell was over powering. 'Jesus,' he muttered, looking at Brother David. 'Sorry.'

Brother David shushed him.

'Shh?' Danny muttered, taking a step back, 'you telling me to shh? Five minutes in here, mate, and I'll be high as a fucking kite... Sorry.'

A man holding a gun turned and glared at them. The blood left Danny's face as he gulped. It was the thug from the night before. The only satisfaction Danny could glean from the whole episode was the two black eyes the gunman sported. Seeing Danny, he snarled, lifted the gun and pointed it at him.

Danny's heart missed a beat. He felt his legs buckle, but Brother David grabbed him with a strong arm as the thug turned away from them. Danny gasped, and Brother David put a finger to his lips as he moved him down the hall.

Slowly Danny looked around. There were at least fifty people in the large hall, most of them teenagers, a lot of girls and a smattering of boys, a few men and women. None of them lifted their heads to show any interest in the newcomer. Some were bent over tables packing small yellow tablets into tiny plastic bags, others were tending rows of cannabis plants, while three small girls packed everything into boxes.

Danny bit down on a gasp. Every face looked devoid of emotion, as if all hope had gone. All of them had large black panda eyes, as if they existed on very little sleep.

243

No way, man, he mouthed at Brother David, who gestured for him to follow. Silently, Danny did as he was bid. They walked to where the three girls were loading the boxes. No one looked at them except the guard. He followed them with his eyes, eyes that Danny could feel boring into his back.

He thought in the last forty-eight hours that he'd gone beyond terror, but this!

This couldn't be happening.

This was England.

This sort of thing went on in third world countries, of this Danny had no doubt. You heard about it on the news. Everyone had heard of the sweatshops spread around the world. But not even those could be half as bad as this stink pit.

Not here. He shook his head in denial.

Not in England.

No way!

They stopped at the end of the table where the girls were stacking the boxes. Brother David pointed to two of them, both blondes. 'Come with me.'

Fear sprang to the dead faces. One of them, the smallest of the trio, with big blue eyes, started to cry.

'Shh.' Brother David gently patted her shoulder. He turned to Danny and nodded at the remaining girl. 'She will show you what to do.' Taking the two girls by their hands, both of them sobbing now as if they knew where they were going was even worse than this, Brother David, his shoulders slumped, walked away.

Danny stared at the girl. Her face was expressionless as she watched her two friends being led away.

He looked around once more at the sad, dead faces surrounding him, and knew he was truly in hell.

CHAPTER SIXTY

Securing the lock on the gate so that Tiny couldn't escape, Smiler followed Aunt May out into the street. She needed to stock up on groceries, as four new guests were due tomorrow, and she'd commandeered Smiler to do the carrying. She and Smiler had had a long talk this morning, and Smiler had been able to tell her a little about his past, something he'd never been able to do before, not even to Mike.

It had made him feel a lot better about himself as Aunt May had stressed, over and over, that none of it was his fault, he had been a victim, and now it was time to put it all behind him. The other stuff she hadn't mocked, telling him there were more things in heaven and earth, and if he believed he was really having visions, well, that was fine by her.

They entered the shop and Smiler picked up a basket, dropping it a moment later. He quickly shook his hand. It felt like he'd had an electric shock. He eyed the basket suspiciously, while cautiously he wrapped his fingers round the handles again.

Aunt May looked at him oddly, as she stood with two bags of sugar in her hands. He heaved a sigh of relief when nothing happened. Catching her eye, he gave a wan smile, then started following her around the shelves. When that basket was filled to overflowing, he took it to the front of the shop and placed it on the counter.

The shopkeeper stared at him, as he filled a knick-knack shelf with small snowstorm scenes of Holy Island. Smiler hurried back to Aunt May with another basket. He didn't like the shopkeeper, he reminded him a little of Snakes, same mean, nasty little eyes. When Aunt May had filled the other basket, they both went to the front of the shop.

'Are you coming to the meeting tomorrow night?' the shopkeeper demanded. He looked at Aunt May over the rims of his glasses while he checked her shopping through his till.

'Not sure,' Aunt May replied, picking one of the snow scenes up and shaking it.

'Why?' he asked, as if it was a foregone conclusion that everyone on the island would be at the meeting in Berwick, and how dare this little old woman say otherwise.

Smiler glanced quickly at Aunt May.

She frowned at the shopkeeper. 'That's my business, don't you think?' She looked at him with one eyebrow raised.

'Well, if you care enough about the island, you'll surely want to be there, I would have thought.'

'Why are you stirring things up?' she asked bluntly.

'Because it's our heritage. The gospels belong

here on Lindisfarne, not in London.' He scowled at her, his hand itching to snatch the snow scene off her.

'Well, guess I'll have to think about it, then.' She put the snow scene as far out of his reach as possible, then paid cash for her shopping, gave him a haughty look, and they left.

'I don't like him,' she said to Smiler, who was carrying the two heaviest bags. 'Don't trust him either, that's why I pay cash. He's not getting his hands on my card.'

Smiler had never owned a card. What very little cash passed through his hands did just that – pass through in a hurry. 'Not too keen on him either, but what can he do with the card?'

'Ahh, see, they can trace the metal strip, and find out everything about you. I heard about it somewhere. They know what clothes you buy, what you eat, where you go, everything.'

'Who's they?'

'You know. Them. The government.'

Smiler shrugged 'I don't think so.' He hid a smile as he changed the bags over, so his left hand was carrying the heavier one, flexing the fingers of his right hand where the handles had dug in, as again he tried not to smile.

Aunt May was deeply into conspiracy theories and regularly talked to people of a like mind on the Internet. He'd found out that much last night, as Mike had gently teased her.

As they slowly walked back to the house, a dark-haired, heavy-set man, dressed in a cream suit, lilac shirt and tie, and smoking a huge fat cigar, passed them. Smiler felt a tingle start in his toes. He began to shake and dropped the bags. He leaned against the wall, sweat streaming from his brow.

'Are you all right, son?' Aunt May asked, her voice full of concern, then sighing as one of the bags of sugar spilled its contents onto the ground.

Smiler shook his head. He stared at the man's back. He felt sick, and couldn't explain why.

Aunt May followed Smiler's eyes. 'He's one of those foreigners up at the castle,' she whispered. They watched as he walked into the shop.

Aunt May took a roll of kitchen paper covered in blue flowers out of her carrier bag, tore it open and handed it to Smiler. Then she bent down to pick up the spilt shopping, glad that the only damage was the bag of sugar.

'Thanks,' Smiler said, tearing a piece off the kitchen roll and mopping his brow.

'What did you see?'

Smiler sighed. 'Nothing.'

'Nothing?' she asked in dismay.

'A ... a blackness.'

Disappointed, she said, 'I felt as if he was creepy.' She glanced quickly up the street, then back at Smiler.

Smiler nodded. 'Sometimes that's all there is. Everything goes black. Other times, things come out of the blackness ... terrible things.'

CHAPTER SIXTY-ONE

Cassie had fought as hard as she could, managing to leave two large scratch marks on Maria's face. But there had been two of them in the back of the car, and a rag filled with chloroform. She hadn't stood a chance. Even now she was still groggy. The large room they were in kept swimming in and out of focus, and she had no recollection of how she'd got there. All she knew was that she was terrified, and wanted to go home. She wanted her mother's arms around her, telling her she was safe.

A big man with long hair and a booming voice kept striding back and forth. Cassie squinted, and realised that what she had first thought was a long coat was actually a monk's robe.

A monk!

Her heart lifted. Monks were good people.

Will he help me? she wondered.

Monks are good people.

He will, he must.

Filled with desperation, she tried to stand up to get his attention. Surely he can see me? He will help... Take me home.

Her efforts were wasted. She was forced back into her seat by someone behind her. Wriggling, she looked round.

A man with a heavily pockmarked face and a black moustache, who stank of stale cigarette smoke, leaned forward and whispered in her ear. 'If you know what's good for you, kid, you'll keep very still and very, very quiet.' Roughly, he took hold of her head and forced it to the front.

'She is not the one you were supposed to bring.' The monk was talking to someone Cassie couldn't see. She stared at him in fear. She could feel the man's fingers digging into her head, and she was terrified to move. 'Where is the one you showed me?' the monk said, his voice rising.

'She ... she wouldn't come. I had to bring this one to fill the quota,' a woman replied, with a tremor in her voice that frightened Cassie even more.

'Huh,' he grunted, his lips curled in an arrogant snarl. 'How much does the other one know?'

'Nothing,' the woman said quickly. 'Nothing at all. The bitch just didn't turn up when she was supposed to.'

'So you picked this one up off the street?'

'More or less.'

'Did she come quietly?'

'Yes, yes,' she answered quickly. 'I know her.'

'Good.' He swung his face to Cassie.

Terrified, Cassie began to sob, quietly at first, then with huge heart-rending gasps. 'Mum,' she whispered between sobs. 'Please take me home.'

Smiling, he walked over to her. 'This is your home now,' he said, as if she was an orphan and had found refuge in a storm. 'We will take care of you now.'

Horrified, she shook her head. 'No. I don't want you to. I have a home.' She was shaking now, her pleas coming out in small gasps. 'Please,' she begged, 'let me go home... Please. Please. Please, I want to go home.'

He stroked her hair, each movement with gentle practised ease. 'Pretty.'

Her eyes bulging in fear, Cassie shivered under his touch. He laughed. 'Frightened little bird.'

'Get off me,' she managed to shout bravely, as she shook her head to get rid of his hand. He only laughed louder, his voice filling the room.

It was then she saw Maria. 'You!' she gasped. 'What have you done? Take me home. I want to go home right now. I want my mum.' She stamped her feet, only to have her right ankle kicked viciously by Tobacco Breath.

'You won't ever see your mum again, little bird.' The Leader's voice mocked her before he turned to Maria. 'Not the one I wanted, but she'll do. Put her to work.' He touched Cassie's hair again. 'Bring her to me tomorrow night. I have business to sort out with that other lying scheming bitch tonight.'

Cassie struggled gamely, but the man behind pinned her arms at her side. 'Let me go,' she yelled, back-heeling him and catching his foot. In response, he pulled her hair hard, forcing her head back until her eyes were staring at the ceiling. Amused, the monk laughed as he moved back to her and stroked her neck, sending shivers of revulsion down her spine.

Brother David stepped out of the shadows, and bowed to The Leader, who barely acknowledged him. Taking a sobbing Cassie by the arm, he led her from the room.

She tried to shake Brother David off, looking

251

wildly about for any means of escape when they walked down a long panelled hallway. 'What ... what are you going to do with me?' she managed, between sobs. 'Why does he want me tomorrow night?'

Brother David, knowing exactly why the madman who was running their lives wanted this child, bit down on an angry retort. He wanted to yell at the panelled walls, rave at the ceiling. Nothing had prepared him for the living hell they had all endured for the last year. And here was another innocent.

His faith was sorely tried as he thought angrily, Where the hell are you, Mike Yorke?

Even though he was seething inside, he kept a calm exterior so as not to frighten her more. 'Don't fret, child. Tomorrow is a long way off. Who knows what it will bring?'

CHAPTER SIXTY-TWO

Mike and Kristina pulled up outside the nightclub. Before they got out of the car, Mike said, 'Forgot to say – I like your hair that way.'

About to open the car door, Kristina paused, looked at him and shook her head. 'It took you two days to notice?'

'Well, no, I mean, it was really short before and now it's long in a ponytail. Just saying you suit it, that's all. You never could take a compliment, could you, Kristina?'

'You used to take plenty for the both of us.' She got out of the car and slammed the door, instantly regretting what she'd said, and knowing Mike didn't deserve that. He was a little vain, but certainly not over the top. So, he flirted a little, but never when he was in a relationship. It's me being a fool, acting as if the last four years hasn't happened and we're still together. God, I feel like such an idiot.

Oh dear, Mike was thinking as he followed her, said the wrong thing again. What the hell is it with her and Jill?

He caught up with her before they entered the double doors. 'So how's Mr Kristina these days?' She gave him a look that would re-freeze the melting ice caps.

'What?'

'Don't say you haven't heard.'

Mike looked perplexed. 'Heard?'

She put her head down for a moment. Slowly lifting it, she met his eyes. 'Tim died over a year ago.'

'Oh... I'm sorry, Kristina, I swear I didn't know.'

She sighed. 'I guess you didn't, Mike. Sorry for snapping at you. But it was over before the first year was out, anyhow. There was nothing there. I realised more or less right off. Still, he was a good man, and it did break my heart when he died.' She sighed again. 'Should we go in now?'

Mike nodded as he opened the door. Putting aside until later what she'd just told him, he became all copper as he strode across the room. Reaching the bar, he took his badge out, and said to the barman and the pretty blonde waitress, 'DI Mike Yorke. Could you both spare me a minute to look at some pictures?'

The barman shrugged. 'No skin off my nose, mate, give us them here.' The waitress stepped close, and the pair studied the three photographs.

After a moment the waitress stepped back and shook her head. 'Never seen any of them before. But a lot of them look the same these days, don't they? Same hair, same clothes.'

'Are you sure?' Kristina asked.

She shrugged. 'Can't really say.'

'How about you?' Mike looked at the barman.

'Well...' He sucked his teeth for a moment, a habit Mike found annoying. 'I think I've seen the bloke in here before. Couldn't tell you his name, though. But the girls look familiar, there's a group of them, they generally sit together.' He gestured with his head towards the far right-hand side of the room. 'Over there.'

'What's up?' The voice came from the far end of the bar, where a door marked Manager was half-open.

'It's the cops,' the waitress said. 'Want to know if we've seen these people before.'

A bald man in a grey suit and a white T-shirt moved along the bar. Mike guessed that it was one of the bouncers. He nodded at Mike and Kristina as he picked up the photographs. A moment later, he put two of the photographs on the bar and handed the remaining one to Mike. 'This girl – a couple of nights ago, she ran out of here like a bat out of hell. No one followed her so, I guessed she must have had trouble at home and someone had given her a bell. The bloke, never seen him before. The other girl, probably.'

'OK. Know any names of the people she was with?'

The bouncer frowned. 'I'm sure they all knock around in a sort of gang, about half a dozen of them.'

Nodding his agreement, the barman snapped his fingers. 'Maria, that's her name. She's always in here. Lives not far from here, actually.'

'Do you know where?' Mike asked.

'Em... oh, bloody hell. Tell you what, if I write it down it'll come to me. Funny sort of memory, if you know what I mean.' He pulled a small note-book out of the breast pocket of his shirt and started writing. He hesitated a moment, then carried on at full speed. With a flourish, he handed the note over to Mike. 'That's it. I had to drop her home one night, she'd had one too many.'

Mike stared for a moment at the note, and thought, Shit. Looking up at the trio, he said, 'Thanks for your help.' Quickly, watched by three pairs of inquisitive eyes, he ushered Kristina out of the bar.

Kristina blinked in the bright sunlight. 'What's all that about?'

'Get in the car.'

When they were both strapped in, Mike said, 'That piece of paper, where the hell is it?'

'I left it on your desk, in a plastic bag. Why?'

'God, why didn't you remind me?'

'Mike, you couldn't miss it.'

'I've never seen it. Must have dropped something on top of it.' He waited until a red Post

255

Office van passed, then pulled out into the traffic.

Kristina shrugged. 'It's meaningless, anyhow. Just a bunch of circles and squiggles. And it's got to be on your desk, because I put it there myself.'

'Hmm. Must have become mixed up with some paperwork. I'll have a good look when we get back.' He stopped outside of Maria's house. They knocked, waited, knocked again, waited some more. Still no answer.

'Guess we're gonna have to come back,' Kristina said, blowing air up into her fringe.

Mike nodded, looked at his watch. 'We best get back.' He moved to the window and, cupping his hands around his face to block the sun, looked inside. In the far corner stood a fifty-inch television set, next to it a state of the art music centre. Expensive-looking furniture and thick, creamy-coloured carpets caused him to say, 'Wow, this Maria must have a hell of a job!'

'Let me see.' Kristina pushed Mike out of the way and stood on her toes to look inside. After a moment taking in the luxurious sitting room, she said. 'Wow's right.'

'Tell you what.' Mike pointed up the street. 'You work up that way to the top, and I'll go down, cross over to the other side. Then we'll meet back here. See what this Maria's neighbours have to say about her.'

Twenty minutes later they met up again, having both drawn blanks.

Mike looked puzzled. 'Can't see how you can live in a place for three years, and not one of your neighbours knows anything at all about you. Even the old biddy next door, who was prepared to tell me anything I wanted to know about everyone in the whole of bloody Berwick, knows nothing about Maria. Only that she's been here for three years, and comes and goes at odd hours.'

'Yeah, doesn't sound like she has a regular job to pay for all of that. She's certainly not a copper, that's for sure.'

Mike laughed. 'You got that in one. OK, let's get back. This note has me puzzled.'

CHAPTER SIXTY-THREE

Smiler got off the bus in the middle of Berwick. The town was full of holidaymakers who seemed to have descended in swarms. He had to see Mike. He couldn't think straight – the pressure of knowing only so much was torturing him. Both girls, who were somehow linked to him, were in grave danger. He had to make Mike realise there were less than two days left. They had to find out where the girls were before it was too late. But all he could see was blood, blood and more blood.

Somehow he had to make Mike believe.

The girls were in some sort of fortress, perhaps a castle. He knew this from the rough cold stone he had felt through their hands, and the vast empty spaces above them. They were together, but not together; in the same place, but unaware of each other.

But where? This coast was littered with castles. It was all so frustrating. He knew, and he believed. This wasn't just something he was imagining, it was real. He knew he could really see things, but Mike could be so stubborn.

Lately the flashes he'd been getting had been terrifying, more intense. It seemed the older he got, the more he was able to see. And the more it was frightening him. He wished to God they would stop, go away, leave him in peace. Aunt May had said it was a gift, and he should be thankful.

He only saw it as a curse.

Arriving at the police station, he was told by the blonde PC that Mike was out. Disappointed, and anxious because time was running away at an alarming speed, he went back into the town centre. He would grab a ham and cheese sandwich somewhere, then go back and wait.

The café he chose was The Baguette in Hide Street. Further down the street, on the other side, he spotted The Flower Room. He would take Aunt May a bunch of flowers. Last night had been so special. He had found out, for the first time ever, how good it felt to really laugh, so much that it hurt. His eyes misted up just remembering. He supposed any flowers would do, she seemed to love them all.

He counted the change in his pocket without taking it out, a trick you learned early on when your life was the streets. Mike had sorted him out with Social Security and now, thank God, he got money on a regular basis.

No more selling himself just to eat.

To be honest, though, it wasn't just to eat. The depraved things he'd let happen to himself had been to feed his drug addiction. And the things that happened before he was addicted were done to him to feed his mother's addiction.

He sighed. So much to be sorry for.

So much to be thankful for.

So much to lose.

CHAPTER SIXTY-FOUR

Danny watched one of the monks and the gunman walk round the tables, giving out little white pills. Eager hands reached towards them, the pills greedily snatched and swallowed at once.

Shit! he thought, wondering exactly what deadly poison the monk was giving out.

How the hell do I get out of this?

Once, when they were teenagers, he and Evan had been tempted to try drugs by a beautiful girl they both fancied like mad. That once had been more than enough. All he remembered about the experience was being chased down the street by every horrific monster fiction writers had dreamed up, and many more of his own creation. Hell, there were even Space Invaders from the actual game bloody well chasing him, with their own special sound effects. He shuddered at the memory.

If Evan, who had seemed untouched by the drugs, apart from being a little hyper, hadn't finally caught him, God only knows what might have happened to him. He was heading directly for the motorway at the time, like a homing pigeon, his way home across two- and three-lane motorways. They had both sworn off it the next day, and had never been tempted since.

This stuff that they were feeding the work force seemed to have a different effect though, he thought, sort of keeping the poor sods like zombies.

He looked at the tablets he was packing, noting with relief that they were coated and probably, he thought – he hoped – would only dissolve in the stomach. He glanced up at the new girl, who was still shaking, and wondered what her story was, what had led her to this hell. Waiting until the monk and the gunman were furthest away, and thanking God that they hadn't started with his little corner, he hissed quietly.

Either she hadn't heard him, or she was ignoring him. He looked at the other girl, her brown hair tied up in bunches which fell halfway down her back. Her eyes behind her glasses were as far away as they could possibly be. Danny felt a stab of pity. She only looked about fifteen years old.

He tore his eyes away from her, knowing in the state she was in there was nothing he could do. She would take the pill with great joy, and probably claw his eyes out if he attempted to stop her. Looking at the new girl, he hissed again. This time she looked up. He used his eyes to get her attention to what the monk and the gunman were doing. She stared at them, puzzled, for a moment then, noticing the delight on the workers' faces as each was handed a tablet, froze in fear.

His heart pounding, anxious not to be heard, Danny hissed again, knowing it was probably the last time he would be able to make such a noise without drawing attention to himself, as the monk and the gunman came closer.

She swung her head towards him. Danny opened his mouth and lifted his tongue up. Keeping his hand on the table, he turned it palm up and pointed with his middle finger towards his mouth.

Misreading his intentions, Cassie stared at him in horror.

Seeing her expression, and understanding what she was thinking, the look on Danny's bright red face was no less horrified.

My God, she thinks I'm a perve!

No no, no, he mouthed, slowly shaking his head. Don't swallow the tablet... Do ... not ... swallow ... the tablet.

He looked furtively round. The gunman and the monk were two tables behind, with their backs to him. Swinging his head back to face Cassie, he did the same mime again, raising his hand to his mouth this time and putting his finger under his tongue.

To Danny's immense relief, a moment later she gave a quick nod before dropping her head and getting on with her work.

Thank God, Danny thought, as the monk reached his side.

The monk handed Danny a pill. 'Oh, thank you so much.' He beamed at the monk, then switched his smile to the gunman, who rolled his eyes as he walked away.

Cassie was handed her pill, and did what Danny had said. Both of them took the pills out of their mouths as soon as the monk and the gunman disappeared through the door.

Quickly, Danny opened one of the plastic bags they were packing and dropped the pill inside. Watching him, Cassie did the same. He nodded encouragingly at her, and received a wan smile in return.

Danny risked a quick smile, then mimed, look dopey.

She got it right this time, and looked at the other girl. She tried a few faces out on Danny, who chose number two. Catching sight of the door opening again, he put his head down and got on with his work.

CHAPTER SIXTY-FIVE

Mike and Kristina walked into the station, to be told Mike had a visitor waiting in his office. He was about to ask who when the desk sergeant, a small, pretty, heavily-pregnant Asian woman, who Mike had never seen before, ducked out of sight and bobbed up again a moment later. Throwing a large brown handbag strap over her shoulder, she said quickly, 'Sorry, got to go... Ante-natal class this afternoon.' She ran round the counter, stopped at the door and gave them a wave.

Mike threw Kristina a look of total disbelief as the regular desk sergeant walked through the door behind the counter.

'Jenna gone then, has she?'

'Oh yeah,' Mike replied with a smile.

'She's a canny enough kid. Been here about a year or so. A bit excitable at the moment, but that's to be expected.' He laughed. 'If you'll pardon the pun.'

'God help us,' Kristina murmured, as she turned and headed down the corridor, followed a moment later by Mike.

As she reached the door, Mike caught up with her. Stretching his arm, he got the handle just before she did. She looked up at his face as the door swung open. For a few brief seconds, they looked into each other's eyes. Then they were disturbed by a low cough.

They both looked to see where the sound had come from. Kristina smiled while Mike, for a brief moment, was shocked.

'Hello, Tony.' Kristina moved first. 'It's been a good few years. When did you get here?'

Tony stood up to greet Kristina with a kiss on her cheek. 'An hour or so ago. You look really well, Kristina. You certainly suit your hair like that. If you want my opinion, girl, you shouldn't ever get it cut again.'

Kristina looked at Mike with one raised eyebrow. Mike rolled his eyes. Over his shock, he walked over and clasped Tony's hand. 'Why didn't you tell me you were coming? I would have met you at the station.'

'It's good to see you, too.'

Mike tutted. 'You know what I mean. Aunt May will be thrilled you're home.'

Kristina didn't see the slight change in Tony's face, but Mike did. He knew him too well not to notice.

Suddenly the room was filled with tension. Kristina felt it, but didn't know the reason – four years was a long time to be out of someone's life, anything could have happened between them. Feeling that they needed some space, she said. 'I've got some phone calls to make, OK? See youse guys in a mo, right?' With a sideways wink at Mike, she walked back out the door.

Gently closing the door behind her, Mike turned to face Tony. 'OK, what is it?'

'Look, Mike, I'm only here for a day, two at the most. There won't be any time. I'd rather you not tell her that I'm up here than have her upset that I don't visit.'

Mike stared at him. He knew there was something wrong, but he couldn't quite put a finger on it. He also knew if he pushed too hard, Tony would close his shell. Tony could be as stubborn as hell when it suited him. Shrugging, Mike said, 'OK, if it's that important.'

Tony was about to thank him when, unable to resist, Mike went on, 'She was very upset that you didn't make Christmas, and what? A couple of phone calls since? Nearly half a year later.'

Tony held his hands up. 'Guilty as charged, but I will make it up to her, I promise. As soon as this business is finished.'

Grudgingly, Mike nodded. 'OK. So what really brings you back home?'

'Sorry, that's classified.'

'For fuck's sake, Tony! Has it anything to do with what I was working on down there?' Mike's exasperation showed as he frowned at Tony.

'Mike, you know how it works. Let's just forget

264

it, eh? A flying visit, that's all. And please don't tell Aunt May I was here. I feel guilty enough as it is.'

Mike relented. 'OK.'

Relieved, Tony went on, 'I've heard about the two murders you have on your hands. Any progress?'

Shaking his head, Mike moved to the window. He needed space to think. There was something odd about Tony, something in his eyes. Something that perhaps only two other people in the world would pick up. He'd noticed it in London, but had been unable to put his finger on the problem.

Instead of answering him, Mike turned and asked a question of his own. 'Have you heard from Dave lately?'

There was a tiny breath of a pause before Tony answered. There it is again, Mike thought. As well as noting the pause, he registered the faint haze over his eyes, as Tony replied, 'Er, yeah, a few weeks ago. Not quite a month. He said he was well... Have you heard from him? He usually writes to us at the same time.'

Mike gave a flat, 'No.'

'Oh. Right then. This business of the march to bring the Gospels back home. Tell Aunt May to keep away.'

'Why?' Mike frowned at the swift change of subject.

Tony sighed. 'That's all I can say, don't let her get involved. And now I have to leave.'

'Talk about a flying visit.'

'Sorry, Mike, it's work. I only took time out to see you, and warn you to keep her away from that lot.'

'But why?'

With a sigh, Tony stood up. 'Later, Mike, OK? All I can say – and believe me, I shouldn't even say this – they aren't what they seem. Just keep her away, will you?'

Mike moved to stand in front of the door. Physically, Tony was no match for Mike. He never had been. He'd tried, once, when they had only known each other for a few weeks. Mike had beaten the shit out of him. Again when they were teenagers, Aunt May had forced her way between them, stopping a second beating just by her very presence. They had settled their differences, with Dave as the peacemaker, and six months later they had become inseparable.

Mike folded his arms across his chest, a gesture Tony knew well. 'If something's happening on my patch, I want to know about it. And I want to know now.'

Tony had the lie ready. It spilled quickly from his lips. 'All right, but you must keep it to yourself.' He raised his eyebrows in a question.

Mike gave a quick nod.

'It's all a cover-up. The lot in charge are using the march to get most of the people off the island–'

'Why?' Mike snapped.

'They're staying at the castle, and plan to rob the place during the two hours everyone's at the meeting. And you know Aunt May, if she takes a dislike to them... Well, I'm worried in case she stands in their way. Anything could happen to her. This particular bunch of art thieves have killed before.'

'She already has.'

'What?'

'Taken a dislike to them.'

Tony's face dropped, and Mike started to believe that his main concern was Aunt May.

'She hasn't been making her mouth go about them, has she?'

'Just to me and Smiler. And,' Mike shrugged, 'probably a few friends of hers. So just how bad are these creeps?'

'We've been chasing them for a good few years. They've pulled quite a few scams, but this time I think we have them. It's cleared with the powers that be. We have temporary jurisdiction over the island.'

Mike was quiet for a moment. Seeing the stubborn set of his chin Tony said quickly. 'It just came through about an hour ago, if you're wondering why you haven't been informed.'

Why don't I believe him? Mike wondered, but said, 'OK, I'll do my best to keep her away.'

'And you've got to promise me you'll keep out of it. The whole business is cleared by the big guys. It may be on your patch, but trust me – it's sorted.'

'Right, whatever.' Clearly unhappy about it, Mike held his hands up.

Tony sighed his relief. 'Right, gotta go, Mike. Take care.' He gave Mike a hug, something he hadn't done for a long time. Surprised, Mike hugged him back. But his mind was working overtime. Far from allaying his suspicions, the hug had intensified them.

As they walked to the outer doors, Tony in front, Mike stared at the back of his head, wondering if Tony was in some kind of trouble. The bit about classified information he didn't buy, not one little bit. Tony was a good cop and hot on protocol. No way would he let slip information like that.

CHAPTER SIXTY-SIX

Mike was rummaging around his desk when Kristina came in, followed by Smiler. She motioned with her thumb over her shoulder. 'Found your mate here, sitting outside.'

'Mike, I have to talk to you.' Smiler stepped to the side of Kristina so that he could be seen.

Frowning, Mike looked up, his hands still amongst the rubbish on his desk.

'What are you looking for?' Kristina asked.

'That scrap of paper.'

'For God's sake, Mike. I put it right there.' Kristina poked the middle of his desk with her finger. 'How could you miss it?'

'Mike,' Smiler said, watching Kristina having a rummage of her own.

'Just a minute, sunshine.'

Both Smiler and the paper were forgotten a moment later, when the phone rang. Snatching it up, Mike gave his usual prologue. He nearly dropped the phone a moment later, shouting, 'What? How?'

Kristina stopped rummaging. She and Smiler stared at Mike, as he went on. 'OK, Jill, calm down. I'm sure there'll be a good reason.' He listened again, then said, 'Give me Billy's address, and I'll send a car for you.'

Kristina handed him a pen and a sheet of paper. He threw her a grateful smile, then listened intently as he scribbled the address down. 'Right, Jill, now that's only about four or five minutes away. See you in a bit.'

He strode out of the room. Kristina and Smiler frowned their puzzlement at each other. A minute later he was back.

'What the hell's going on?' Kristina demanded, as he came back through the door.

'Jill's youngest girl. She's gone missing.'

Before Kristina could say anything, both she and Mike were startled by a loud thud. Smiler had fainted.

'Jesus Christ,' Mike said, rushing to pick him up.

Together they got him into a chair, then Kristina went for water as Mike tried to bring him round. Gently he patted his face. Smiler blinked. A moment later, his eyes shot wide open. 'You've got to help her, Mike.'

'Help who?' Kristina asked, holding the glass of water to Smiler's lips.

Smiler shook his head. 'I don't know, it's all confusing.' He took a sip of water and looked up at Mike. 'It's gone. But I think they, she... They are in a castle, or something like one.'

'Something like one, eh?' Mike tutted. 'Have you any idea how many castles there are in Northumberland? Or even how many buildings that look like a castle?' Answering his own ques-

269

tion, he went on. 'Bloody twenty-five of them, that's how many. And that's not even counting the lookalikes, nor the ones in Durham, for God's sake.'

Smiler was about to say just how many there were of either description, when Jill came rushing in. Mike gave Smiler a look that plainly said, not a word about this.

Looking sheepish, Smiler nodded.

Jill was totally distraught. Kristina jumped up from her chair by the computer and coaxed her to sit down.

'Smiler, bring some coffees from the machine, and an orange juice for me.' Mike handed him some change. As Smiler left, Mike turned to Jill. 'Right, give me a quick rundown.'

'When she didn't turn up at Billy's, he waited half an hour, then phoned the school. She hasn't been there all day.' Jill took a deep breath. 'Then Jayne turned up, and said she hadn't even seen her this morning. She said, she said that Cassie got the early bus to go shopping, for ... for a birthday present.' She looked up at Mike. 'For me.' She shook her head. 'Truly, Mike, Cassie wouldn't do something like this. She's a good girl. Something's happened to her, I know it has. I just know it. She just wouldn't stay out at all. She's not streetwise or anything like that.'

She started to sob, and Kristina put her arm around her. 'Shh. She'll be fine... Don't worry, we'll find her.' Kristina looked up at Mike. 'Won't we, Mike?'

Cupping his chin in his hand, Mike scratched day-old stubble as he stared at the top of Jill's head. Then at Kristina, who was urging him with her eyes to say something.

He cleared his throat. 'Of course we will. Have youse two had a row lately? Or something like that? Can you give me anything at all to go on?'

Jill didn't even look up. She just shook her head. Smiler came back with three coffees on a tray. Taking one, Kristina put extra sugar in, stirred it, then handed it to Jill. 'Here, love, drink this.'

Mike waited until she'd taken a sip. 'OK. Kristina, you stay here with Jill. I'll go to Billy's house, see what he has to say. But before that, I'll give a description to the patrol cars. They might spot her. Of course, she could have gone present-hunting after school, forgotten what time it was.' He shrugged.'Who knows, she may even be back at Billy's now.'

Jill shook her head. 'No,' she said quietly.

'OK, come with me Smiler.'

Stopping at the desk, Mike and Smiler gave a description of Cassie to the desk sergeant, who relayed it to the patrol cars. Quickly Mike and Smiler went to the car. Mike started the engine. Suddenly, Smiler said, 'It's Cassie.'

Mike felt the small hairs on the back of his neck stand up. He pulled out onto the road before saying, 'What do you mean, It's Cassie?'

'I saw her. She's one of the girls.'

Mike's face was grim as he stared at the rush-hour traffic.

'Mike,' Smiler said a moment later in a hushed voice. 'There isn't much time... One more sunset.'

271

CHAPTER SIXTY-SEVEN

Brother David fussed around in the study, knowing that The Leader always watched the local six o'clock news. He had knocked and walked in, on the pretence that he had to find some important documents that must be sent off in the morning, or they would be getting a visit from their sister priory in Durham.

A visit had already been made three months ago, a visit that ended in tragedy. Three brothers had died that night, murdered and made to look as if their car had gone off the road and into a tree.

Ignoring the irritated glances he kept getting from The Leader, he continued with his search.

When the newsreader had finished, and there had been no mention of a body found in the Police Station yard, he headed for the door. He was stopped in his tracks when The Leader said, with a touch of sarcastic irritation, 'Finally found what you're looking for, fool?'

'Sorry, sir,' Brother David said humbly, staring at the carpet, praying as hard as he could to be allowed to go.

'Get out.' The Leader waved his long bony hand at him.

'Thank you, God,' Brother David muttered under his breath, as he practically ran out of the door.

Where are you, Michael? he thought, making

his way along to the factory.

Why haven't you come?

Surely he's read the note by now.

Please God, hear my prayers. These children need your help.

He knew at least two of them might not make it to the end of the week, they were so wasted, so frail. He'd thought hard about breaking his vows and attempting to murder The Leader, but the two henchmen were never out of his sight. His sacrifice would be pointless. No way could he succeed against the three of them.

Their only hope was Michael Yorke.

Reaching the end of the corridor, he pushed the heavy oak door open. Brother Andrew was giving the poison out tonight. He worried about Brother Andrew, wondered how much more he could take. He had Brother Josh watching every move he made. If Brother Andrew committed suicide, then two children would lose their lives, and help might be just around the corner.

Stepping silently into the great room, he stood at the back and watched Brother Andrew and the guard make their way around the workers. His throat hurt with wanting to cry, as the kids eagerly reached out for the drugs. He blinked hard to stop the tears that were building up behind his eyes.

No emotion must be shown, ever. They had learned that lesson in the very beginning. Emotion brought painful beatings. Some of the brothers and some of the kids still carried the scars from months ago.

His interest was piqued a few minutes later

273

when Brother Andrew reached the newcomers. Brother David was certain he saw the young man and the girl palm the drugs. The act they put on a few minutes later was very convincing.

His heart lightened. Had his prayers been heard?

Had God sent him some allies?

The Leader gorged himself on roasted chicken and fine wine. Sprawling on furs, he toasted himself in front of the unnecessary roaring log fire. Sweat ran down the faces of his two guards, but neither of them dared complain. There was another guard who watched while The Leader and these two slept. He would be wakening soon to take their place. But before then The Leader had some fun planned.

He spat into the fire and laughed at the flames. Without turning his head, he said, 'Bring the one called Shelly.'

Immediately the Chinese guard turned and left. Entering a door midway down the panelled hallway, he roughly shook the sleeping Shelly.

Still half-asleep, she cried out. Pulling her knees to her chin, she stared in horror at the guard. Her hands were tied together in front of her with a length of thick rough rope that already had her wrists chafed in places.

'What?' She blinked, saw who it was and begged, 'Please. No more.'

He laughed as, with one arm, he hoisted her off the simple cot bed and pushed her, crying and sobbing, down the corridor.

PART THREE

CHAPTER SIXTY-EIGHT

7.30 am

Mike opened his eyes, and knew instantly that there was someone else in the room. Someone very close. Someone trying hard to be quiet.

Keeping perfectly still, and controlling his breathing, he listened intently. He could hear short, shallow breaths and guessed whoever it was, was very near the bottom of the bed on his right. He listened for the sound of a gun cocking.

Nothing.

Even the sound of breathing had stopped or, more likely, someone was trying very hard to hold their breath.

OK, Mike thought. In one fluid motion, he shot up with the quilt in his hands and threw it over the figure. 'Right, you bastard. Who the hell are you?'

A muffled sob, followed a moment later by, 'It's me. Smiler.'

'Bloody hell. You scared me to death. What the hell are you doing?' Mike disentangled Smiler from the quilt, then glanced at the bedroom clock on his dresser. 'Good God. It's half-past seven!' he said in disbelief, as he reached for the light switch.

'I know. I'm sorry.'

'You're sorry? Two bloody hours, that's all the sleep we've had.' He sighed. 'OK, what's wrong?'

He sat down on the edge of the bed and looked at Smiler.

'I think she's dead.' Staring at the floor, Smiler started to sob. 'It was terrible, Mike... She's not there any more.' He glanced up at Mike, his eyes full of tears, 'It's like there's a black hole where she should be.'

Patting Smiler's shoulder, Mike said, 'Right, mate, who are we talking about here?' He rubbed his eyes with his other hand, feeling totally lousy. A night on the booze never left him feeling this bad. They had been up most of the night searching for Jill's daughter, with no success. Aunt May had spent the night at Jill's house. Mike guessed she'd have had less sleep than any of them, and he knew he must catch her sometime today to warn her about going to the meeting tonight. There was something mighty suspicious about the whole thing. He put all those thoughts out of his mind when Smiler started agitatedly cracking his knuckles.

'OK, Smiler, chill, eh?'

Suddenly Smiler stopped, and Mike felt overwhelmed with a feeling of dread at the tortured look on his face.

'She's screaming, Mike,' he said a moment later. 'Really screaming, and ... and I don't know which one it is, because one of them's gone.' Burying his head in his hands, he started to rock back and forth.

8.30 am

Quietly closing the door behind her, Aunt May walked along to her own house. Jill was sedated,

278

old Dr Monty had said she would sleep until well past midday. Far from the teenage rebel persona she had adopted over the last few months, Jayne had proved to be a rock, and was now dozing in a chair by her mother's bed.

She was surprised to see Smiler standing at the gate with Tiny. Patting the dog's head, she said, 'Mike up yet?'

Smiler nodded. 'Yeah, he's cooking breakfast. I'm just taking Tiny out for his walk. No word yet?'

Sadly Aunt May shook her head.

Smiler sighed. 'I wish I could see more, Aunt May. If this is the gift you say it is, why can't I see exactly where she is? Why can't I make Mike believe? It's worse than useless.' Without waiting for her to answer, he turned and headed up the street towards the churchyard. Watching him go, Aunt May felt sad for him. She wished she could help. Sometimes the poor kid looked as if his very soul was being tortured. But she had no answers. She'd read much on the subject mainly out of curiosity, but also because of some very strange things she'd experienced herself. Since Smiler had arrived she'd dug some of her old books out to re-read, hoping for what, she didn't know. One thing she did know was that this world should be treated with an open mind. Hiding behind closed doors got you nowhere fast. Smiler carried on past the church, using the same route down to the beach that Mike regularly used. Although the causeway was open, the sea was still swirling around the small island of St Cuthbert, making it impossible to cross over. Instead, he sat down on the rocky beach and stared at the islet and St Cuthbert's cross.

He recalled everything he'd read about St Cuthbert. How he was tormented by demons on the islet, and on Inner Farne, where he also spent time as a hermit. The demons did their best to cast him into the ocean, but nothing they did discouraged him. When the devils had been driven from the island through faith and prayer, angels came and helped build a cell and a chapel.

St Cuthbert had the power of second sight, because he was a good holy man. He'd first seen an angel when he was eight years old and tending sheep. He also had the power to perform miracles. He healed many sick and diseased people. Once he changed water into wine. Even on his deathbed, he healed a servant, and his miracles continued well after his death. In 1942 his relics, resting in Durham Cathedral, saved the city from the bombs of the Luftwaffe by shrouding the city in thick fog on the night of their raid.

Smiler hung his head, his thoughts heavy. St Cuthbert had been a good man, who had been given the gift because of his goodness. If this is truly a gift, as Aunt May says, then why has it been given to me? A useless, worthless ex-druggie. I'm no good to anyone.

Mike's right, it's all my imagination. A backlash from all the shit I pumped into myself. I might as well be dead for all the use I am to anybody.

Slowly he rose and headed towards the pounding waves, tripping over pebbles and standing on sharp rocks, noticing neither as he reached the shore.

10.30 am

A low moan escaped from Shelly's lips as she slowly opened her eyes. Her body felt as if it was being squeezed inch by inch. There was no part she could favour, the pain was everywhere.

'Shut up and get up, you have work to do,' a disembodied voice said behind her.

She lacked the strength to turn her head, but she knew it was the Chinese guard, and cringed inside. When The Leader had finished inflicting his own torture, he had handed her over to the two guards, who had repeatedly beaten and raped her through the night.

'Here.' He placed her insulin pen and a bowl of cereal on the small night table. 'Five minutes.'

She heard the door slam and the key turn in the lock, and sighed from the soles of her feet.

Last night The Leader had told her, as he laughed in her face – she shivered, remembering the spit that had landed all over her – that she had twenty-four hours to live. She had only been given a stay of execution because the workforce was depleted. A new shipment of peasants was due later tonight. She had thought at the time, what a strange thing to say, but realised that it fitted in with what she knew. Most of people in the world were peasants to the families.

Easing her feet off the bed, she groaned as she sat up, and instantly felt dizzy. Knowing she'd already used up probably half of the five minutes just getting off the bed, she injected herself, before hastily swallowing most of the cereal. She was drinking the milk from the bowl when he came for her.

10.40 am
Danny was facing the open door, and was shocked when Shelly walked through, accompanied by one of the fiend's brutes. He watched as she hobbled towards him. She looked twenty years older. Her face was grey. He could see huge bruises on her arms and legs. Immediately he felt sorry and angry at the same time, sorry for the physical wreck she had become in a few short hours, and angry at the people responsible. He knew nothing of the families, nor the yoke the whole world had been under for centuries. His anger was directed at The Leader. His brain had worked overtime, figuring out ways he and Cassie could escape. They had lain with their heads together, whispering, until they fell asleep out of sheer exhaustion.

The thug with the gun was pretty lax really, probably thinking that his charges were little more than zombies. Danny had told Cassie to be ready, and in the two hours after their breakfast, a slice of bread thrown at them as if they were animals, she had hardly taken her eyes off him.

He figured he could probably take the thug from behind, but how the hell to get out of here? No matter how hard he tried, he couldn't come up with a working plan.

Shelly was moving towards them. Danny was saddened to see that the closer she got, the worse she looked. His throat tightened. He put his head down so the over-developed freak with her would not see his eyes.

'You.'

Danny knew he was talking to him. Still he kept his head down and muttered a meek, 'Yes.'

'Show her what to do.'

Danny nodded. When he was certain the freak had gone, he looked at Shelly. Are you all right? he mouthed, even though he could see she was far from all right.

Is that a bite mark on her cheek? Jesus!

Slowly she shook her head. Danny ached to hold her. No matter what she'd done, she did not deserve this. He knew then that he still loved her, and felt totally inadequate at his inability to protect her. 'Just fill these boxes with the packets of poison,' he said quietly, aware that Cassie was watching. Then he whispered, 'They'll be round later with some shit. Don't swallow it, OK?'

She nodded, staring at the packets of pills. Danny knew the nod was automatic, a reaction from someone who was already dead. His spirits sank. Shelly knew more about these people than anyone here. If she was reacting like this, what hope did any of them have?

12.15 pm

'Where's Smiler?' Mike asked Aunt May, as he closed his mobile and slipped it into his pocket. Officially today was his day off, but he had been in contact with the office every few minutes, driving Kristina crazy.

Aunt May shrugged. 'Never seen him, nor the bloody Shetland pony, for' – she shrugged again – 'a couple of hours. Any news about Cassie?'

Mike sighed. 'No. She was spotted looking into a jewellery shop window at about five to nine yesterday morning, by the postman. Before that, a couple of kids saw her at half-past eight. Nothing since. I'm going in to work anyway. We're going to the school, question some of the kids who know her.' He looked at Aunt May. 'There's not a lot more we can do.'

Aunt May nodded. 'I'll pop round and see Jill.'

'You do that. Tell her ... tell her we're doing everything we can to find Cassie.'

Aunt May nodded. She left through the back door as Mike headed up to the shower.

1.30 pm

Simmonds glared at his oldest son. 'I've told you, he's completely reliable. Everything is going according to plan. By tonight the fool in Northumbria will be dead, along with that interfering copper.'

His son Giles was a younger version of himself, with the same petulant mouth, now down-turned at the corners. He said, 'As long as he knows what's riding on this. Seeing as you failed to push through the deaths of his whole family, we've lost out on their empire.' He slammed the book he'd been holding onto the coffee table. 'Really, Father, things aren't going according to plan.'

'We have to tread carefully, surely you can see that? If any of the families get wind of what we're planning, then we will be the ones murdered in our beds.'

'Huh.'

'Huh, you say? Why do you think the Norwegian family were wiped out in the fourteenth century?'

Giles shrugged. 'That was then. This is now.'

'This is now?' Simmonds snapped. 'How many times do you need to be told that we are all in danger? Until the real Lindisfarne Gospels are found and hidden with the Historian, every one of the families is in danger. Thank God everyone thinks the ones in London are the real thing. If the genuine gospels were ever found, with the real truth of the world in them, we would be hunted down and torn to pieces.'

Giles shrugged.

Seeing his usual uncaring attitude, Simmonds snapped, 'That is why the whole operation up north is being supervised by your brother Michael. If it's hidden where we think, then they'll recover it tonight while most of the islanders are in Berwick. Here.' Simmonds got up from the settee and walked over to a sixteenth-century chest. Using a tiny key taken from a chain around his neck, he opened a compartment at the back of the chest and drew out a wad of notes, which he handed to his son. 'Do what you do best. The casino's open now.'

With a look of contempt, Giles snatched the money from his father's hand and, without a backward glance, walked out.

Simmonds gritted his teeth. If Giles didn't look so much like him, he would swear he was not his son. Even so, he'd still had a secret DNA test done which unfortunately had proved positive.

Michael was so much better material, just like his bastard peasant daughter, who was a rising star of the stock market. A little helping hand, unknown to her, had not gone amiss. He smiled.

If Giles ever bumped into her, it would be like looking in a mirror. He would guess right off who she was.

Picking his phone up, he dialled a north-east number.

3.00 pm

Shelly stared at the half-full box. She had no idea how many bags she had put in. Each one had to be counted, and she found it hard to concentrate, especially with Danny's eyes on her most of the time. Guilt weighed heavy on her mind, and pain wracked her body with every breath she took. Every time she moved, her nerves screamed in agony. Not for the first time she would have to empty the box out and start again.

Sighing, she tried to tip the box up, and couldn't find the strength. Suddenly the box was taken out of her hands. She watched as the deadly packets were tipped onto the bench. Looking up, her eyes met Danny's. 'Sorry,' she whispered – not for the box, but for the horror she had dragged him into.

Understanding, Danny give her a quick smile. He hadn't forgiven her, and wasn't sure if he ever would, but his heart ached for what had happened to her. He was still looking at Shelly when Cassie nudged him. He winced, and felt his knees wobble as pain washed over him. She had caught him in the ribs. He hung onto the bench. To give in meant to be dragged away. Already, four kids and one of the women were lying in the corner.

He felt a breath on his neck, and froze as the man with the gun said, 'Just give me any excuse to waste you.'

'Sorry,' Danny whispered, getting on with his work. He looked at Cassie and pulled a face.

As the gunman walked back to the middle of the room, Brother David and four other monks came into the hall, each carrying a tray with six bowls of soup. They delivered these to the top four tables, then went out for more.

'We should complain to the union about this, we get served last every time,' Danny whispered to the girls. Despite their plight, it raised a ghost of a smile from Cassie and Shelly, but the girl with the glasses and the long brown bunches just looked vacantly at him.

Tutting, Danny got on with his work, still racking his mind for ways to escape, while Cassie dreaded every passing minute, wondering exactly what was in store for her tonight. Shelly already knew.

4.15 pm

Mike and Kristina looked at each other as the boy turned to go. When he reached the door, Mike said, 'Tell the next one to wait, we'll come for him when we're ready.' The boy threw them a quick smile and a nod as he closed the door behind him.

They had been at it for hours and, after interviewing most of the school, they were down to the last four. 'He seemed like a nice kid,' Kristina said, smoothing the creases out of her pale blue linen dress.

Dry-washing his face with his hands, Mike replied. 'Yeah, but like most of them he never really knew Cassie. She hasn't been here long enough to make much of an impression on them.'

'Well, there's only a few left. Might as well get it over with.' When Mike nodded, Kristina got up and went to the door. She smiled at the four teenagers, three boys and a chubby girl with short red hair, and beckoned for the girl to come in.

When she was seated in front of them, Mike said, 'So, what's your name?'

'Amber.' She looked from under her lids at Mike.

Guessing that she was quite shy, and probably bullied for her weight and the colour of her hair, which was really quite beautiful, Mike said gently, 'All right, Amber, I guess by now you'll have heard what this is all about?'

The girl's face flushed as she nodded. 'I ... I saw her get into a car... I was late and I ran past her.'

Mike and Kristina looked at each other. 'At last,' Kristina muttered.

'OK.' Mike smiled at the girl. 'Take your time and tell us everything you can remember. Even if you think it's not important, it might be.'

She paused for a moment, then said hesitantly, 'I ... er ... I didn't really see much. Cassie was looking in the shop window when the car came up the road and turned. When I passed, she got in the car.' She shrugged. 'That's all, really.'

'What colour was the car?' Kristina asked.

Amber bit her lip. 'Oh, dark, I think. Black or dark blue.'

'Did you notice the number plate?' Mike raised an eyebrow, hoping for the practically impossible.

She shook her head. 'No, sorry. I never looked.'

'It's all right, Amber... Why would you? Did you see who else was in the car?'

'A girl, and two men.'

'Seen any of them before, Amber?' Kristina put in.

Turning to Kristina, Amber went on, 'Not the men, 'cos it drove off too fast. I think I've seen the girl before though, but I can't remember where. She's not in our class. I think she's too old, she might have left school.'

'Did Cassie get into the car willingly, or did it look like she was forced?'

'I think she just got in, like she knew them.'

'OK, Amber, you're doing great. Now, can you tell us what the girl looked like?' Mike asked, leaning eagerly across the desk, praying that fate was finally dealing them a good card.

Amber chewed her lip for a moment. 'She's got long black hair, and face rings.'

'Maria!' Mike said, turning his head to look at Kristina.

'Sounds like it to me. Amber, you've been a great help. Thank you.' Kristina smiled, and, basking in the praise, Amber beamed back at her.

When she had gone, Mike shrugged his jacket on. 'Come on, Kristina, we might catch her in the house this time.'

'What about the rest of them out there?'

Opening the door, Mike said to the three boys, 'Any of youse lot got anything to tell us? Do you even know Cassie?'

The boys looked at each other, shrugged in turn, then shook their heads. Stopping himself from asking if any of them had tongues in their mouths, Mike said, 'Right, lads, you can go now.'

He watched as the trio slumped away. Turning back, he waited while Kristina slipped a white bolero over her shoulders, then together they walked out to the car.

6.30 pm

Aunt May was looking out of her window as the coach arrived to take the villagers to Berwick Town Hall for the meeting. She still had time to go, and was actually in two minds. But she was worried about Smiler. He'd been missing most of the day. The bread had almost disappeared, nothing left but a crust, and she didn't know if Smiler had been back and had a snack, or if Mike had taken sandwiches to work with him.

Should I go?

No. Can't stand the bloody poncy idiots.

Anyhow, I can't go unless I know Smiler's safe.

She was about to slip her old blue cardigan on and have another wander round the village, when Mike walked in.

'Oh, thank God you're back.'

'Why, what's wrong?' Watching her heading for the door, Mike left his jacket on. He already had a feeling that this was something to do with Smiler.

'Did you take sandwiches to work today?'

'That'll be a yes.'

'Then Smiler's been missing all day. And that bloody Tiny.' She couldn't keep the worry off her face as she looked at Mike.

'Ahh, fuck.'

'Uh-hmm.'

'Sorry, Aunt May, it's been one of those days. We actually have a lead, but can't flaming well find her.'

'Oh, dear. So nothing at all?'

Mike shook his head.

'I've been with Jill most of the day. She's in a right bloody state, the poor lass.'

'Yeah, I bet. Look, we better go and find our own missing ones.'

As they stepped out of the door, the bus went past. Aunt May stopped and watched. Noticing that it was full, she muttered, 'Bloody fools.'

Pleased that she hadn't gone, but still not sure why, Mike hid a smile as they walked to the centre of the village. When they had reached Stables coffee shop, Mike said, 'You carry on round the streets, I'll go down onto the beach.'

'Right, then. See you back here,' Aunt May answered, as she turned and walked off in the opposite direction.

6.50 pm

Aunt May had searched every street and alleyway, looking into back yards and every other place she could think of. She decided to go and look around the old monastery. The monastery was built in AD 635 for the Irish-born St Aidan, and around the early seven hundreds the Lindisfarne Gospels had been created there.

Aunt May was thinking of the Gospels when she reached the monastery. Most of the villagers' hearts were in the right place, but she just didn't trust these strangers, who had turned up out of the blue and riled people up. A worthy cause, yes, but what were these people really after?

Although well-preserved in some places, the monastery was still a ruin. A large ruin though, with plenty of hiding places for a boy and a dog who didn't want to be found.

She was just entering the main gate when she heard whispering voices. Pausing, she listened intently. It sounded like there were at least three of them. Then came the sound of digging.

Her heart rate increased. What are they doing? she wondered, as she hid behind one of the ancient walls and peeped round. Too late, she heard a sound behind her. She spun round, and saw a rush of movement. A moment later the blow to her head rendered her unconscious. Slowly she slid down the wall, first scraping the skin off her cheek, then snagging her blue cardigan on the rough stone.

6.55 pm
Mike had walked the full length of the beach towards Beal. He'd bumped into a lone man out with his dog, and remembered why the place seemed so deserted. Most of the islanders were at the meeting. Now back where he started, he set off in the other direction. As he turned a rocky outcrop, he noticed some markings in the flat damp sand. At first he ignored them, but they seemed to be everywhere, stretching from the land, across the sand to the water's edge. Frowning, he studied the nearest set. They looked familiar, but no memory of them came rushing to his mind.

Moving on, he was puzzled. The markings seemed to go on and on. He scanned the beach, and spotted a small boy doodling in the sand with a large stick or twig. Mike frowned. Could that be Smiler? He knew for sure a moment later, when a large dog came out of the sea, ran up to the boy and showered him with water as it gave a gigantic shake. The boy ignored the dog, and carried on with his frantic scrawling.

Mike sighed, pleased he'd found Smiler, but upset at what he was doing.

Looking at the marks again, and shocked by the amount, all in rigid lines of five, Mike muttered, 'The poor sod must have been at it for hours.' He looked back along the beach at Smiler. With a deep sigh, he headed off towards him.

When he reached him, Smiler was again talking in unintelligible quick time. 'Smiler,' Mike said, gently touching his shoulder. 'What's all this?' He indicated the marks in the sand – then found himself staring at them.

'No, can't be!'

At the sound of Mike's voice, as if someone had pressed a switch, Smiler stopped talking and scribbling.

'Mike!'

But Mike was walking back and forth, studying each identical section of marks from different angles. Suddenly he shouted, 'Dave!' Spinning round, he faced Smiler. For a moment he stared at him in wonder. 'How?'

Smiler shook his head as Tiny, hearing Mike shout, came bounding up. The dog jumped up to be patted. 'Yes, yes, hello, Tiny.' Mike stroked his

293

head, but his eyes were still on Smiler. 'How?' he asked again.

'I don't know. Those symbols have been burning in my head all day. But...' He looked around. As far as the eye could see the sand was covered in them. 'I don't remember doing any of this,' he muttered, his voice shaky, his eyes wide and staring. Frightened at the scale of the markings, he ran his fingers through his hair. 'What does it mean?'

'It's something we made up as kids. See the backwards-facing D? That's for Dave. The three interlocking circles are also his sign. The number of wavy lines above them means danger. The more lines there are, the more danger he's in.'

Smiler looked at the signs again. 'Looks like he's in a hell of a lot of danger, then.'

Taking his phone out, Mike dialled Kristina. When she answered he said, 'That missing note, can you describe what was on it?'

'Looked like nothing more than a bunch of circles and some wavy lines. Why?'

'Send a couple of squad cars, packed with as many cops as you can squeeze in, to the monastery on the mainland. ASAP, no sirens or any noise. I'll explain when I see you.' Without waiting for an answer, he snapped his phone shut.

Hurrying away, Mike said over his shoulder to Smiler, 'You go and find Aunt May. She's worried sick about you. She'll be somewhere in the village.'

He took off at a run, leaving a puzzled Smiler staring after him.

7.15 pm

Brother Josh's lips moved in silent prayer as he walked down the hall. Shelly spotted him, and knew instinctively that he was coming for her. She froze, watching every step he made. She knew, in those steps her fate was sealed.

Cassie was also watching him. She couldn't begin to imagine that they would kill her. She hung onto the hope that they would be rescued. But she also had a good idea of what was going to happen, and to her it was a fate worse than death. She started to sob.

Danny looked up, then stared from one girl to another. His heart rate speeded up. No way could he stand still and let this happen to either of them.

What to do?

His mind raced, rejecting everything he thought of. He knew that at this end of the hall were two sheds connected to the main building, where most of the pot was grown. He'd spotted a door from one of the sheds which led into the garden. But how the hell to get out of the garden, with those friggin' electronic gates controlling everyone who enters and everyone who leaves? Shit!

Brother Josh reached them.

Where's the prat with the gun? Danny looked quickly round, but couldn't see him. As Brother Josh took each girl by the arms, Danny reacted in typical Danny fashion.

7.20 pm

Mike stopped the car behind a thick hedgerow,

where he knew he couldn't be seen from the monastery. Taking a minute to whip off his white T-shirt, and shrugging into a black one which he kept in the car for emergencies, he quickly and quietly jumped out of the car, locked it, and ran along the road. The body had been found early yesterday morning in the yard that was used by a lot of policemen. Mike had a feeling that, if he was right, Dave wanted more than one person there when the body and the note were discovered. That had to mean there was someone in the station he didn't trust. The CCTV camera had shown nothing, and still showed nothing four hours later, when someone went outside and had a look, and found the camera lens covered in grey tape.

Kristina had said there were thirty seconds of tape, showing a large man wearing a hood, who kept his head down as he ran across the yard. A minute later, the tape went blank. Whoever it was had shoved the large black dustbin under the camera to reach it.

It must have been Dave. His habit could have been mistaken for a hoodie.

He reached the door in the wall, which was also hidden from outside by overgrown ivy. He had to rummage amongst the leaves until he found the door, and was pleased that it was unlocked. Obviously Dave's doing.

Again, he wondered what the hell was going on, and why the note had disappeared. He froze. 'Shit,' he whispered, 'The note disappeared after Tony was in the office... Where the hell does he fit into all of this?'

Frowning, he opened the door, He remembered that it used to squeak, but no. It opened silently. Thank God. Dave must have oiled it. Closing the door behind him, he rearranged the ivy, then, hugging the wall, he ran to the first of the sheds and peered into the window just as Brother Josh reached Danny and the girls.

7.21 pm

Danny launched a fist at Brother Josh. It connected with the end of his chin, felling him immediately. Shocked, for a moment Danny could only stare. Too late, the option for action was lost as the gunman walked in.

'What the fuck?' He ran down towards them, his gun pointed at Danny.

Shaking, Danny held his hands up. 'He ... he just collapsed, honest to God, he fainted or something. Yeah, that's what must have happened, he fucking fainted, didn't he?'

Cassie nodded. 'Yes, that's what happened, he must be poorly. Do you think he's poorly?' Her eyes were a picture of innocence as she looked at the gunman.

Ignoring her, he snarled, 'Get out of the way, bitch. You!' He poked Danny in the ribs with his gun. Danny gritted his teeth, doing his best not to show any pain. 'Pick him up.' The gunman sneered in Danny's face.

Trying hard to get a grip on his temper, Danny bent down and hauled Brother Josh to a standing position. He managed out of sheer stubbornness, but the pain made him feel like fainting. What stopped him was the fact that he knew, if he hit the deck, Ugly Fart Face Gunman wouldn't waste the opportunity to get a few more kicks in. One more blow would probably crunch his rib cage to bits. He shivered inwardly at the picture. Can you walk with no ribs?

Christ, can you do anything with no ribs?

'Wait here,' the gunman snarled at Danny. Turning to the girls, he said, 'Follow me.'

'No.' Cassie backed away. 'No. I want to go home.'

He looked suspiciously at Cassie, before stealing a quick glance at Shelly, who stood with her head down. She was swaying, and looked as if she might collapse at any time. Taking a step forward, he thrust his face into Cassie's, grabbed her arm and shook her hard. 'You been taking the goodies?' He frowned at her. 'Or palming them?'

'She's been taking them,' a voice said from behind him.

The gunman swung round. 'Where the fuck have you been?'

'I got here as soon as I could,' Brother David answered.

Gently, he took hold of Cassie's hand. He shot a puzzled look at Danny, who was still holding Brother Josh up, and was about to ask what the problem was when the gunman snarled, 'Get on with your business.'

Trying to conceal his worry, Brother David said, 'Don't be afraid, child. Come with me.' He felt a self-loathing so intense, as Cassie pleaded with her eyes for his help, that for a moment he was unable to move – until a poke in the ribs with the gun spurred him on.

He could save this one. She was still fit and strong enough to make a run for it. Just along the corridor, and they could disappear. But how many would that madman take vengeance on? A new shipment was due in an hour. Just about every one of the children here was now expendable. He thought hard as he walked along the corridor. Reaching the door to freedom, he passed by. As much as he wanted to save this one child, his conscience would not allow him to have even more blood on his hands.

It had not taken Mike long to suss out exactly what was going on. The smell would be enough for anyone. He'd watched what had transpired between the gunman, the two girls and Danny, seen how gaunt Dave was, and the heartbreaking state of the others in there. It all brought his blood to boiling point.

Taking a wild guess, he ran round the side of the building, praying he'd remembered rightly that there was a door on this side of the building and not the other.

He spotted the door only because it was slightly ajar. Dave's doing, he wondered, or a trap? Slowing down to minimize any noise, he reached the door. His back flat against the wall, he used his left foot to push the door open.

Silently it moved inwards. Well oiled, again. It had to be Dave. He took courage in the fact that Dave obviously had enough faith in him to think that he would understand the note. Pushing off from the wall, he spun into the small corridor that led into the larger one. Three strides took

299

him to the next door. He put his ear to one of the panels. After a moment he heard a noise, two separate pairs of feet. He guessed rightly that Dave and Cassie had already passed by, so these must be the creep with the gun and Shelly.

Judging the right moment, he flung the door open, and threw himself onto the shocked gunman.

7.30 pm

Smiler and Tiny had walked round the nearly deserted island, and found no sign of Aunt May. Frustrated, Smiler turned for home. 'Not even a whiff of her,' he muttered to Tiny, then stopped in his tracks. 'That's it!' He looked at the dog. 'Time to show if you're worth your keep, boy. Come on.'

At a run, he headed for Aunt May's house. Practically falling through the back door, he grabbed one of Aunt May's countless wool cardigans off a peg. 'Here, boy find.' He had no idea if Tiny was any good at fetching or finding, but if there was any chance it might work, he had to give it a go. He rubbed the cardigan on Tiny's nose. The dog barked, then grabbed a mouthful of the cardigan, thinking he was playing tug-of-war.

'No, no.' Smiler carefully disentangled the dog's teeth from the wool. 'Find.' He rubbed the cardigan over Tiny's nose again, repeating, 'Find!' as he guided Tiny towards the back door.

Outside, Tiny sniffed the ground. Suddenly he started barking loudly and set off at a run, yanking the lead out of Smiler's hand. Catching him,

300

Smiler allowed Tiny to lead him around the streets. The dog paused now and then, before setting off in a different direction that led him back to the same place. Smiler guessed that perhaps Aunt May had passed over the various points more than once.

That Tiny had the scent was obvious, but they seemed to be getting nowhere. Smiler was becoming increasingly worried. The feeling that something was very wrong with Aunt May was growing stronger by the minute. His heart was heavy, and there was an ever-increasing blackness in his head that was starting to frighten him.

'Come on, good dog. Find... Find Aunt May, Tiny, good boy.'

Tiny shook himself, turned round and, nose to the ground, hurried off in the direction of the ruined monastery. 'OK,' Smiler said, 'we'll try over there. We've done just about everywhere else.'

Tiny sniffed around the entrance, then suddenly took off again, dragging Smiler with him. Reaching the wall where Aunt May lay, Tiny put his head back and howled. His heart pounding in his chest, Smiler walked round to the other side of the wall.

7.31 pm
Wrapping his left hand around the gunman's mouth, Mike gestured with his head to the amazed Shelly, urging her to follow him as he dragged the struggling man back into the passageway.

He'd noticed that a lot of the people had a

length of rope hanging from their right wrists, Shelly included. Shrugging off the thought his mind provided for this, he gave the gunman a punch to the side of his head, knocking him out completely. Letting him fall to the floor, he reached for Shelly's wrist. Wide-eyed and trembling, she shied away from him.

'It's all right love,' he said gently, 'I'm a police officer.' For a moment, her eyes met his. Mike could see in their depths that she wanted to believe him. But he knew she was also getting ready to run. That was easily read in her posture. 'No, Shelly, keep calm. Trust me, I'm here to help.'

Still not one hundred percent convinced, she said hesitatingly, 'How do you know my name?'

'I told you, I'm a policeman. I've been looking for you... Your brothers, Gary and Liam? They reported you missing.'

Taking a deep breath, she relaxed slightly.

'OK, now give me the rope, so that we can tie this joker up.'

Looking down at the gunman, she curled her lip as she lifted her hand for Mike to untie the rope. In less than a minute he had it off her wrist. Flipping the gunman over, he quickly tied his hands. Standing up, Mike shed his jacket then, pulling his T-shirt over his head, he ripped it in half, then once more. Balling the thickest piece he shoved it into the man's mouth, then stretched one of the longer strips over his mouth and tied it at the back of his neck.

'OK.' He looked at Shelly. 'Give me a brief rundown about exactly what the hell's going on here.'

Danny was still holding Brother Josh upright. He was showing signs of coming round now. Danny was anxiously biting his lip when Brother David entered the hall, with a puzzled look on his face. He strode down to Danny and Brother Josh, just as Brother Josh let out a huge moan.

'What? Who did this?' Brother David stared in horror at the state of Brother Josh's face.

Danny swallowed hard, and said meekly, 'Er, me.'

'You!'

'Er, yes.' Danny looked wildly around for an escape route, even though he knew there was none, because this brother looked a hell of a lot tougher than the other.

'Hmm. I can probably guess why.' Brother David sighed. He hooked an arm under Brother Josh's arms, and started to lead him away. Half-way down the hall, he turned back. 'Where's Shelly?'

Shrugging, Danny muttered, 'Happy Face took her away.'

Brother David stopped. 'How long ago?'

'Just after you took Cassie.'

He gasped. He'd looked into the room she was supposed to be in, after delivering Cassie up to the monster, hoping to take her hand in prayer. It was the least he could do. But she hadn't been there. He glanced quickly around the room. The gunman, who had never once in all the months he'd been there told them his name, was nowhere in sight.

Suddenly his heart soared. Could Mike be here?

Could it be possible that he'd finally got the message? 'Come with me,' he said. 'Quickly, now.'

'OK,' Danny answered. Anything was better than standing here filling the endless bags with the endless piles of pills. He actually wondered how long he would stay sane at this rate. Perhaps the poor sods swallowing the poison had it right after all. Sweet oblivion!

Mike had listened in amazement as Shelly gave him a garbled tale that made the hairs on the back of his neck stand up. He had to stop her once or twice to clarify something, and although a lot of what she said sounded like fiction, there were so many plausible things that made the whole story ring true.

The gunman had regained consciousness, and was now glaring at Shelly. He started to struggle, and kicked at her. Mike gave him another tap on the head with his gun, sending him spiralling down into blackness again.

Opening the gun, he checked it for ammunition, satisfied there was a full clip. He turned his mobile phone off. He needed no sudden noise to alert the fiend and his cronies.

He judged Kristina and crew should only be five minutes, max. Turning to Shelly, Jesus Christ, she looks like she's dying, he thought, and said gently, 'Wait here. I doubt he'll wake up for a good while now, but if he does, keep him quiet any way you can.'

She nodded, and slid down the wall to sit next to the gunman. She didn't have the strength to do anything else.

Mike crept along silently. Having visited the monastery more than once, he had a good idea of the layout of the place. He prayed he would be in time to save Cassie. He moved four doors along the corridor. This room had a big bay window that he could easily climb out of. He needed to be outside. Surprise was his best weapon, and it could not be achieved by creeping along corridors, where at any given moment four or five doors could open at once, spilling God knows what into his space.

Cassie stood in front of The Leader. She was shaking with fright as he smiled down at her. Cassie's eyes were not on his face though, but on the large knife he held in his left hand. They were alone in the room. The stone floor was cold on her bare feet. Her shoes had been taken away the moment she got here.

'You look good in your school uniform. Have any of the boys told you that before? Of course they have.' Without waiting for an answer, he moved closer, one slow step after another. 'A beautiful girl like you must have many boyfriends.' He was in front of her now, his feet inches away from hers, his body even closer.

Mike dropped silently to the ground. Bending over, he ran to the window he wanted, reaching it just as The Leader flicked Cassie's hair off her shoulder with the knife.

Breathing deeply, Mike used a calming technique to still the anger building in his blood. He had to wait for a distraction, the man was too close to the girl. One wrong move on Mike's part, and the bastard could easily slit her throat in seconds. He looked through the gun sights. One shot to the bastard's head was all it would take, and whatever spell he had these people under would be broken. Mike had dealt with cults before. He knew that sometimes all it needed was a drastic sharp shock for most to come to their senses. Some, however, were lost forever, and he strongly doubted if those poor souls in the packing sheds would ever make it back to some semblance of normal life. But Cassie could be saved.

'If he would only step back for a moment,' Mike whispered. 'That's all, one moment.'

7.50 am
The ambulance hurried over the causeway. Inside, Smiler had tight hold of Aunt May's hand. She was unconscious, and so pale, he thought, as the nurse cleaned the blood off her face. They hadn't been very encouraging when they had arrived, saying very little until Smiler, crazy with worry for the woman who in a short time had become his surrogate mother, demanded to know what they thought. A lot of head-shaking went on between the two ambulance people, with a serious whisper– 'We won't know until we get her to the hospital.'

Why whisper? Smiler thought. It's obvious that she can't hear you!

They passed through Beal, turned left onto the motorway and, sirens blasting, headed towards Newcastle.

Smiler took out his mobile and looked at the time. Fifteen minutes since he'd phoned Mike and left a message. What was he doing? Mike never switched his mobile off.

As he looked back at Aunt May, a feeling of blackness descended on him. He didn't know if it was for Aunt May, the two girls in his head, for Mike, or for all of them.

Mike gently put pressure on the trigger. Then, startled, he swung the gun away as the sound of gunshots rang through the building. He ducked out of sight. Leaning against the wall, he slowly rose again until his eyes were peering over the sill. The room was empty, and the sound of gun-fire even louder.

He tried opening the window. To his surprise it slid upwards easily enough. This one he didn't put down to Dave, but to the warm summer night. It only took a moment for him to hoist himself inside. Reaching the open door, he peered round. Someone was running along the corridor. He realised who it was the moment they passed. Stepping out behind the running figure, he said, 'Wait.'

Still running, Danny swung his head round. Recognising Mike, he stopped and heaved a huge sigh. 'Jesus, man, the fucking cavalry at last. Where the hell have you been? Do you have any fucking idea what's going on here? There's a room full of friggin' zombies back there. Call yourself a copper, with this going on under your fucking nose for a year or more?'

'Shut up,' Mike said as he reached him. 'Do

307

everything I say when I say it.'

'Yeah, I can live with that.' Pleased that there was someone to take charge, Danny fell in step with Mike as they headed towards the gunfire that was coming from the large dining hall.

'Just one thing,' Danny said, as they reached the heavy oaken doors.

'What?' Mike snarled.

'Shouldn't we be running the other way?'

Ignoring him, Mike slowly opened the door a few inches. Right in his line of sight, he could see Dave, his arms around Cassie. Both of them were huddled under a large table. His eyes tight shut, Dave was praying, his lips moving as guns blasted back and forth. Suddenly he opened his eyes, and stared at Mike.

Mike gave him a nod. His face wreathed in smiles, Dave cuddled Cassie closer and whispered something in her ear.

'What's going on?' Danny asked from behind Mike.

'Can't you guess?' Mike hissed in exasperation.

'Well ... well, yes, I suppose. What we've got here is a bunch of fucking nutters.'

Ignoring him again, Mike rested his gun against his shoulder, barrel pointed at the ceiling. He risked a glance. Half a dozen men were firing at each other, ducking and weaving about, shooting at anything that moved. He noticed the one they called The Leader, hiding behind two huge guards. He swung his head the other way and gasped when he saw Tony taking aim. The Leader went down. Suddenly the harsh sound of sirens filled the air.

'Thank God for that,' Danny said, actually managing to make it sound like a genuine prayer.

Mike looked back for Tony, caught him running across the room, making for a door further down the hall than the one that Mike and Danny were standing in.

Knowing where Tony was heading, Mike spun round. Nearly knocking Danny off his feet, he took off at a run. Not wanting to be left behind, Danny followed him, muttering, 'I knew we should have gone this way.'

When they reached the small corridor which led outside, where Mike had left Shelly and the gunman, the door was wide open and either the light bulb had blown, or Tony had taken the time to switch it off.

Was he waiting in there for them, hiding in the dark, ready to kill again?

'God, what's that smell?' Danny wrinkled his nose.

'Shush, Danny... Shelly?' Mike said quietly. There was no answer. He turned to Danny and mouthed, 'The light switch is on the left of the door. When I step in, switch it on.'

Danny gulped, but nodded as he moved to stand side by side with Mike.

Stepping into the corridor, Mike quickly swung his gun from side to side, as Danny flipped the switch. Both of them gasped loudly, and Mike dropped the gun to his side. There was blood everywhere. Up the walls, pooling on the floor – even the light shade was splattered. Danny's hand suddenly felt damp and sticky. Not daring to look at his fingers, he shuddered, and quickly wiped his hand on his jeans.

'Dear God!' Mike said.

Danny followed Mike's gaze. 'Oh, no. Oh, no.' Sobbing, he fell to his knees.

Shelly and the gunman lay propped against the wall. Their throats had been cut. The gunman's body had been savagely sliced open, his intestines spilling onto the floor. Not only had they fallen out of the gaping wound, they had been helped out, dragged along the floor and stamped on, as if a petulant child had, after being punished, wrecked his room. Mike looked around in horror. He thought he'd seen the worst thing ever when he had seen what had been done to Alicia, but this was worse than anything he could ever have imagined.

Bending down, he checked Shelly for a pulse, guessing that it was only because the bastard was pushed for time that she hadn't suffered the same fate as the gunman. If she had been sitting where the gunman was, then it would have been her insides scattered all over the floor.

He tried every pulse point he knew, and was about to give up when he tried her left wrist again. He felt a faint pulse. He snatched the gag out of the gunman's mouth and used it to put pressure on Shelly's wound. 'She's alive, Danny ... Danny?' Mike turned. Danny was flat out on the floor behind him.

8.35 pm

As a fleet of ambulances left the monastery for the hospital, Mike and Kristina stood over the dead body of the gunman. Cassie was on her

310

way, physically unscathed, to her mother, and a traumatized Danny had been taken to his friend Evan's flat. It was touch and go with Shelly, but the ambulance crew were doing everything they could to stabilize her. If she made it to the hospital, she stood a chance. Dave and the other brothers were all being interviewed.

9.00 pm
A pathologist that Mike had never met before had been sent up from Newcastle to fill in for Jill. The woman, who had been on her knees staring at the gaping wound in the gunman's throat, stood up. She stretched, with her hands on her hips. Long and lean. Mike could not help but admire her lithe shape. Morgane Westwood was a beautiful woman, with thick, raven-black hair tied at the nape of her neck, and large violet eyes. But Mike was distracted only momentarily. His mind was in a place far different from the claustrophobic walls of this small space. He was wondering how Tony could have done this cold-blooded murder. The Tony he knew would be incapable of such a callous act.

Why?

The only reason he could come up with was to silence Shelly and the gunman. Both obviously knew too much, but too much about what?

The information Shelly had given him had been garbled, to say the least. A group of families, stretching back God knows how many centuries, who controlled everything, even down to the global credit crunch that she insisted was coming this winter and would affect just about every country in the world. Dave certainly knew nothing about the so-called families. He only knew the tyrant who had ruled their lives, thinking of him as a cult leader.

Actually, the more Mike thought about it, the more frighteningly possible it did become.

'No,' he muttered, arguing with himself. 'Pure fiction.'

'Sorry?' Westwood said, giving Mike an odd look.

'Nothing, just thinking aloud.'

'He does it a lot,' Kristina snapped, walking in. 'So, can you tell us anything before you take him away?'

'There's one thing I need to ask you.' Ignoring Kristina, she looked at Mike.

'Go ahead.'

'Is this body in the same position as you left it?'

Pretending not to notice the scowl on Kristina's face, Mike answered. 'Near enough. He wasn't going anywhere, and Shelly barely had the strength in her to move.'

'Then I'm pretty sure the murderer is left-handed.'

'You can tell that? How?' Kristina asked.

'The angle that the throats have been cut.' She used a slashing movement with her right hand to demonstrate. 'A right-handed person would slash from right to left, a left-handed person from left to right.'

'Tony is right-handed,' Mike said quietly.

'Tony who?' Westwood asked.

Before Mike could answer, Kristina asked. 'Why would he slit him open like that? I mean, he had to be in a hurry.'

Shrugging, Westwood looked down at the body, before giving Kristina a quick appraisal and saying, 'Heaven knows.'

'Because he's taking the piss. He knew Shelly had spilled her guts, and he in his arrogance was going to spill hers. Only not enough time. But he's left her a warning.' Mike gritted his teeth as he took out his mobile.

'Shit, no reception in here. Kristina, phone from outside and get an armed guard on Shelly, now.'

Nodding, Kristina hurried outside.

'This bastard thinks he's invincible.' He looked at Westwood. 'Everything, I need everything you can get me, the smallest detail. OK?'

Westwood nodded. She pulled a white mask from her pocket. The smell in the confined space was becoming unbearable. Before putting the mask on, she said, 'I assure you, you will get everything I can possibly come up with to catch this renegade.'

Kristina came back in, and shot the pathologist an odd look, wondering at her strange choice of word for the murderer.

Before she could comment, Mike said, 'Come on, Kristina.' Turning, he left the room.

'What's up?' she asked, catching up to him in the main corridor.

'I need to talk to Dave.'

'You mean, Brother David?'

Mike paused slightly, a breath of a movement, that no one who didn't know him well would not have noticed. But Kristina knew that Mike had never really accepted the fact that Dave had

313

chosen the holy life.

They reached the door where Brother David was being interviewed. Mike gave a single knock, and opened the door when he heard someone say, 'Come in.'

'Excuse me,' he said to the officer, a pale-faced young man with a huge gap in his front teeth. 'Can I have a few words?'

'Certainly, sir.' The young officer nodded at Brother David, who looked up at Mike, a question in his eyes.

'This Leader, is he left-handed or right-handed?'

'Left-handed,' Brother David replied without hesitation.

'Do any of his followers look like him?'

Again Brother David's reply was quick. 'Actually, yes, and I know what you're thinking. Once or twice ... certain mannerisms have seemed strange, different, if you know what I mean. It wasn't Tony, was it?' His last words were said with relief. He had prayed over the dead body, and could still see the horrific picture behind his eyes. He waited anxiously for Mike to say something.

Before Mike could reply, Kristina's mobile rang. Fishing it out of her pocket, she said, 'Hello.' She listened for a moment then, her face grim, she switched it off. 'Mike, turn your phone on.'

Frowning, Mike took his mobile out. Message after message from Smiler. 'Shit. What the hell?' He listened to the latest frantic message.

Slowly he put his phone away. Staring at Brother David, he said, 'Aunt May is in Newcastle Hospital. She's been hit on the head. It's serious.'

314

When they got to the hospital, Mike spotted Smiler smoking outside the gate. Stopping the car, he jumped out. Kristina, climbing into the driver's seat, said sarcastically, 'I'll park it.'

As she drove off, Brother David looked at Smiler, who was wiping his face, and staring at Mike with undisguised relief. Mike had told him as much as he knew about Smiler on the way over.

Mike held his hand out for a cigarette. 'So what the hell happened?' He puffed raggedly on the cigarette as Smiler told him how he and Tiny had found Aunt May.

Five minutes later, the four of them were around her bed.

Aunt May lay unmoving, wired up to various machines. Mike was about to look for a doctor, because Smiler had very little information as to her condition, when the doctor in charge walked in.

Knowing what questions would be asked, the doctor said, before any of them could speak, 'I'm afraid she is in a coma.'

'No!' Brother David said. Stepping closer, he took hold of her hand and began to pray.

'She's had a massive trauma to the back of her head.'

'So when will she...' Mike looked hopefully at the doctor.

'I'm sorry, I really don't know. It could be an hour from now, tomorrow, or—'

'Never.' Mike cut him off.

Kristina gripped his arm. 'She'll come through this, Mike, you know how tough she is.'

'That's always a help in these cases,' the doctor said. 'And he's got the right idea.' He looked at Brother David, who was still praying.

Mike sighed, and chewed the inside of his bottom lip. He wanted to cry like everyone else, but tears would get him nowhere. He needed action.

'You stay with her, Dave.'

Brother David nodded, and made the sign of the cross as he said, 'You do what you have to do, Mike. I'll be here waiting.'

Mike nodded at him. For a moment, their eyes locked. Then Mike turned away. 'Come with me,' he said to Kristina and Smiler.

An hour later, they were on Holy Island, walking through the cemetery towards the monastery. Smiler had been babbling the whole way here about the Lindisfarne Gospels, how they had been dropped overboard into the sea centuries ago, then found later completely intact. Knowing that it was his way of dealing with things, Mike had let him get it out.

Now, though, as they reached the spot where Smiler had found her, Mike held his hand up for Smiler to be quiet.

Silently, they gazed down at the spot. Mike guessed rightly that the brown marks trailing down the ancient walls were Aunt May's blood. As he stared at the bloodstains, he vowed to capture the bastards responsible, no matter how long it took, or wherever it took him. He would search every nook and cranny of the world until he had the weasels in his hands. Then they would regret ever having been born.

'Someone's been digging here.' Kristina knelt down. 'It's pretty deep. Wonder if they found what they were looking for?'

Mike wasn't listening. He was watching another helicopter, only this one was leaving the island from the field near to the castle. He watched until it was a speck in the sky, and smaller than the birds that had become airborne with it.

'Mike,' Kristina said, as she rose and pointed at the hole. 'Look.'

Mike looked down. He had seen the hole, but now that Kristina had moved and wasn't casting a shadow over it, he noticed a tiny glint of gold. He picked it up, and sighed heavily. The gold was a small Celtic cross. He, Tony and Dave had scraped together the cash that first year at Aunt May's by doing as many jobs as they could – running errands for anyone, cleaning fish. Anything that they could do, they did, and bought it for Christmas for her. She never took it off.

Wrapping his fist around the cross, he again vowed silently to hunt down whoever was responsible for harming Aunt May, and God help the bastards when he caught them. It was obvious that the freak who had taken over the monastery was linked to this business.

And so was Tony.

His first stop was London, the first link was Tony. And he just better have the right answers.

The publishers hope that this book has given you enjoyable reading. Large Print Books are especially designed to be as easy to see and hold as possible. If you wish a complete list of our books please ask at your local library or write directly to:

Magna Large Print Books
Magna House, Long Preston,
Skipton, North Yorkshire.
BD23 4ND

This Large Print Book for the partially sighted, who cannot read normal print, is published under the auspices of

THE ULVERSCROFT FOUNDATION